'I could not.'

'I wanted you there. I wanted to see you,' Duncan whispered, close enough for Marian to feel his breath on her face. Then he kissed her neck, the heat of his mouth sending chills through her. Still she dared not move. 'I wanted to taste you.'

He leaned down until his lips met hers. It was only a moment before the kiss changed from tender to possessive and she lost the ability to think or to move. Heat raced through her and centred itself in that place deep inside. Soon Marian discovered that her limbs had lost the ability to support her and she leaned towards him.

She'd been completely prepared to fight him away. Now she was not so certain. He slid his arms around her, touching her stomach, then her breasts. The caresses excited her, making her shiver.

Was this passion, then? Was this what made men lose their minds and what brought clans to war?

First published in Great Britain 2009
Harlequin Mills & Boon Limited,
Eton House, 18-24 Paradise Road, Richmond, Surrey TW9 1SR

© Theresa S. Brisbin 2008

ISBN: 978 0 263 86800 5

Set in Times Roman 10½ on 12½ pt
04-0909-77862

Harlequin Mills & Boon policy is to use papers that are natural, renewable and recyclable products and made from wood grown in sustainable forests. The logging and manufacturing process conform to the legal environmental regulations of the country of origin.

Printed and bound in Spain
by Litografia Rosés, S.A., Barcelona

POSSESSED BY
THE HIGHLANDER

Terri Brisbin

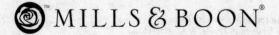

Terri Brisbin is wife to one, mother of three, and dental hygienist to hundreds when not living the life of a glamorous romance author. She was born, raised and is still living in the southern New Jersey suburbs. Teri's love of history led her to write time-travel romances and historical romances set in Scotland and England. Readers are invited to visit her website for more information at www.terribrisbin.com, or contact her at PO Box 41, Berlin, NJ 08009-0041, USA.

Recent novels by the same author:

THE DUMONT BRIDE
LOVE AT FIRST STEP
  (short story in *The Christmas Visit*)
THE NORMAN'S BRIDE
THE COUNTESS BRIDE
THE EARL'S SECRET
TAMING THE HIGHLANDER
SURRENDER TO THE HIGHLANDER

I'd like to dedicate this book to my friend Mo Boylan.
She was one of my first fans when my first book
came out in 1998 and she remains my friend now!
To over 10 years of friendship! Thanks, Mo, for all
your support and help and for having fun with me, too!

Many thanks go out to my writing colleague
Jennifer Wagner for her willingness to listen
as I rambled on and on about Duncan and Marian
and their dilemmas…and for her help in
making it all make sense! Thanks, Jen!

Chapter One

"'Tis said that her breasts fill a man's hand with their creamy fullness."

"Or his mouth!" another in the back shouted.

"I heard the tale that her legs can circle a man's girth and pull him into heaven's very grasp." This from the youngest of the group. "And her hair falls in raven waves down her back." Duncan swore he could hear an almost wistful longing in the voice of a boy on the verge of manhood.

"Nay, 'tis the palest of blond hair," called out another.

"I heard as red as...Hamish's!" said Tavis.

They laughed at that bit of overblown if confused imagery, but the chuckling quieted quickly and Duncan realized they were all thinking the same thing.

"Aye, laddie," Hamish called out then as he tossed his head, making his dark red hair flow down his back. "And I heard the tale that her hair was all that covered the lass's charms when she were caught by her da, the old laird, wi' two men or mayhap three in her bed."

Duncan was tempted to warn them off, but Hamish began singing just then. It was a quick little tune that was familiar to all of them, but Hamish changed a few of the words and turned it into something bawdy about the sexual delights offered by the woman in the Robertson clan called the Harlot as well as her various physical attributes. Duncan let a few more minutes of merriment to go by before he finally intervened.

"'Tis one thing to say such things among ourselves, but talk like that could ruin all my efforts to negotiate with the girl's brother," he said, meeting the gaze of each one in turn. "Discretion is one of my important tools and I expect that you will guard your tongues. She is ruined and she was exiled. There is nothing else to say of her."

The men behind him grumbled under their breaths, but he knew they would follow his orders. He'd chosen them for that very reason—he needed to know he could count on their obedience during the possibly contentious negotiations that he faced. One wrong word, one wrong act, one untoward glance even and the months of preparation and preliminary work would be undone.

The sun broke through the clouds just as the men reached the point in the path where they could look across the valley to the beginning of Robertson lands. Lands that spread for miles from here in the Grampian Mountains out to Perth near the eastern coast of Scotland. Lands that held villages, acres of thick forests, well-stocked rivers, rich farmland and rolling mountains. And thousands of fighting men who had stood at Robert the Bruce's back decades before.

Aye, the Robertsons were well-stocked and well-armed and that simply added to the appeal of the proposed alliance. For a moment, Duncan shielded his eyes from the sun and searched across the valley for the road leading to the keep.

"You can make camp here and wait for my return," Duncan said as he turned to face them. "It should take no more than three days."

"He just wants the Harlot to himself," Donald said, with a laugh.

Duncan could not stifle the curse that burst out of his mouth. The men nodded in acceptance of this new warning, except for Hamish. Damn him, he simply winked. Hamish knew too much of Duncan's recent dissatisfaction with life and with women to not make some comment, but he wisely left it at the wink.

"At midday three days hence ride to the western edge of the village and meet me," Duncan said as he turned his horse and began down the path to the village in the distance.

His men knew their duties and he did not doubt that they would have a small, unnoticeable camp set up by dark. And he would be well on his way to meet the man from the Robertson clan who provided him with details and news not easily found about the clan and their new laird.

The old laird's passing two years before had been the opening he needed to begin negotiations. But, it had not been without hard work, determination and the complete support of Connor MacLerie. As Duncan passed through a thick copse of trees, he followed the path of a stream as it moved downhill and onto Robertson lands. From the maps he'd studied, he knew that he would reach a village in another two or so hours of riding.

As he rode, he reviewed his plans, his questions for Ranald, and the provisions of the treaty he carried for his laird. Contingency plans and alternate demands were already prepared, for Duncan believed and had learned through experience that triumph came from planning and thorough preparation and left nothing to chance.

Planning and preparation were the keys to a successful campaign of any kind whether it be an alliance or a war. And since everyone knew that the relationship between the clans could go from alliance to war in moments over nothing more than a word spoken wrongly, he'd spent the last months readying himself for this series of meetings.

The land leveled out before him, but the trees stayed thick, blocking most of the sunlight where he rode. Watching for the place where the stream split and each branch curved away, one making a path to the still-distant keep and one flowing farther down and off toward the east, Duncan knew he was approaching the meeting place outside the village. When the low stone bridge came into sight, he slowed his horse to a walk and approached it slowly and quietly.

By the look of it, he'd arrived a bit earlier than planned, so after he watered the horse, he took the skin of ale from his bag and drank deeply. Seeing a small break in the trees, he dismounted and walked his horse there. Searching inside the bag for his supplies, he found the wrapped piece of cheese and hard crust of bread he'd brought along. Ranald would see him well-fed, so this would be enough to keep his stomach from growling until then.

A short while passed and Duncan found himself on edge, the importance of these talks no doubt the reason for it. Leaving his horse tethered in the small clearing, he strode toward the bridge to see if he could catch sight of Ranald. Without crossing, he searched along the path that led toward the village for any sign of him.

None.

'Twas not like Ranald to be late or to miss a meeting. Duncan decided to give the man some time before leaving and returning to his men since he could not travel on to the Robertson's keep without them. Pacing near the bridge, just out of sight of the path, he waited. The only sounds he heard were those of the forest creatures and a few birds flying overhead…and the sound of his jaws and teeth as he ground them.

No matter his reputation for a boundless supply of patience when in the midst of difficult negotiations, Duncan was, in reality, a man with little of it. And, as the time passed slowly, that fact was made new to him. The scream, when it came, seemed so out of place as to be in his imagination.

Tilting his head and listening intently so as to discover the scream's origin, Duncan turned around and waited for only a moment before another one came. This one was not as loud, but he was able to locate it and began to trot over the bridge toward the sound. Turning off the path, he pushed through the trees and found himself behind a small stone cottage. Listening as he made his way to one side, Duncan crept to the corner and looked around it toward the front of the building.

Never expecting the need for it, Duncan realized his sword remained on his horse, so he reached down and drew forth his dagger. More a short sword than a knife, Duncan relied on it many times and in many scrapes and trouble. He took a quick step away from the cottage and used a huge tree a pace away as cover to find the trouble.

And there it was—a woman struggling in the arms of a man who was much taller and stronger than she.

Duncan took a moment to assess the situation and realized that the woman did not appear to be in imminent danger, but she certainly was not welcoming such an embrace. Her kerchief loosened as she fought off the man's hold and fell to the ground revealing a wealth of brown hair, but now he noticed she did not scream. Actually, as he observed them, he noticed that she purposely turned them so that the man faced the path and not the cottage.

A sound drew his attention then and, as he looked at the side of the cottage, he met the gaze of a small child. A young girl, who could have been no more than five years and who had the palest blond hair he'd seen, peered out of the small window. He read the fear in her wide eyes and trembling mouth and tried to allay it by smiling slightly and raising his finger to his own lips to warn her to stay quiet.

Now he understood why the woman turned the man's attention from the cottage—to protect the child within. Duncan stood up and stepped out from the shadows. He cleared his throat loudly and waited for the man to acknowledge him. It took only a moment and the man took pains to position the woman between them, even as she pivoted to turn from the front of the cottage.

"'Twould seem the lady wishes not for your attentions," Duncan said quietly. "Leave her in peace now." The man stopped at his warning but did not release her.

"I think ye should no' meddle in what's no' yers to hiv a concern aboot," the man called back to him, dragging her a few steps back to separate them more.

Watching the woman, he noticed that she seemed more disgruntled than fearful. A calm look of purpose filled her face and, although she did not relax in the man's hold, neither did she now struggle as before. She whispered something only the man could hear as though warning the man of something.

"Release her and go on your way," he repeated, this time moving his dagger between them to show he was armed.

This was the last thing he needed now and especially when negotiations were tentative. He would not hesitate to protect the woman if necessary, but it would raise questions about his private presence here without knowledge of the laird. Duncan hoped the man would simply believe he would not hesitate to use the weapon and hoped he would not be forced to. "Release her."

Although he looked ready to offer argument, the man dropped his arms and pushed her away from him. Without a backward glance, he ran down the narrow path and into the woods.

Duncan stepped forward to catch the stumbling woman who regained her balance before he could help. She grabbed her kerchief from the ground, shook it out quickly and efficiently wrapped it around her hair before turning to face him. Her glance at his dagger reminded him he still held his weapon at the ready. He sheathed it and then took a closer look at the woman before him.

She would reach only as high as his chest, if she were close enough, and was younger than he thought. Her clothing made her appear older and wider…at first glance. Duncan knew her hair was long and a muddy shade of brown. Her eyes were the feature that most impressed him, both with their clear intelligent gaze and their deep icy-blue color.

But it was her mouth that distracted him from his purpose. Full pale red lips that she now licked with the tip of her tongue.

"I thank you for your help, sir. He was more nuisance than danger," she offered, without moving toward him. Once more he noticed that she positioned herself away from the cottage.

Like any good mother would, drawing the danger from her daughter to herself.

"Your scream said otherwise, mistress…" He waited for her to explain.

"Laren surprised me, 'tis all." She nodded to the path and then looked at him. "You are not from the village." The woman searched the area around her cottage and then looked down at the path. "What would bring you to my door?"

"I am a visitor, mistress," he answered calmly. 'Twas the truth of the matter so why not use it?

"Then, surely your business lies elsewhere?"

Her words were clearly a dismissal, but from the expression in her eyes, Duncan knew she'd only just realized that she could have exchanged the so-called nuisance for something truly dangerous…if his intent had been such as that. But, his intent should have been to avoid identification by any of the Robertsons before his official arrival at their keep.

"And, now that you are safe, I will take my leave, mistress. You can see to your daughter without fear," he reassured her as he turned away. But not before she gasped at his words and took a few steps to put herself between him and the cottage now. "She waits for you inside. I but saw her at the cottage window as I passed," he explained. "I will make certain that Laren has gone before continuing on my journey."

He watched as she ran inside the cottage and heard the bar drop behind the door a moment later. A stout bar from the sturdy sound of it. Duncan searched the area around her cottage to convince himself that the man had left before retracing his steps back to the main path and the bridge. Crossing the stream, he went down the road to check his horse and his belongings before returning to wait for Ranald at their prearranged place.

But in those next minutes before his friend appeared, his thoughts were filled not with alliances and treaties, but with the image of one woman who tried very hard not to let her true appearance show through.

And he knew not even her name.

Marian cursed herself a fool as she tried to catch her breath. In spite of her attempts to remain calm, her heart raced and her chest hurt from the fear. Not of Laren, who truly was more a nuisance than a danger, but of the stranger who'd stepped in to save her from harm. Before she could think on his dark gaze and tall stature, a small voice cried out to her.

"Mama!" her daughter cried before running into her skirts and wrapping her small arms around her legs. "Mama…" The words drifted off and were replaced by sobs.

"Ciara, my sweet," she soothed, peeling her daughter loose and pulling her into her arms. "We are well, my love," she whispered, smoothing the pale hair back and out of her eyes. Marian sat down, arranged Ciara on her lap and rocked her until she stopped crying.

When Laren surprised her while she worked in her garden, Marian had ordered Ciara inside. They had practiced such a thing from the time they'd returned to Dunalastair from her father's distant holdings in the south. Living apart from her family, alone without the protection of a husband or father, could present dangers of a sort she wished to avoid. Even if most had not realized who she was, a woman alone with a child could be a dangerous thing to be.

Ciara knew to run into the cottage and hide next to the cupboard, if need be. Marian had always prayed it would not be necessary, but today had shown her she could probably not escape her past. Ciara quieted in her arms and Marian loosened her hold just a bit. Kissing her on the head, she whispered to her of her love and her pride that Ciara had followed her instructions. So, her daughter's words came as a surprise and reminded her of that which she was trying to avoid thinking on—. the stranger who had come to her aid.

"Mama, who was the man?" Ciara asked, rubbing

her eyes and lifting her head from Marian's chest. "Is he gone?"

"That was Laren, my sweet, and yes he is gone. He will not bother us again, I think," she said, trying to reassure the child.

"Not him, Mama. The nice one who smiled at me."

Marian lost her words, for she would not have thought the man who stepped forward to help her could smile or be nice. His face was filled with stern, angry eyes and chiseled, masculine angles that had no softness and certainly no smiles. With his huge dagger drawn and dark expression she feared she would be his target once he'd disposed of Laren. He'd stood taller than even her older brother Iain and was broader in the shoulders than even Ranald the blacksmith here in the village. A shiver raced through her.

Formidable might be a more accurate way to describe him.

Yet, even at the moment when she knew he was aware of her fear, she did not feel in danger. His sheer physical presence overwhelmed her, but not a sense that he would attack her. 'Twas obvious that her daughter was simply having the fanciful thoughts that young children seemed to have at times.

"I dinna ken him," she whispered to Ciara, whose head began to drop against her.

Growing fast, but still a bairn in so many ways, her daughter still napped most days. Now that the excitement was past, Ciara began sliding into sleep in her arms. Marian gathered her back close and hummed a soft tune to guide her way to sleep. A few minutes later, she carried her to the bed and laid her on it. After watching Ciara settle in and covering her with a woolen blanket, Marian lifted the bar on the door and went back outside to make certain no one was there.

The late summer breezes moved through the trees, but there was a hint of something cooler in the air. In just a few weeks, the clan would prepare to harvest most of the crops they'd planted in the surrounding fields and the drovers would plan which herds would be moved from the hills to winter grazing and which would be slaughtered or sold. Marian looked over at her own garden plot and knew she would be busy picking and drying the herbs she grew for use in the coming winter.

Walking around the perimeter of her small cottage and garden plot, she looked for any signs of incursion, or of the stranger who has walked in and out of her life so quickly. Nothing looked amiss, her garden lay peaceful and no sign of trampling appeared. Marian lifted her head and listened to the sounds of the day as it passed. Birds flew overhead, trees rustled in the wind, clouds floated across the sky, just as they should on this September day.

If not for the racing of her heart and the blood pounding through her veins, even she would have thought it a usual day in Dunalastair. Marian tried to concentrate on those tasks she still needed to complete, but all she could do was think of the stranger who had stepped in to protect her.

All she could see in her mind were his eyes—so dark to be almost black—gleaming in anger at Laren and then with intensity at her when he mentioned seeing to her daughter inside the cottage. And it was those expressions along with his strong and masculine stature that now made it difficult to breathe.

For not once had she, the Robertson Harlot, ever found a man to be so intriguing to her. Never had she let down her guard in the last five years and allowed herself to be affected by a man. 'Twas so much danger in even considering such a lapse in control to occur that it never occurred to her to be on guard against such a thing.

She'd expected the nuisances of men such as Laren, at least once the news of who she really was got out. Her brother would give orders that would frighten away any serious approaches.

But she'd never expected the danger to come from such a stranger, and, after looking into his deep, dark eyes, she knew he was more dangerous than any who had come before him and any who would come after. It was the memory of his eyes that plagued her all through the day.

Chapter Two

Duncan spied the bridge as they rode toward it on the road and his stomach tightened. 'Twas the way of it when he approached a new series of negotiations. His gut was ever his weakness, but his thoughts were clear and focused for now. His two days of visiting and talking with Ranald revealed no surprises that should cause problems with the laird.

Indeed, he discovered that the Robertsons were as strong and well-managed as his reports had said. Word was out now that once this alliance was in place, the laird would seek a new wife from the northern clans to further cement and strengthen their position as the guardians of Scotland. Some worrisome rumors still floated about regarding the new laird some years ago—while his father still lived—and, as Duncan knew from his own laird's experience, rumor and innuendo could destroy a reputation quickly. So, a move toward a new marriage, after his first one ended in the death of his wife in childbirth, was a good one on the laird's part.

One of his men called out and Duncan looked at the road ahead of them. A contingent of heavily armed Robertson warriors awaited them on the other side of the bridge. Straightening up on his own mount, he warned his men before going on.

"You have your orders and know the importance of what we do here. From here on, report anything untoward to me. Bring your questions to me. Agree to nothing in Connor's name."

"Do we need yer permission to piss then, too, Duncan?" asked Hamish from behind.

"Aye, Hamish, e'en that," he replied without breaking a smile. "More importantly, watch your drink and watch out for the lasses. Those two things can cause a man more trouble than almost anything else."

He took their grumbling as assent and nudged his horse forward. Adjusting the tartan and badge on his shoulder, Duncan led the MacLeries over the bridge and into Dunalastair. The Robertson's man greeted them formally and invited them to follow to the entrance of the keep still some distance away and Duncan nodded and accepted the welcome.

It was only as he found himself searching the faces of the villagers who'd gathered to watch their arrival that he realized he was looking for her.

He'd carefully controlled the growing curiosity within himself to ask about her when he stayed with Ranald. He did not stray from Ranald's croft or smithy and did not seek out neighbors or villagers in order to remain anonymous. But, the urge to know more about her increased until now he found himself examining the face of everyone who stood watching along the path.

And not finding her.

Cursing himself for not remaining on task, he realized he'd slowed his pace while he had gawked. Caelan, the Robertson who led them, turned back to say something, but his gaze moved off to something in the shadows along one of the other paths. Following it, Duncan discovered the woman he'd been thinking about and the little girl. They stood back, away from the other villagers, far enough to be out of the way, yet close enough to see what had drawn the Robertson soldiers to the village.

The girl was tucked deeply into her mother's skirts, only her head was visible as she said something to the woman. The woman leaned down and answered the child without ever taking her eyes off Caelan. Glancing back at the laird's younger brother, Duncan noticed the protective gaze and began to wonder if the woman was Caelan's leman. Just a few moments after he'd found her, she disappeared into the maze of cottages, dismissed by just a nod from Caelan.

If he'd forgotten his own instructions, he found himself reminded of them by a very distinctive clearing of the throat by Hamish. The others took it up for only a second, but he knew that his attention to the woman had been noticed by them, too. He quelled the minor rebellion with a glance of his own and then quickened the pace to move along the path faster.

Forcing his thoughts on what awaited them at the keep, Duncan was able to think on numbers of men the clan could call on in battle and the number of cattle the Robertson clan owned and how many meetings and talks faced him in the next few weeks. And he would later pride himself that he only thought about the woman with the pain in her gaze and the lovely child at her feet once during the ride to the keep.

Holy Mother, protect her!

Marian clasped Ciara's hand in hers and practically ran toward her cottage. Making it a game so her daughter would not object, she sang a ditty and counted the stones along the way. The words sounded strange to her, but it was the beating of her heart that almost blocked out every sound around her.

Caelan! Caelan was there!

She'd mistook him for someone else as he rode by the place where she stood, backed enough into the shadows of the surrounding crofts to be unnoticeable to anyone. The noise of the soldiers' arrival at the bridge, the excitement of the news of the MacLerie's man's entrance into the village and the purpose of his presence all fueled the gossip that swirled through the small village.

Visitors were always of interest, but a man who carried with him the tidings and power of the one still called, though in whispered tones, the Beast of the Highlands, was something that would stir anticipation and storytelling for weeks to come. Curious, Marian had followed some of the women to observe their arrival.

Then, the first shock had hit her.

The man who led the MacLerie soldiers was the stranger who'd chased Laren away just three days past! Oh, he was dressed better now, with his clan badge gleaming on the plaid he wore over his shoulder, but she would have recognized that face and those eyes anywhere. Now he had eight warriors at his back as he rode into Dunalastair. He had not seen her yet, so she ducked back a bit, drawing Ciara with her.

Then the second shock of the day—her youngest brother Caelan led the soldiers to the keep. She'd heard he had returned recently but had not seen him anywhere near the village. Her father had sent him off to foster with a cousin near Skye about three years before... before...before everything had happened five years ago. He must have nigh on ten-and-six years now and be almost a man. Iain must have great faith and trust in Caelan to allow him the honor of escorting such a guest into Dunalastair.

Marian reached her cottage and sat down on a stool she kept near the entrance to her garden. Usually a place for her to clean the plants she harvested or the cuttings she culled, she plopped down and tried to calm her racing heart. When Ciara touched her wet cheek and asked why she was sad, Marian realized she'd been crying all the way from the road when she first saw Caelan. Wiping the tears with the back of her hand, she took in a deep breath and let out a ragged one before she even tried to speak.

"I am not sad, my sweet," she said, pasting on a smile she neither wanted nor felt. "'Twas simply the excitement of seeing so many horses and men and everyone gathering around."

"Did you see the big black horse?" Ciara asked. "It was the biggest horse I have ever seen!"

Marian laughed then, for Ciara loved horses. In spite of not having one at her disposal as she had in her father's house, she'd passed her love of them down to her daughter just by stories and sightings.

"He did seem to be the largest one." Marian wiped the last of the moisture off her cheeks and smiled then. "I thought brown was your favorite color?"

"I used to like brown," she answered, her eyes bright with merriment as she talked about something she liked. "But I think black is the prettiest now."

Marian paused and realized that there had been only one black horse among all of them, and that had been *his* horse. The MacLerie's man. Now she knew who he was but still had no name for him.

Ciara began to chatter about horses, and that horse, and Marian took up her shovel and began where she had stopped before they'd gone to watch the soldiers cross the bridge. Digging into the dirt, she lost herself in her work and tried not to think about the man on the black horse and what trouble he could bring to her doorstep.

Duncan lifted the satchel of parchment scrolls, charts and sheets from the back of his horse and searched for a certain one before turning back to follow Caelan into the keep where the laird awaited him. Handing the leather bag to Hamish to carry, they walked inside and up the stone steps to the second floor where the corridor led to a large chamber. Those waiting on their arrival milled around the whole of the room, which was about half the size of the one at Lairig Dubh.

Still, it was clean and tapestries depicting folk tales and myths of their country's past covered the walls. A huge hearth stood at one side and next to it was a dais with a long table that ran its length. In front of the table, at the top of the steps leading to it, sat a huge wooden chair, engraved and carved with symbols, he knew, from the Robertson clan badge. And in it sat Iain the Bold, son of Stout Duncan and now second chief of the Clan *Donnachaidh* or Robertson as they preferred to be called.

Standing behind him and at his side were the other three remaining sons of Stout Duncan—Caelan, Padruig and Graem—as well as other clan elders and councillors. With Hamish at his own side and the others behind them, he walked quickly to meet the laird. All conversation stopped as they approached the dais.

"Greetings, my lord," he began with a deep bow. "I bring regards and a personal message from the MacLerie." Duncan moved closer and held out the scroll.

The Robertson laird stood and walked down the steps instead of summoning him forward. He took the scroll and tucked it inside his shirt and then held out his arm in greeting. "Welcome to Dunalastair Keep, Duncan." The laird's grasp was strong and sure as they clasped arms and shook. "I offer you and your men the hospitality of my home and hearth as we discuss the future of the alliance between the Robertsons and the MacLeries."

As clapping and cheering exploded throughout the hall at his words, Duncan took a moment to assess the laird. The reports he'd received were very close to the reality of the man. The laird was a tall man, nearly as tall as he, and a young man, too, having followed his father into the high chair of the clan at nly five-and-twenty years old. Young, yes, but clea. 'y well-liked and secure in his clan's backing. Duncan sensed no hesitation or divide among those at the laird's side and had learned of none in his investigations.

A servant came forward with a mug of ale and offered some to his men as well. The Robertson climbed the steps so that he could be seen by all in the hall and raised a cup of his own. Duncan waited, preparing his own words.

"I welcome you, Duncan MacLerie, and bid you to be at ease in my hall, my keep and my village. You and your men are welcome to move freely among the Robertsons as the talks commence that will surely make us allies and friends."

Duncan smiled and met Hamish's gaze. No sign of suspicion there, a good omen then, for Hamish had the instincts of a fox in seeking out any sign of subterfuge or dishonesty. The laird came down the steps, leaned over and spoke close to his ear, so he could hear it above the din.

"Your reputation is quite well-known here. Duncan the Peacemaker you are called for all the times you have averted war and battle between factions, clans, even countries. I am honored by your presence in this matter."

That was not expected. Duncan nodded his head, accepting the compliment without allowing it to swell his head. He recognized it for the strategy it was. When the cheering quieted, Duncan raised his own mug as did his men.

"On behalf of Connor MacLerie, Earl of Douran and chief of the Clan MacLerie, I thank you for your welcome and the hospitality you offer and promise to use all good counsel so that our clans may be united in the bond of friendship and treaty." Raising his cup higher, he called out, "A Robertson! A Robertson!" His men joined in and then so did everyone else in the hall, which echoed with the chant for several minutes.

The laird smiled and drank deeply of his cup. Waving Duncan onto the dais, he brought him and the others to the long table. Trays and platters of food, breads, cheeses, fruits and cooked meats filled the table and the laird directed them to stools around it. Once they had gained their seats, servants circled the table and the guests, filling cups, serving food and seeing to their needs.

"Your journey was a good one, Duncan?"

"Aye, my lord," he replied, tearing off a piece of bread. "The weather held and the winds, when we needed them, were fair and strong."

"Did you come directly here from Lairig Dubh?"

The question was asked in a convivial tone, but it was a test nonetheless. The Robertsons wanted to know who else he was negotiating with and who their competition was. The truth was the easiest way.

"Nay, my lord. We traveled to both Glasgow and Edinburgh on the earl's business before heading north to Dunalastair." Duncan caught Hamish's eye as he took a mouthful of ale from his cup.

"So you having been traveling since…?"

"Since midsummer's day, my lord."

"We are friends, or are soon to be friends. Please call me Iain, as those in the clan do," the laird offered.

He passed the test, apparently, for the laird nodded to several of his councillors.

"As you wish, Iain," he replied.

"Let me make you known to my brothers, the sons of Duncan the Stout. This one you have met—" he patted the man next to him on the shoulder "—my youngest brother Caelan." Duncan nodded as Iain continued, "He has only just recently returned from his fostering with the MacLeans."

Point taken—an established relationship with the powerful MacLean clan of the isles.

Duncan watched Caelan and realized he was much too young to be husband or lover to the woman he'd met…and he was gone when the child was conceived, if Duncan knew anything about calculations. The little girl was nigh on five which meant she could not be his. Not certain why this was important to him, Duncan turned to the man seated next to him as the laird continued the introductions.

"That is my brother Padruig and his betrothed next to him, Iseabail of the MacKendimens."

The MacKendimens were a small, but not inconsequential clan near Dalmally, not far from Lairig Dubh. Another connection made and acknowledged. Duncan the Stout would have been proud of Iain's neat handling of showing their strength without ever raising a weapon. With a nod to both of them, Duncan waited for the last brother to be introduced.

"And that is Graem," Iain began, with a tilt of his head at the last brother who was seated opposite of Hamish, "who has been invited by the Bishop of Dunkeld to take up studies under his tutelage."

And that was the final connection—to one of the most powerful and important bishops in Scotland, giving the clan a link to the Church. The sons of Duncan the

Stout were well-established and connected to important clans, big and small, throughout Scotland. And the clan was one of the oldest families in the land, tracing their heritage back to the Celtic lords of Atholl. Their heraldry and position had been announced more effectively than calling the roll of ancestors. Duncan admired the efficiency with which Iain had established their position.

Iain may only have been laird for just over two years, but he was firmly in command and knew his mind. From the expressions of the others seated at the table, they were proud of him as well and would back his efforts and decisions.

Duncan recognized a challenge made and he could feel the blood in his veins begin to pulse in anticipation of a good fight. He relished nothing more than a worthy adversary across the negotiating table and now knew that the next few weeks would test his abilities on every front.

"We will begin on the morrow, if that suits you, Duncan?" Iain asked.

"Aye, 'tis fine." Duncan was anxious to get into the thick of battle.

"My steward will see to your comfort," he said. An older man came forward and stood at Iain's side. "If there is anything you need, Struan will see to it." Struan bowed and, after asking about their preferences for rooming, left to make the arrangements.

The rest of the meal passed pleasurably, but Duncan discovered he did not even remember what he ate or drank, though the latter was sparsely done. He wanted and needed time to make his final review of the possibilities and their offer before night fell. He could not wait for the thrill of the process. And like a child with a wrapped gift sitting before him, Duncan found that he could not wait for the day to be over and the negotiations to begin.

Duncan would look back, at some time later, and laugh over his misbegotten anticipation and excitement of what was to come. And five days later, in the middle of a heated discussion, and for the first time in all the treaties he'd negotiated, Duncan the Peacemaker lost his temper.

Chapter Three

"You cannot be serious," Duncan shouted as his fists pounded on the table, scattering documents and scrolls in the wake. "You already agreed with that provision nearly two days ago!"

He sensed his control slipping and could not pull himself back. Never had he felt as though the very ground beneath him lay coated with oil and his feet could find no purchase. Hamish glared at him…again. The Robertsons's chief negotiator glared again. Even the laird, who usually stood by silently and watched the proceedings, glared. The thing that Duncan did not understand was what had sent him down such a course that resulted in his anger.

"I was under the impression, sir, that all matters were still negotiable until the laird signs the final treaty. Is that no longer the way we are proceeding?" Symon asked, turning to Iain, again, for confirmation.

Duncan leaned back in his chair and took a deep breath. He gathered and straightened the documents and scrolls he'd scattered and decided that what he needed most was a short time away from Symon before his control snapped completely, for he feared Symon's neck would be the next thing in the room to snap. Having made the decision, he pushed back from the table, bowed in Iain's direction and walked to the door.

"The weather has cleared and I feel that a short break now might clear my head. With your permission, Iain?"

Without waiting for permission, Duncan pulled open the door, followed the corridor and then the steps down to the lower floor and made his way to the stables. He had spoken the truth, for the last four days had been one torrential rainstorm, complete with winds and lightning that split the sky and rumbled over Dunalastair with fierce power. This morn had dawned clear and crisp as though the storm had raged only in their imaginations. And mayhap it had?

He reached the stables and his horse greeted him with the same snorts and stamping he'd just offered to Symon, telling Duncan that they both needed a good run to burn off some of the tension that built within them. Readying the horse himself, it was only a short time before they both raced toward the keep's gate and out through the village. Crossing the bridge, Duncan let the horse have his head for a short time. Using muscles that had been too long unused, Duncan brought the mount under control and laughed as the exertion revived his body and his spirits. A short time and distance later, he turned around and headed back to the keep.

As he rode, he tumbled this morn's work over and over in his head, searching for the problem. There had been significant progress and then he felt as though they hit a stone wall. Each word, each provision was contested. Reviewing it brought him no clarity and he continued to assess the strengths and weaknesses in his offer. When next he looked up, he was sitting on the path that led to the woman's cottage without any knowledge of how he'd gotten there.

He knew he should leave and return to his duties and to the keep where others waited on his return.

He knew he should avoid her for she was like every other distraction that pulled him from his task.

He knew there was nothing remarkable about her, yet something drew him to her and something enticed him to discover more about her.

Duncan shook his head at such nonsensical thoughts. He must be more tired than he thought if he lost his concentration so easily now. Mayhap if he learned her name, her appeal would lessen? 'Twas a chance that it was the mystery of her that made her attractive to him? He'd nearly talked himself out of staying to speak with her when the door to the cottage opened and the woman came out.

Once more struck by the way she looked from a distance and how differently she appeared up close, he watched as her daughter followed a few moments later and skipped along in her mother's shadow, through a gate and into a garden next to the croft. Their soft and completely feminine laughter floated to him where he sat, still on his horse, in the shadows of the tree-lined path.

He'd watched and listened to Connor's wife, Jocelyn, as she played and frolicked with her son and, more recently, her daughter and his heart did the same thing now as then. He felt as though a fist wrapped around it and tightened. With each soft peal of laughter or each word spoken in love and encouragement, the grasp grew tighter and tighter in his chest. A longing so strong he could not breathe filled his heart and soul.

His horse must have sensed the tension, for it began to shift and become skittish beneath him. When he gathered the reins to try to calm it, he dropped one and cursed at his stupidity. Sliding from his seat, he collected the reins and prepared to mount again when he noticed the silence around him. Glancing toward the garden, he did not hear the two any longer. Had they seen him and gone inside?

'Twould be untoward for him to deliberately approach the woman, so he decided it was time to leave. Duncan chose to walk the horse back to the keep and he was just about to when he saw the blond little head peek over the stone wall that surrounded the garden. He could not help the smile that tugged at the corners of his mouth. Some whispering followed and then he spied her pale hair again. Finally he settled on a new approach, damn it all.

"Good day," he called out, as he hobbled the horse near the path.

Silence followed his call. Tempted to give up but not willing to, he tried once more. "Good day."

"Good day, my lord," the woman said as she rose from her hunched-over position and stood at the gate.

"I am not your lord," he said, shaking his head. "My name is Duncan."

Marian knew both of those things, but fought not to reply with the sarcasm she felt. If the truth be told, she was higher in precedence than he and could rightly be called "my lady." But that life was so far away that she dared not even think of it. "The Peacemaker," she said instead.

"Just Duncan," he answered as he walked toward the gate. "And you are called…?" he asked her.

She hesitated for a moment, dreading and anticipating the sound of her name on his lips, but she answered in spite of her fears. "I am called Mara."

The gate opened and Ciara ran out. She stopped a few steps from Marian and her eyes widened as she caught sight of his horse. Her mouth dropped open in awe and although she tried to say something, no words could be heard. Then only one.

"Pretty," she whispered on a sigh.

"Ciara," Marian called. "Come away now with mama."

Ignored because of the animal, Marian grew nervous and held out her hand to her daughter. "Ciara, my sweet, come to mama now." She took a step, but Ciara was faster and bolted in the direction of the horse. Marian froze in fear.

Luckily the man called the Peacemaker did not. With little effort, he leaned down and intercepted her daughter before she could pass. And, in an effort that was made apurpose, he lifted her up and swung her around to make it seem a game. By the time he'd circled her around once, Marian reached his side.

"My thanks, sir," she said, reaching out to take her from him. Instead he gathered Ciara in his arms and took a step toward his horse. "Sir, please!"

"Fear not, Mara. I would but show her the horse. If you would permit it?" he asked before taking another step.

Marian watched as Ciara settled into his arms, leaning against his chest and examining everything in her world from this new height. Pointing to the horse, she uttered that word again. "Pretty."

Then, the daughter who never talked to strangers and never strayed more than a step from her side abandoned her completely.

"What is his name?" she asked the man, even as she leaned toward the horse, forcing Duncan to move or risk dropping her on the ground. With a quick nod of consent Marian freed him and then followed right behind as they approached the horse.

"He has no name. I call him 'horse'," he answered.

Ciara laughed then and for a moment Marian could not decipher the expression in his eyes when he watched her daughter laugh aloud. The same ones she thought were so hard and ungiving melted, and yet now she witnessed a longing there so strong it made her knees almost buckle beneath her. And then it was gone as quickly as it happened. He carried her closer, but stopped a few paces away.

"We must let him learn us or he will try to run," he explained in a calm voice. "Let him learn your smell."

Ciara giggled then as though that was the funniest thing she'd ever heard. The horse's ears pricked up and he snorted once and then again, watching them get closer now.

"'Tis true, lass. We all smell funny to horses and you have to let them learn what you smell like before you get close."

She watched as he took her daughter's hand and held it out to the horse. Whether it was her daughter's scent or its master's that it recognized, the horse calmed and gently nudged both of them. Ciara turned back to her with the greatest smile on her face.

"He would become your friend if you gave him something to eat," Duncan said seriously. "Horses like food."

"I have none to give him," Ciara said.

Shaking her head, she looked around as though she would find something on the ground. Before she could answer, Duncan reached beneath his cloak and took out the stub of a carrot.

"Ah," he said, "here's just the thing."

Under his guidance, Ciara took hold of it and held it out to the horse, who first sniffed it and then pulled it into its mouth. Ciara laughed again, claiming it tickled.

In that moment, Marian's world tilted before her.

No man had ever held her daughter so. No man had made her laugh this way. No man.

Now, there she sat in the arms of a stranger, feeding his horse and giggling over the way its wet tongue felt against her palm. Marian stumbled then, just a step or two, but enough that he noticed it and he reached his free hand out to steady her.

"Are you ill, mistress?"

"Nay, sir. Not ill, just a bit dizzy," she said. Marian reached up to take Ciara from him, but he shook his head and stepped back.

"You cannot carry her if you are unbalanced." He noticed Ciara staring at her, the enthusiasm of the horse now waning as she must have picked up on Marian's concern. "Your mama is worried about us being so close to such a big horse. Come, let's look at him from a bit further away then."

He walked toward the cottage and crouched down to lower Ciara to her feet. Instead of letting her go, he spoke softly to her, telling her about how old the horse was, and how many teeth it had and its favorite foods. Marian felt as though she'd regained her balance by the time he stood and smiled at her.

"I am sorry if it made you worry. I meant no harm," he said.

Looking at Ciara's face and the pure joy that shone there, she knew he had not. "My thanks for such kindness to my daughter."

"'Twas nothing, Mara." His voice poured through her and he turned his attention to her as he had to her daughter just minutes ago. "'Tis not often I find a woman, although she is a wee bit younger than most I speak with, who likes my brute of a horse as much as I do."

She laughed, for she doubted he ever had trouble finding women to talk to…or flirt with…or do the other things men and women do together. Marian met his gaze and wondered how she ever thought him stern or forbidding.

His eyes flashed with amusement as he watched Ciara talking to herself merrily about the horse. Marian was close enough to notice the small flashes of gold in their centers. And she noticed that his hair, worn loose around his shoulders, that had seemed all one color, now caught the sun as it shone through the trees above and gleamed with all the shades of brown.

When the direction of her thoughts struck her,

Marian began to tremble. She purposely did not allow herself to notice such things and went out of her way to disguise any such attractive traits in herself so they would not be noticed by others. Being noticed meant trouble. And it was trouble she neither welcomed nor could afford.

"My thanks again for this small treat for my daughter, sir. We must not keep you from your duties any longer." Marian reached out for Ciara's hand and grabbed it when she did not move quickly enough.

"Ciara, thank Sir Duncan for letting you feed his horse."

"Duncan is fine, Mara. She can call me Duncan."

Ciara mumbled her thanks, still in awe of the horse and its owner and, with a nod, Marian led her to the cottage door.

"Mayhap Ciara can suggest a name when next I visit?" he asked.

She hurried inside, hoping her daughter had not heard his words. Closing it behind them, she resisted the urge to drop the bar and secure it. Such an action could be construed as an insult, since he'd offered nothing but pleasant company to her and her daughter. Even as Ciara went searching through her small box of toys for the horse made of sticks, Marian walked to the small window that faced the front of the cottage and peeked carefully through the covering to watch him leave.

He untangled the reins from the horse's legs and pulled himself onto its back. The strength in his arms and legs was obvious as he brought the strong horse under control and turned it toward the village. If she'd thought him only a man of meetings and discussion, she'd been so very wrong. Duncan the Peacemaker was first a warrior and then a negotiator.

Marian watched as he leaned down and said something to the animal that made it rear up and shake its head and snort. Instead of trying to overpower the animal, Duncan laughed loudly and patted its head and neck in approval. Then just before he guided the horse into the path, he turned and nodded in her direction.

Had she been so obvious in her observation of him? What must he think of her gaping and gawking at him through her window? Shocked, she backed away but she knew it was too late. Her transgression had been witnessed. Luckily Ciara was completely engrossed in playing and reliving every moment of her horse experience and so she missed the embarrassing display her mother was making.

Tugging the kerchief from her hair and loosening the braid to allow her hair to fall freely, Marian moved about the cottage finishing tasks left undone when they'd been drawn out by the first flashes of sunshine in days. Now, she worried over the results and thought on his parting words.

Mayhap Ciara can suggest a name when next I visit?

A shiver pulsed through her body and claws of fear pulled at her as she considered all the dangers inherent in his words and possibly in his intentions, too. She knew how men thought, but her daughter did not. If Ciara became attached to this man, it would break her heart when he left…as he no doubt would.

She must discourage him somehow. Discreetly of course and in a way that did not offer insult to his honor.

Although she kept apart from the machinations within the clan, even she understood the importance of his work and the alliance his laird offered her brother. Marian must turn his attentions from her, for whatever reason they were focused on her mattered not, and keep it on his duties and responsibilities.

She must convince him that she was not worthy of or interested in his concern and she must do it in a way that seemed like his idea. Regardless that he had stepped forward to help her rid herself of Laren. Regardless of the kindness he'd shown her daughter. Regardless that, as the clan's honored guest, he should be granted any, *any,* measure of hospitality that gained his attention.

Discourage without insult.

Ignore without insult.

Direct his interest without insult.

Marian knew these were the tasks before her and she prayed that she was up to it. For the sake of her daughter and everyone she loved and for the multitude of sins she bore, she must be.

Duncan returned to the keep with a clear head and a much lighter spirit than when he'd left. Leaving the horse with a boy in the stables, he trotted to the great hall and found those he'd left behind readying for the noon meal. He climbed the dais, bowed to the laird and sat in the stool left open for him.

If anyone wanted to redress him for his abrupt departure earlier, none did. Platters of food were passed and cups filled and then simple and congenial conversation followed as they ate. Soon they all rose and prepared to return to the laird's solar where the discussions were being held.

Mayhap he had been the problem? Mayhap his own attitude had been at fault and this short break would improve the business still ahead of them?

He spied Tavis in the corridor as he walked behind the laird and called him over. Tavis's talent was just what he needed for a special gift he would need within the next few days. With a few instructions and a warning to speak of it to no one, Tavis headed off to find what he needed.

Duncan smiled then, thinking on the expression the child's face would wear when she saw the surprise he was planning. And, if he did that, made the little girl smile, mayhap he could draw one from her mother as well?

Chapter Four

Duncan allowed three more days to pass, three long, unending days, before he permitted his thoughts to drift from the numbers and the clauses of the treaties under discussion to the woman and the wee child who lived at the edge of the village. Yet, for every step forward the negotiations took, they fell two behind. If the pattern had not repeated itself three times so far, he would have doubted his assessment. But, even Hamish had noticed it.

This time, Iain had suggested a break, with some hunting to refresh their larder and their spirits. His men agreed rapidly, as he knew they would, for they tired of their close quarters and good behavior. A hard ride and some good hunting would burn off the building tension. That and the feast that the laird had announced for two days hence. Fearing that he'd kept them on too tight a hold, Duncan accepted the invitation and extended it to the MacLerie men.

The day was fair and the storm clouds that built on

the horizon in the morn seemed to drift in other directions, giving them the perfect conditions for their hunt. The Robertsons seemed a congenial lot—mock battles of their hunting skills carried them through the day, with each clan proving themselves as worthy adversaries. Even the laird brought down a stag, to the wild cheering of his men. Duncan allowed him his moment of triumph, deciding that he and the tentative negotiations did not need him to demonstrate his own prowess in the hunt. By the time the sun began to slide down toward the dusk, the group was heading toward the village and the keep behind it.

It was as they rode over the bridge that Duncan's attention shifted for only a moment, but it was time enough to be noticed by Hamish. Feeling under his cloak for the toy, he took leave of the laird, announcing his intention to visit with his clansman Ranald. After the others traveled on ahead, he did indeed go to the smithy's cottage, for he had questions on his mind and could trust Ranald for honest answers and discretion.

A mug of ale and a short conversation later, and Duncan headed to the cottage off the path. Along with the carved wooden toy, he also carried several game birds caught this day. A gift for Ciara and her mother.

He shifted on the horse as he realized how much planning he'd put into this supposed casual visit to the girl and her mother, but after that brief moment of doubt, Duncan continued down the path. Listening to the sounds around him, he did not hear the sounds of laughter that had greeted him previously. Nor did he hear any sounds of a struggle. Dismounting and tethering his horse to a tree, he walked toward the front of the cottage.

A glance and a listen told him that Ciara and Mara worked not in their garden. He strode over to the stone wall that surrounded it and peered into the enclosure. Examining it without the distraction of the women who cared for it, Duncan noticed that, though small in size, it was efficiently laid out and well-cared for. He recognized both some cooking and healing herbs that Jocelyn and her women used in Lairig Dubh, but there were many he did not. Still, the signs told him that the garden's keeper was organized and dependable in its care.

Still hearing no sounds from the cottage, he returned to its door and knocked softly. When no reply came, he called out their names softly and still heard no response. He should have turned and walked away…and taken it as the sign he needed to tarry no longer in this interest. But, something made him stay, reach for the latch and open the door.

The cottage was small, but clean and dry. Several mats lay strewn over the packed dirt floor and a small palette was positioned in the farthest corner from the door. A cupboard and another trunk sat on the other wall. There was a small hearth in the far wall and, in the middle of the room, a small round table with two stools. Again, simple and efficient, in its contents and care. It was the few items on the table that made his chest tighten.

A child's meager toys, made of sticks and cloth, sat in a pile there, as though waiting for their owner to return. One was a doll; another was a horse. Duncan smiled, knowing that the one inside his cloak would please the girl. And for some reason still to be deciphered, that pleased him.

Now, looking around the room, he acknowledged for the first time to himself, that this was what he wanted. No more traveling from one end of Scotland to the other on the clan's business. No more always living and traveling in the middle of tension and danger and strife. His life had been and still was about peace at any price, but that did not mean he did not wish it to be different, with a wife, some children and lands to tend.

In his heart, Duncan the Peacemaker wanted to be nothing more than Duncan the Farmer.

Oh, Connor and Rurik would get a hearty laugh out of that. They would double over from laughing so hard at such a thought, but Duncan knew it for the truth it was. And now, standing here, in the quiet of this plain cottage, he believed it for the first time.

He was so caught up in contemplating his future that he never heard their approach. It was the girl's gasp that drew him from his thoughts and made him realize he was an intruder here.

"My pardon," he began, looking into the shocked eyes of the mother. "I was looking for you and thought you might be inside," he explained.

Marian took Ciara's hand, knowing that her daughter would run to him. The man had been the subject of her childish ramblings since his last visit here and now that he stood before them, Marian did not discount her daughter's infatuation. His very size made her reluctant to enter the cottage, for he nearly touched the roof of it when he stood at his full height. It was Ciara's other infatuation that saved her.

"Sir, can I see your horse?" her daughter asked.

A smile filled his face, once more softening his gaze and his eyes, as he nodded. But before he agreed aloud, he looked to her for permission. She was prepared for this, having thought through all sorts of scenarios after his last visit and knowing she must guide him into disinterest before it became dangerous.

Marian was prepared to wave off such an invitation…until she looked at her daughter's face.

Never had she seen such an expression in Ciara's eyes—wonderment and anticipation blended and practically shone like the sun there. Was it the attention of such a man that enthralled her daughter? Was it the simple interest in a lively animal? Or was there something else happening here? With a worried twisting in her stomach, she gave in without a word. All it took was a slight nod, and Ciara grabbed the Peacemaker's hands and dragged him outside toward the horse.

Marian followed along, all but forgotten by both of them, or so she thought, until they reached the horse. Having seen it rear and rage, its docile stance now made her nervous. But, from the confident way that Ciara strode at Duncan's side without hesitation, her daughter carried none of that fear. Although the horse raised its head and watched their approach, it stood still as they moved closer.

Duncan crouched down and whispered instructions to the girl before he took her to the horse's side. She was as sure as anyone he'd seen in her manner around the animal and even the horse's great size did not scare her off. He smiled and turned to her mother.

"With your permission, I would let her ride," he said.

And he waited. He knew Mara was uncomfortable with even his presence, but he was counting on her desire to please her daughter to see this through.

"She is so small. I…" Mara shook her head. Though, if he could read her expression, she seemed less opposed to the idea and more fearful of it.

"Come," he said, holding his hand out to her, "you get on first and place her in front of you."

If he had thought her afraid, he'd been wrong. Duncan watched as the idea took hold within her and, in a second, he was no longer certain if she'd hesitated at all. Mara accepted his hand and stepped toward them.

She'd surprised her daughter as well, for the girl's mouth dropped open, her eyes widened and then she uttered one word filled with such awe and appreciation and wonderment.

"Mama."

Duncan left the horse tethered to the tree and stood by the saddle. He lifted his foot and placed it in the stirrup to give her something to leverage herself up. Surprising him with her ability, Mara stepped on his foot and climbed into the saddle. Patting the horse's neck, she seemed as much at home on the animal as he might be. After a moment of adjusting her skirts around her, she held her arms out for her daughter.

And she smiled.

The corners of her mouth curved up and the whole countenance of her face changed. Her appearance brightened and he discovered another woman instead of the stern one he'd met. This one seemed younger than the other and there was a mischievous glimmer in her eyes that made him question his first, second and third appraisals of her.

"You have ridden?" Although a statement, it came out as a question.

"Aye, sir. But, it has been many years since then."

Her body adapted to the horse's shifting as though she were born to it, regardless of her claims. Duncan reached down and took Ciara up in his arms and then handed her to Mara, who settled the girl before her. Their heads bent together and they whispered words he could not hear, but could guess. He stood back and watched them for a few moments and the tightness in his chest returned.

Marian dared not meet his gaze, for his eyes had taken on that soft look of yearning that she'd glimpsed before. He stepped away from them and, after a few minutes of letting the horse accustom itself to their weight (though together they did not weigh as much as he did) and presence, he tugged the reins free of the tree and turned to face her.

"Shall I walk you or would you like the reins?" he asked.

It was a quiet question but it caused a yearning of her own to creep into her heart.

When she lived here those years ago, a daughter of the laird surrounded by all the honor and comforts of such a position, riding had been her passion and her talent. Her brother told her she rode better than any man he knew and that had been a source of pride to her. Now, though, owning or riding a mount such as the one she'd had or one such as this would bring too much attention to her and would remind too many of her past. So, she exercised the self-control that had served her this long and wrapped her arms around her daughter.

"We would be pleased if you would control the horse, sir," she said softly.

"Oh, yes, Duncan," Ciara said. "Please?"

Her daughter knew nothing of her past, and she intended to keep it that way now. 'Twas safer for all involved. Mara held on to her and watched with a feeling of pride as Ciara sat confidently before her, reaching out to pat the horse's mane and to ask the Peacemaker an unending string of questions. So many in fact that he finally laughed a loud at them.

When they reached the end of the lane to her door, he turned, thankfully, not toward the rest of the village, but away and down the path that led to the bridge and off into the forest. He walked quietly at their side, guiding the horse to a slow and even gait. He continued across the bridge and down the road and then stopped just out of sight of the bridge.

"How was that, Ciara?" he asked. "Did you enjoy riding my horse?"

"Oh, yes," she said in that soft, childish tone. "And Mama did, as well."

"Did she now?" he asked her daughter while shifting his gaze to hers.

Marian swallowed and then swallowed again, trying to clear her throat of the tightness that had taken control. She did not understand the how or why of it, but a glance from this man made parts of her feel alive and awake. Parts that had never been tempted to feel anything, now pulsed with some sense of anticipation. Regardless of her past, regardless of her lack of experience in such things, she had the urge to touch her mouth to determine why it tingled so. Finally she blinked and freed herself from his gaze.

"Aye, sir. And my thanks for such a pleasant ride." She smiled and kissed the top of Ciara's head before handing her over to him. "'Twas an uncommon treat for us."

Ciara babbled on to him as he lowered her to the ground, nodding or shaking his head in quick succession as the questions and comments flowed unabated. Ciara, as much as she, was unused to the presence of such a man in her life. Pretending to be a widowed cousin of the laird extended a certain protection and excuse to their lives and, except for the occasional incursion of someone like Laren, the men of the clan gave them no troubles or even attention. What Iain had said, or what orders he'd given, she knew not. But, the result was that Ciara knew very few men at all.

Duncan stood and held out his hand for a moment before dropping it to his side. Marian shook her foot free of the straps on the other side of the horse and was preparing to climb down when his words stopped her.

"In spite of his sometimes-brutish behavior, the horse is usually well-mannered," he began, reaching out to stroke the horse's head. He held out the reins to her. "If you would like to ride him down the road a bit, he wouldna mind."

Of all the things he could offer, this one was truly temptation. She forced her hand to stay on the edge of the saddle and shook her head.

"I could not do that, sir. But I…" She was about to thank him when he interrupted.

"You have the skills. Any man with eyes in his head

could see that." He held the leather straps up closer. "I will keep watch on the lass while you go a bit down the road and back."

How could she fight this? How could she resist such a simple and innocent pleasure? Ciara, once more, decided her answer before she could.

"Oh, Mama!" she exclaimed from the ground, where she stood safely at the man's side. Marian noticed that he kept her close enough to shield her from any such movements by the horse. "Ride the horse, please!" That expression of awe filled her face again and Marian was unable to refuse and make that look go away.

"May I?" she asked, just to be certain she did not misunderstand. "And you will wait here with Sir Duncan for a moment or two, Ciara?"

Her daughter, fearless as she was, slipped her hand into Duncan's larger one and nodded. "We will watch you."

Marian nodded and took the reins from him. The two of them stepped back, still hand in hand, but now her daughter stood silent. Wrapping the leather straps around her hands, through her fingers and on her wrists as was her custom when riding, Marian brought her knees forward and leaned down to gain a better balance. With a touch on its sides, the horse began to trot down the pathway.

It felt familiar within scant moments: the feel of being atop of horse and using her legs to control it and the motion as they moved along the road. Glancing back, she saw the two standing there, waving to her and a wild thought entered her mind.

But, did she dare?

She laughed then, something of the old Marian filled her and then, with more pressure and a flick of the reins, she gave the horse its head and held on as the black stallion took it. The trees raced by her. The wind tore her kerchief from her head and loosened her hair from its bonds, but she cared not. Leaning down closer to the horse's head, she whispered words of encouragement as it sped up even more. It was a glorious animal.

Marian soon realized she must go back. The daylight was dwindling and tasks lay before her. And she should feel guilty about leaving her daughter with the MacLerie's man, but she knew down deep inside that he was trustworthy or would not be who he was.

Still, this small pleasure would sustain for years. Now, she must return before anyone witnessed her behavior. Gathering the reins in and drawing the horse to a slower speed, she guided it back toward the bridge and her daughter. Retrieving her kerchief from the branch that captured it on her passing, she returned a bit slower than she'd ridden away.

Marian arrived at the bridge and slowed the horse to a walk, allowing it to cool from the run. Looking around, she could not find either the Peacemaker or her daughter. Tamping down the urge to panic, she guided the horse back toward her cottage, looking ahead as she rode. When she saw them standing at the edge of the trees, she slowed the horse to a walk and approached them slowly. Once more Ciara surprised her by waiting at Sir Duncan's side and not running up to the horse.

Her cheeks held color now, whether from exhilaration or the pleasure of the ride, he knew not. Duncan watched as she changed before his eyes, from a vibrant young woman who obviously enjoyed riding to someone much older and more staid. As she wrapped the kerchief back over her hair and tied it, Mara became a different person.

He'd only seen glimpses of it before and those had heightened his curiosity about the woman. Ranald would give no more information about her than that she was a widowed cousin of the laird's, recently returned to live there with her daughter. His reticence gave Duncan pause and now, after watching this, he knew there was much, much more going on here.

Mara tugged the horse to stop and he walked over to help her down. Her waist was slight in his hands, narrower than her clothing gave the appearance it would be. He guided her to her feet and would have let go, but she stumbled and he grabbed her to keep her from falling. This time, his hands did not land on her waist, but higher, where he could feel the fullness of her breasts.

Breasts she hid from the rest.

Breasts that would fill his hands, if he but moved them a wee bit higher.

His body shivered then and he grew hard at the feel of her womanly curves in his grasp. Mara stilled in his hold and he knew that she felt the growing hardness positioned between them. In that instant, an awareness of her as a woman took hold of him that shocked him in its simplicity. He'd been intrigued by her, amused by and interested in many things about her. But, now, on a more visceral, more primitive level, he was aroused by her.

It may have only been a moment, but it stretched on

for a piece of forever, broken only when the girl's voice called his name. Releasing her from his hold, Duncan stepped away from Mara and turned to her daughter.

"Mama, look what Sir Duncan gave me!" Ciara squealed. Holding her hand out, she showed her mother the horse that Tavis had carved at his request.

"What is this?" Marian asked. Her gaze met his and he saw a myriad of questions in it. Then she took the horse from Ciara and examined it.

The sight of her fingers following the smooth curves of the wood sent alternating waves of heat and ice through his body now, which seemed to recognize the pleasure that would be gained if such a caress slid over it instead of the wood. Duncan inhaled sharply trying to break the growing spell that surrounded him now.

"One of my men makes them for his wee sisters and brothers. I thought Ciara might like one," he offered.

"You are kind, sir, but we cannot accept this."

Her eyes hardened in that moment and she shook her head. Ciara gasped and then reached out for the toy.

"Mama!" she cried. "Please!"

He tried to figure out what had happened and how this innocent gesture had gone wrong. Then the truth struck him. A gift given to a woman who lived without the protection of a man meant one thing.

"It is only a small toy for the child, Mara. I meant no disrespect by it," he explained in a low voice. He neither wished to make the situation worse, nor did he wish to undermine her authority in her daughter's eyes.

Mara looked at her daughter for a moment and relented. She handed the toy back to Ciara and motioned with a tilt of her head.

"Thank you, Sir Duncan!" Ciara chirped. "Thank you!"

Before he could answer, Mara interrupted. "Ciara, take the horse in and let it meet your other toys."

Ciara laughed aloud and left them both, as she skipped back to the cottage and her other toys, intent on introducing a new plaything to the existing ones. He watched her path for a few seconds before turning back to face her mother.

After the physical reaction his body had shown to her nearness, Duncan suspected that his gift had not been all that respectful. Not the carved toy, but the chance to ride his horse.

He'd read her desire to ride free of his presence and even that of her daughter in her face whenever she glanced at his horse. It was like seeing a secret past flitting over her features, moments and memories of pleasure and happiness now held deep inside and only let loose when she thought no one saw or recognized them.

But he had.

His years of reading expressions during negotiations and interpreting them, ascertaining weaknesses and strengths, had not stopped simply because she was a woman and not involved in the meetings. He'd seen the desire and the aching want there on her face, in her eyes, and allowing her that short pleasure seemed an easy thing.

But his body had interpreted the basic, raw part of the offer and she had, too. In spite of his inability to see it, both gifts came with an expectation. He should apologize. 'Twas the right thing to do. But the awareness between them made it difficult to deny its existence.

"Mara," he began, but she stopped him with a shake of her head.

"Sir Duncan," she said quietly, "let me be candid with you. I returned here with the laird's permission and have tried to lead a circumspect life with my daughter."

He thought her choice of words strange, especially since she sounded much more educated than a poor widow living on the laird's beneficence. But he waited for more.

"You are an honored guest of the laird's and I would not offer insult or be inhospitable to you or in any way threaten the success of your work here, but…"

She glanced at him and then away, taking in and letting out a deep breath, as though fortifying herself for the rest of it. Still he waited.

"But your presence here and your attentions to me and my daughter, regardless of your intentions, can bring only problems to us all."

Well, at least she'd allowed that his intentions might be simply innocent ones. Practicing the patience he was known for, Duncan let the silence go on, knowing she had more to say. It was her touch, her hand placed on his arm, that nearly undid his control.

"There can be nothing more between us, sir. If you seek only a fleeting amusement, there are others in the village who would gladly provide it to such a man as you." She paused then for another breath. "And I know that you cannot seek more than that, for your duties to your clan and your laird will call for your return and you will be gone from these lands. And a woman like me has nothing to offer you."

Part of him wanted to argue each point with her. He

did not seek only amusements of the flesh. His actions did not ask for that. He would not simply engage her in something meaningless and then return to Lairig Dubh and she insulted him with such an accusation. However, his pride stung with the truth of her words and he took a moment to think a bit before speaking.

"I did not mean to insult you, mistress," he began, as he stepped back and added some space between them. Her hand dropped from his arm, but the heat of the touch still pulsed through his skin. "In all candor, I did not think of the consequences of my visits to you or my gift to your daughter. Since I have no wish to cause trouble for either of you, I will not seek your company again."

Duncan turned to leave, but she stopped him—again with her hand on his arm. Facing her, he now read fear in her expression. And he did not like it.

"Your pardon, sir, for my boldness. I did not mean to insult you or your kindness to my daughter," Mara said, bowing her head in a gesture of submission that did not fit her and that he wanted not to ever see her perform.

He knew as she did, that she would not, indeed, *could not* refuse him any request he made. Duncan had the laird's welcome and they both knew it extended to anything or anyone in the laird's control. And that meant her. If he'd wanted her in his bed, naked and there for his pleasure, she would be there with the laird's blessing.

That was one thing he would never do. One limitation he had set for himself early on in his experience. He did not use women for his comfort no matter that he could. Reaching over he lifted her chin with his fingers and waited for her to meet his gaze.

"You have nothing to fear from me, mistress. Truly. I take my leave of you and hope you will give my fare-wells to your daughter."

He offered a slight bow and turned away then, even as so many unspoken words entered his thoughts. Some of them would explain his actions, some would simply muddy the waters between them now. Duncan listened as he walked to his horse and mounted it, hoping deep inside that she would call him back.

But she did not.

The pragmatic man within who'd never before been distracted from his duties understood and accepted her actions for what they were—the sensible thing to do for both of them.

Marian watched him leave before returning to her own duties that waited inside the cottage. Dinner, some mending and sewing, taking care of Ciara and more. The strength drained from her and she strug-gled to complete even the simplest of tasks. Ciara seemed to know she was out-of-sorts and did not press her for too many songs or stories before sliding under the blankets on her pallet and into the sleep of the innocent.

But sleep did not come to Marian.

She tossed and turned, feeling every bump in the pallet beneath her. Deep in her heart, grief and anger grew until she could no longer deny that it raged within. The only warning was the burning in her throat and eyes before the tears began pouring out. Marian tugged the end of the blanket up and held it against her mouth to capture any noise that might wake Ciara.

Once the grief was loosed, it would not go quietly back under control. The years of loneliness, the ongoing humiliation, the loss of family and friends broke through and she sobbed at the pain. The worst of it were the feelings that this stranger had caused, feelings that could never be part of her life. Desires and yearnings for a life of her own, buried these last five years, now tore free. For a husband and children.

Some minutes later, when the tempest calmed, Marian turned over and looked at the one thing that had made it all worthwhile. Ciara was the one joy in her life and made every moment of suffering and every lost possibility bearable. Reaching over to smooth her daughter's hair away from her face, she knew she would bear this sorrow as well.

Iain nodded to the villager to come forward. Leaning over he listened to the man's words and then sent him on his way with another nod. Turning to his steward, Iain grinned with the smile of the vindicated.

"So, his interest in my sister grows then," he commented.

"Aye," Struan answered. "Do you think 'tis wise not to interfere?"

"The MacLerie's man has done nothing that needs my intervention, Struan. At least not yet. And especially since not many know she is my sister."

Struan bowed and moved away, leaving Iain alone. Glancing around the room at the others present, he realized that so much had changed since that terrible night five years before. His brothers had grown, he had inherited the clan leadership from his father and had instituted many changes that were beneficial to them. These negotiations were only one of them.

Still, the guilt that Marian carried the burden of his own actions had weighed on him lately. He'd allowed her to return, hoping that a solution would come to him about her future. None had until just these last days.

The Peacemaker's interest in her was intriguing. He was not known to turn his attentions from his work while negotiating. He did not seek out the company of women while traveling on his laird's business. So, the turning of his attentions to any woman was remarkable. That the woman was Iain's own sister made it even more so.

Iain drank deeply from his cup and thought on the possibilities. A few hours later, as the fire in the hearth burned down to only embers and the chamber emptied around him, he still sat deep in thought.

Chapter Five

Duncan listened but could not believe the words he heard. The Robertson's man had just relinquished his objections to a primary clause in their treaty and given in to Connor's demands on several other issues as well. They'd made more progress in hours than they had in the days since their arrival there. And if there was a reason, Duncan could see it not.

Still, he found himself pleased by the concessions made so far and he felt the temptation to continue to press for more. If the Robertson was feeling generous, why ever not? When Hamish nodded at him, Duncan knew his friend noticed the same thing.

"…and I have ordered a feast for tomorrow eve to mark our progress," Iain finished.

"A feast? Pardon my inattention, Iain. A feast on the morrow?" he repeated.

"Aye. Many of my people have voiced an interest in meeting the MacLerie's emissary and his men, so I thought a feast would give them that opportunity."

Something in this offer made Duncan prickle with unease. "Truly, Iain, though I, and my men, appreciate this sign of friendship, this will distract us from our purpose." He turned and looked at the others in the chamber. "Mayhap we should finish our work and celebrate the results then?"

Iain walked to his side and put his arm on Duncan's shoulder. "I assure you I will not be dissuaded from my purpose in this. We are a few measures from completing the agreements and may even be done by tomorrow eve."

Duncan recognized defeat, but he also kenned when and when not to argue with a powerful man. With a nod, he acquiesced to the plans.

"Dinna worry so, Duncan," Iain said as he stepped away and waved his steward out of the chambers. "I will leave you all to your task and you will not be bothered by the preparations."

But Duncan did worry. He was fighting a battle within himself to keep his own thoughts and attentions on the dozen or so clauses yet to be agreed to and off the woman whose mournful eyes plagued him even now. Hamish approached and he leaned close to hear his words.

"Do ye have some fear or concern over this feast that I should ken aboot, Duncan? Something I should be taking a look at?"

Duncan brought a parchment up in front of them as though pointing something out to his man, but truly to cover their words. "'Tis not his words, but something in his manner, that is amiss. I cannot give you an exact thing, but…"

Hamish nodded. "I get yer meaning. But I've sensed

nothing from him that I wouldna—he is nervous aboot the treaty, but no' more than I would expect."

"Be alert, Hamish."

Duncan lowered the parchment back to the table and sat in his chair. "Well, sirs, shall we proceed then and hopefully finish our business in time for the laird's feast?"

There was a certain amiable air in the chamber as they worked through the rest of the day. Duncan chose to eat in the solar and organize his thoughts and strategies for what he believed would be the final day of negotiating with the Robertsons. Although most issues were resolved, a few important ones remained to discuss.

As was his practice, he walked through his concerns one by one in his thoughts until he was clear on his path. What surprised him, though, was what, or who, waited there in the silence as he cleared his path of actions for the morrow.

Mara filled his thoughts then and through the night and the next day. Unlike any other woman he'd encountered, she presented more questions than she answered. The flush in her cheeks as she rode his horse toward him aroused him more than any woman had in…months. The way she humbled herself to beg him, nay there was no doubt she begged, to turn his attentions elsewhere and spare her and her daughter from any scandal. The false face she presented to the world intrigued him rather than angering him. Mara was a riddle, a puzzle full of twists and turns and unexpected secrets, that called to him.

And he excelled at solving riddles and puzzles.

That thought tugged at him the next day as the keep

and village bustled around him, preparing for the feast ordered by its laird. Duncan worked by rote through his tasks, and as he suspected, the final clause stayed just out of reach through the day. They would need to meet on the morrow and finish. Within a sennight, they could all be home in Lairig Dubh.

Now, seated in a place of honor next to Iain, Duncan cast a glance across the crowded hall looking for the one person he'd like most to speak with. Deep inside, he'd known she would not attend, but his damned heart had held on to a spark of hope. 'Twould most likely be the last time he'd see her and to see her smile and possibly to share a dance would have been a good thing.

He noticed that his men were seated in different parts of the hall, each one involved in some measure of flirting or enjoying some woman's company and Duncan suspected that his men would be sleeping outside the keep this night. Even Hamish conversed with a woman, though Duncan kenned that Hamish would never stray from his faithfulness to his Margaret. Since all the women seemed to be offering their companionship freely, he had no problems with whoever among his men wanted to accept that.

He drank deeply from the cup in his hand and shook his head. Mayhap that was exactly what he needed tonight? His journey all over Scotland this summer had been long, the negotiations tenuous at times and lengthier than he'd expected, and a night wrapped around a willing and welcoming lass would not be the worst thing he could do.

"Are you looking for someone, Duncan?" Iain asked as he motioned for a servant to fill his cup once more.

"Try this mead, one of the villagers makes it and it is the smoothest brew I have ever tasted."

One mouthful proved Iain's words true, but Duncan took another to avoid answering the question. It worked for only a few seconds.

"Do you seek someone?"

This time Iain's voice was pitched lower and seemed to coax a reply from him he did not want to give. But it was there, in his thoughts.

Mara was not there tonight.

He'd searched through the crowd, looking from face to face and she was not there. Something flashed through him—disappointment? Lust? Longing? It must have been written on his face for Iain leaned in closer and spoke.

"I would not have the man upon whose favor the success of our negotiations rests to be unhappy here…or to have *any* need go unmet, Duncan. Speak her name or say what you need and I will order it done."

Some insane desire sparked within him at that moment. He wanted to call out her name, call her to him and demand what he wanted from her. The thought of bedding her, peeling off her garments to see what truly lay beneath them and making her blush with the same pleasure that riding his horse had given her was one thing. And the urge to say it and demand it grew so strong, he drank another mouthful of the tasty brew to keep the words from flowing out.

He heard Hamish cough then and knew it for their signal, but his head swam now with thoughts and desires of Mara and the warmth brought by the mead. And again Iain plagued him.

"Well, Peacemaker, what say you? Is there someone that you fancy? Someone I can call to your chambers to offer you a night of pleasure? There are many who would be willing."

Duncan's body responded to the words and the offer. His cock hardened as it had when he held Mara in his arms and he'd noticed her ample breasts almost in his hands. That part of him had no indecision in it—it was ready and able for her touch and her taking. All he had to do was speak her name.

"...speak her name," Iain urged temptingly in a whisper.

He shook his head, grasping the now-empty cup as he fought the battle within. A servant reached over his shoulder and filled the cup. Heat poured through him, but he tossed the mead down and watched as the room swayed before him.

Mara was not here. Mara was the name he wanted to scream.

Mara...had begged him not to.

He knew he could drink all night and not be affected, but this felt different. The villagers seem to melt together as they moved to the music that swirled around him. Tavis waved to him, but Duncan found that his hand did not move fast enough and Tavis had already moved past him when he did raise it.

Waves of heat surrounded him and he knew he needed to get out into the cool night air. Duncan tried to make his legs move, but they would not. The only part of him moving was the hardness between his legs, for it pulsed and throbbed and reminded him of what he really wanted this night.

Mara.

Pushing the hair back from his face, he leaned away from Iain who seemed not to notice the heat at all. Though he moved slowly, Iain's face twisted and smeared into something not quite a face at all. But his voice never stopped echoing through Duncan's head.

"You have but to speak her name and it will be so."

"Speak her name…."

"Her name…"

Duncan stood then, fighting the words, fighting the heat, fighting the urges that grew and filled him and threatened to explode. His stomach tumbled inside and he felt the need to empty it…and soon. Searching for the door that would lead him out of the hall and the keep, Duncan found, not Hamish, but Iain at his side.

"Come, friend. You look to need some air," he said, while guiding his steps down from the dais, through the celebrating crowds, along the corridor and out through the door.

The cool night breezes gave him some ease, but did not clear his head as he'd hoped. And the growing desire to touch Mara did not lessen, either. He cared not where their path led, so he allowed Iain to guide his steps away from the keep and into the quiet of the village. In a moment or some while later, they stopped.

"She did not come tonight," Iain said.

Duncan looked up and realized they stood before Mara's cottage. No light shone in the window and no sounds could be heard.

"She knew you favored her, yet she did not come as commanded," the laird said. "She was told you wished for her presence at the feast, but she spurned you."

Something was not right here. Part of him, the logical, calm part he relied on, was being pushed back and held at bay by some wild madness within him. His chest hurt and his breathing labored, his muscles trembled and his desire raged stronger by the moment. And the object of that desire lay just behind the door of this cottage.

"Mara is her name, Duncan. Say her name."

Duncan took a step toward the cottage and felt her name on his lips. He just wanted to see her, to hear his name on her lips, to understand the strange and powerful feelings surging through him about her. Looking around, he found himself alone, standing just yards now from her door. The moonlight poured through the trees, dappling the ground at his feet and even the patterns seemed to urge his feet forward. The wind moved through the leaves and once more the voice whispered.

"Just say her name…."

Unable to resist it any longer, her name poured out of him into the dark of the night.

Marian sat up at the sound. More like an animal bellowing in pain than a man speaking, she drew the blankets up around and over Ciara before climbing from the pallet and going to the door. Checking the bar, she knew the door was secure against most dangers, but what lurked outside this night? Grabbing her cloak from a hook, she wrapped it around her shoulders and peered into the darkness through the small, high window.

The light of the nearly full moon made much in the

area around her cottage visible to her, but she did not need light to recognize his voice when he spoke. The MacLerie's man.

"Mara!" he called again, leaning over with his hands on his knees.

Sweet Jesus! He would wake not only Ciara but the entire village if he continued bellowing like a wounded bear. Deciding to take a chance that she could quiet him better face-to-face, she slid the bar up and set it aside. Lifting the latch, she opened the door a bit so she could speak to him.

"Sir Duncan," she whispered. "My daughter sleeps within." Marian stepped out and tugged the door closed behind her. "As does the rest of the village. Can we not speak of what concerns you in the morn?"

He stood up then, rising to his full height that made him tower over her and he strode directly to her. More than anything, she wanted to scamper back in the cottage, close the door, drop the bar and gain any protection that the croft could offer, and she did try. But, he moved too quickly. He blocked the door with his foot, making it impossible for her to close it. His hand slid up the edge of the door, making any thought of keeping him out a hopeless one.

"Please, my daughter…" she began in a whisper. Glancing at the pallet and seeing no movement there, she stepped forward to block his view into her home.

"I need to see you, Mara," he said in a low, gruff voice. "Come out, so I can see you."

He stuttered his words and Marian suspected he was in his cups, but that did not make him less dangerous. But, her choice was clear—her safety or her daughter's—so she released her hold on the door and stepped away. His gaze was hot as it passed over her, from her head to the toes that peeked out from beneath the bottom of her chemise. She tugged her cloak closer around her and walked outside.

Marian could see him out of the corner of her eye and she watched as his hands curled and relaxed, curled and relaxed and then again. He allowed her to walk past him and then he followed where she led—away from where her daughter could see or hear them. She suspected how this would end and she did not want Ciara to witness it. When she reached a small clearing in the trees next to the path, she stopped and turned to face him.

His eyes were wild, but there was a sadness and longing deep inside them that made her heart hurt. Her chest tightened and she found it difficult to take in a breath as she waited for him to do something. When his touch came, the tenderness of it was the true surprise. With only the tip of his finger, he traced the edge of her chin and then her mouth. His hand shook as he did it and her body began to tremble beneath his touch.

"You did not come," he said.

"I could not."

"I wanted you there. I wanted to see you," he whispered, closer now, close enough for her to feel his breath on her face. Then he kissed her neck and the heat of his mouth sent chills through her. Still, she dared not move. "I wanted to taste you."

He lifted her face to his and leaned down until his lips met hers. It was only a moment before the kiss changed from tender to possessive and she lost the ability to think or to move. Now, heat raced through her and centered itself in that place deep inside. He guided her face to one side and she felt his tongue pressing against her lips. Opening her mouth to him, Marian discovered that her limbs lost the ability to support her and she leaned toward him.

When he'd called out her name and told her to come out, she'd been completely prepared to fight or reason him away. Now, though, she was not so certain. He slid his arms around her, touching her stomach, her thighs and then her breasts as he did. Instead of giving her the strength to resist, the caresses excited her, making the place between her legs throb in some unrecognizable way.

Was this passion then? Was this what made men lose their minds and what brought clans to war?

That thought cleared her senses and she dragged her mouth from his, drawing in several ragged breaths.

"We must not do this, Sir Duncan," she said, hoping he could still see reason in the muddle of the desire.

"I willna hurt ye, lass," he whispered, kissing her softly once more. His arms loosened not their hold on her and his hands never stopped their teasing caresses. "Tell me ye dinna want this and I will walk away." His mouth took hers again in a kiss that filled her with wicked thoughts of the act to come.

Though she doubted his ability to do that, Marian was more shocked in that she did not want him to walk away. She wanted to feel the rest of the passion that a man and woman shared, a passion she knew was not meant to be for her. He wanted her now, the proof of his desires stood hard between them and he rubbed it against her belly even as her own body readied itself for him. Her breasts felt heavy and the tips of them tingled and tightened beneath her chemise. He drew back this time and watched her mouth, waiting for the word she would speak…the word she wanted to say.

She would never remember how it happened, for in the next instant everything changed. Marian never spoke the word, for he stumbled and fell against her, taking her down to the ground beneath him. Tangled in her chemise and cloak and still wrapped in his arms, she could not protect herself in the fall. His dead weight landed on her, forcing the breath from her body, but it was the unseen rock under her head that took her senses away.

Chapter Six

He'd seen a man's head shatter once in battle, the force of an ax crushed the skull and everything inside it poured out in a bloody gush. Duncan thought that must be happening to his own head at this moment for the pain was so strong, it made him want to vomit. His guts heaved and he rolled to his side and let it happen. Truth be told, he had no choice in it. When his stomach calmed, he climbed to his feet.

And found himself surrounded by Robertson and MacLerie men carrying torches. None looked happy as he would have expected after such a feast. And no one met his gaze, staring instead at something on the ground next to him. Pushing his hair back out of his face, he rubbed his eyes to clear them and turned to see what they were staring at.

Mara lay on the ground, in only her chemise, not moving. Her garment was hiked up nearly to her waist and pulled down as well, exposing her legs, arms and most of her breasts to those watching. Her cloak lay in a heap next to her, so he quickly leaned over and placed it over her. He paid a dear price for such quick movement, too.

"Mara?" he said, touching her cheek. She breathed but did not move. "Mara, you must wake up." This time he tapped gently on her face and her eyes began to move under their lids.

"Get away from her, MacLerie," Iain shouted as he approached, dragging Duncan from his place next to her and nearly throwing him to some of the waiting Robertsons. "Have you not done enough to her?"

In addition to the pain that circled and crushed his head, a thick fog of confusion filled his thoughts. He could not remember most of the feast, could not remember leaving the keep or coming here. And he most certainly did not remember seeing or doing anything to Mara. He held his head in his hands and tried to bring forth memories of what had happened here, between them. There was only darkness in his head.

"I…I…" he stuttered out. He could give no explanation for he had none. Hamish stood across from him, arms crossed over his chest, in the wide stance of a warrior and Duncan knew he was in no danger, but that did not help matters.

Turning, he watched as Iain helped Mara to her feet and spoke words only she could hear. She kept touching the back of her head as though hurt there. And she never looked at him or any of the other men while the hushed conversation took place. A few moments later, Iain confronted him.

"You have dishonored my sister, MacLerie. I expect that you will make things right."

Nothing could have shocked him more. Mara would not meet his gaze so he could find no truth there. The grumbling among the men grew louder until Iain stopped it with a shout.

"This is Marian Robertson, my sister and the only daughter of Stout Duncan," Iain declared. "And you have dishonored her."

"Ye canna dishonor a whore," one of Duncan's men shouted in reply and then he spit on the ground. It had taken such a short time for them to make the connection and identify the woman who stood trembling before them—disheveled and half-naked. But, 'twas a challenge to be sure.

It was only another moment before chaos reigned in the small clearing. Duncan had no sword, but he pushed his way through the men to reach her. He needed to know what had happened. Just as he reached her side, so did her daughter.

Shaking in fear, Ciara cried out for her mother and clutched at her even as Mara, Marian, wobbled precariously. Duncan watched as she tried to shield the girl from the fighting with her own body. Duncan reached out to get them both out of the way of fists and swords, when Iain's shout stopped them all.

But it was Iain's expression that was more shocking than even this situation for he'd lost all color in his face and just stared at Ciara as though seeing someone long dead.

"Order your men to stand down, MacLerie," he said on a ragged breath. "We will handle this at the keep in the light of day and not out in the shadows of night."

With a nod, he gave the order; a nod that made his

head pound even more, reminding him of all he could not remember.

"Marian, get inside and take the child with you," Iain ordered.

She glanced at him then and he saw not guilt or anger there but pity. Leaning down she took Ciara by the hand and guided her back inside the cottage. He heard the bar drop into place and waited.

"Escort *the Peacemaker* to his chambers and place a guard," Iain said.

He would have answered both the threat and the insult, for it could not be missed in the tone or words of the laird, but Duncan realized there were too many gaps in his knowledge right now. He needed to be clear-headed before he could answer the charges made tonight or find a way out of the dilemma in which he now stood. One thing was obvious—Marian was deeply involved.

"And place one at her door as well," Duncan said, not demanding but making it plain to everyone there that he wanted her protected through whatever happened. And he could not be certain from which direction danger could come.

"Very well," Iain accepted with a nod of his head.

Duncan allowed himself to be escorted to a horse and back through the village to the keep. With the way his head swam and the pain and nausea kept threatening to overwhelm him, he had no choice really. Hamish would make his way to Duncan's chambers as soon as he got the men organized and under control. He knew which of the men had called out the insult and he would be apprised of his error. An error that should never have happened.

Like so many other occurrences that night.

* * *

Morning did not dawn bright the next day, but the rain and thunder seemed more appropriate than a shining sun would have. Word spread throughout the village and keep of the incident and every man and woman waited for the outcome. Hamish appeared at his door, but it took some wrangling before he was permitted to see Duncan.

"They were as shocked as we at finding out who she is," Hamish admitted as he closed the door behind him. "The laird only agreed to allow her back after his da passed and only on the condition that she live a proper life with the child."

"Ranald did not tell me of her."

"Chances are Ranald didna know the truth. Verra few did."

Duncan walked over to the tray of food that had been delivered to him and tore off a piece of bread, the only thing his stomach could tolerate this morn. The pain in his head was not so raw now, but the remnants were strong enough to threaten to return at any moment…which led him to believe…

"I was drugged," he said in a voice soft enough not to be heard by guards listening at his door. "At the feast."

"Drugged, ye say?"

"I have a tolerance for drinking, Hamish. Even you have lamented about how much I can drink and still stand," he began.

"Ye are the only mon I know who doesna piss down his legs by the end of a night's revelries, Duncan," Hamish complimented.

"But last evening, I could not stand or walk without help. Without the laird's help." Duncan had been sorting through what he could remember. "He offered me some special mead, but I remember now that he did not drink it."

"And we were all distracted at the same time," Hamish added. "I tried to signal ye."

Duncan remembered the cough, but also remembered not being able to respond to it due to the confusion and the single-minded focus in his thoughts at that moment—Mara. Marian. He sat down on the bed and chewed another bit of bread.

Marian Robertson. The Robertson Harlot.

"I need to speak to her," he declared. She was the only clearheaded one present last eve who could tell him, reassure him, that he had not harmed her. He would not believe himself capable of such a thing, but since he had no memory of the events after he'd begun drinking, she was the only one who could confirm his behavior.

"The laird said you were not to leave this chamber until he called for you." Hamish stood then and touched his hand to the place where his sword should be. "And we have been denied the freedom of movement for now."

"To make certain we do not upset his plans before they're finished," he said.

Now that the drug was wearing off, he could think again. When he examined the last few days here, he could see some of the strands of the web being woven around him. Whether Marian was part of it or at its center mattered not, she was another of the strands. He would wait until the laird revealed his plan before condemning her.

"Has he sent word to Connor?"

"Nay. I wanted to send Tavis off last night, but he said to wait," Hamish said.

"If he'd been surprised by this, he'd have sent off to Connor straightaway. Nay, Hamish, this reeks of plotting."

Duncan walked to the small window in his chamber and opened the wooden shutters to peer out into the small yard beneath it. He preferred the air to flow in, regardless of the rain or wind. Breathing in deeply, he knew there was more yet to come.

"What will ye do, Duncan?"

"Wait to hear the offer."

"What offer?" When Duncan offered a grim smile, Hamish nodded. "Ah, the one that includes marriage to his whore of a sister?"

"Did you consider that there could be certain benefits from such a wife as that?" Duncan asked of the only person he could ask such a question.

Hamish snorted in reply. Duncan tried to make light of the stories they'd heard since he kenned that the reputation did not fit the woman he knew. He suspected that even more of it was just bluster to avert attention and the truth. The words now offered insult to the woman he knew would be his bride. And until he discovered the truths that stood hidden from him, he must stop such conjecture.

"I'd prefer not to hear my betrothed wife called that particular name, Hamish. Tell the men."

"So ye are resigned to it wi'oot an offer being made then?" Hamish walked over and smacked him on the back. "Is there no way oot then?"

Duncan thought about it, but the situation was clear in his mind even when many things still remained muddled. The drinking, the drugging, the helping him to her door, the convenient discovery of them lying together. Iain had marriage between Duncan and Iain's sister in mind and the only way out without a bride was to leave Dunalastair without a treaty between their clans. Everyone involved, including Duncan, kenned that leaving without such an agreement was an unacceptable ending to this charade.

The Peacemaker was gaining a wife even as the clans gained their alliance of power and property.

'Twas midmorning when the knock came at her door. She'd removed the bar early to give the guard some food and had yet to replace it. She feared no intruders this morn, even if there had been no guard. Marian tugged the door open and found Iain there. Stepping back, she gave him room to enter. And she allowed herself to savor the look of him while he walked into the cottage.

Other than passing by on his way through the village or a chance appearance, she'd not seen or spoken to her brother since the day she returned. And even that had been with others present where all pretenses had to be kept up. Now, she was alone with him for the first time in more than five years. Well, almost alone.

Iain stood watching Ciara at play for a few minutes before turning to her. His eyes glimmered with unshed tears and she knew he, too, had been thinking of the past. He held out his arms to her and Marian ran into his embrace. They hugged for what must have been hours and she found that, when he released her, it had not been long enough. It would never be long enough for two siblings who had once been so close. Iain took a few steps away and looked at her.

"How does your head fare this morn?"

Marian reached up and touched the robin's egg–size bump on the back of her head. "It hurts," she admitted. She was in no mood to soften the truth.

"I can have Margret bring something to ease it," he offered.

That was when she realized what she'd tasted in Duncan's kiss. It was a potion that the cook at the keep made to ease pain, especially head pains. She'd taken it before, even grew some of the herbs used in it. Now, his behavior made sense.

"And what did you use to mask the taste of it? The honey mead that Old Innis brews for you?" she asked without hesitation. Would he lie to her or answer in truth.

"The mead's hearty taste masks it well, I think."

Marian closed her eyes and shook her head. Iain had staged the whole incident. "Why, Iain? Just tell me why?" Opening her eyes, she lowered her voice so that Ciara's attention would not be drawn to them. "Have I not paid a high enough price in these last five years? I have kept my promises to you."

And she had—living quietly, not drawing attention to herself or her daughter. For five years, but especially since returning to Dunalastair these last two. She'd even changed her appearance so she would evoke no memories of the Robertson Harlot in the villagers who saw her or in her family.

"I do this for you, Marian. This is not a punishment."

"You would marry me off to a man whose honor you have smeared. You would make the whole treaty contingent on his acceptance of the Robertson Harlot. And I am certain that part of this will force him to take me with him and not allow us to live apart."

Iain approached and took her hands in his. "Aye to all of that. But, he *is* an honorable man, Marian. And he *is* attracted to you. I do not think he is capable of mistreating you. Given a chance, I think you could find happiness with him."

"Attracted, Iain? Present a drunken, drugged man with a half-naked woman in the middle of the night after his lust has been stirred." She ignored his raised brow and continued, "And true attraction has little to do with it."

She crossed her arms over her chest, trying to resist the memories of her own weakness toward Duncan and the attraction she felt for him. No matter, she'd accepted that the temptation he presented to her and her empty life had been only that. Now, she was a burden to be borne by him and she had no doubt that any attraction was gone.

"He lives by his honor, Iain. He lives and breathes it. His success for his clan and his laird are based on it. Now, you give him no choice but to take me or face ruin and failure."

She watched as Iain changed before her eyes into someone resembling their father. He stood tall and took a deep breath and then spoke. "I am laird here, Marian, and this is my decision. You will marry him."

When he was in such a mood, he was inordinately stubborn and immovable in his decisions or opinions.

But, she'd been in tougher situations before and had learned he was not the only one in their family with nerves of steel.

"A handfasting," she said.

"Marriage with the Church's blessing, Marian."

"A handfasting with a dowry to be held by his laird," she insisted, crossing her arms and straightening her stance.

"Marriage with his laird holding your dowry," he countered.

"Handfasting or nothing, Iain. I will not consent to a marriage."

"Are you daft that you would spurn an honest marriage for a temporary bonding that ends in a year-and-a-day?" Iain stood with his hands on his hips and shook his head at her. "Think of your daughter, Marian."

"I am, Iain. I think only of her protection and her life."

Her words had the desired effect on him. He swallowed and swallowed again before he could speak. "I will also send something to the MacLerie to be held for her."

"How long do I have?" she asked, looking around the small cottage that had sheltered her and trying to determine how long it would take to pack everything she would need for a new life. Considering that the treaty was nearly complete, she kenned she had little time here. With the clues falling into place, she saw the extent of Iain's plan even if he spoke not of such a thing.

"The ceremony will take place this evening and you will leave in the morning."

She gasped at the speed of the arrangements. When she would have argued, he held up his hand and shook his head.

"Take only the clothing you need for the two of you. Everything else will be packed and sent to you."

"But, Iain. My plants. The garden," she began.

"Margret will see to them. And, Marian?"

She could not believe Duncan agreed with such speed and wondered at the price paid for it. "Yes?"

"Make arrangements for the child to stay with someone here in the village. Your first night of wedded life will be spent at the keep and it's best for her not to be seen there."

Marian could not find the words to use in argument now that that particular arrangement had been declared, and her thoughts turned to surviving a wedding night with an angry husband. But Iain did not wait on them. He turned and walked to the door, tugging it open. Before he left, he asked one more question.

"Why that color?"

Marian touched her hair, realizing what he meant.

"'Tis the easiest dye to make to cover it. And it seems to straighten the curls as well. More efficient than other things I have tried."

"Come at midafternoon. All will be prepared."

Marian fretted through most of the day, packing things she thought indispensable for the trip and avoiding the emotions and fears she did not wish to face at the moment. The most difficult moment was when she tried to explain to Ciara about the changes coming into their lives. But Ciara did not hesitate in her apprai-

sal or excitement in the plan to go with Sir Duncan and
live in his village for some time. Of course, all the child
could think of was how the journey would be accomplished and she was won over by the horse alone.

If it were only that simple to put her mind at ease
over the coming days and the thought of being under
the control of a man who did not want to be married,
or even handfasted, to her. She tried to convince herself
that she truly did not fear him, for he had been kind to
her daughter when there was no need to be so.

Indeed he seemed to be a man who was not driven
by his emotions and he would understand the situation
better than she. So, even if he wished to bed her, she
could not believe he would be ruled by any anger he felt.
At least, that was the basic plea in the prayer she offered
in that scant second.

Marian made arrangements for Ciara to stay with
someone in the village, one of the other young women
who had a daughter, and walked to the keep. Just before
she reached the gate, she turned to take a final look
around. She'd grown up here and faced disgrace here.
She'd returned thinking she would live here and raise
her daughter, but now everything she'd hoped for and
dreamed of was changed.

Once their year-long commitment was finished, she
would take the money Iain was sending and leave to
find another place to live with Ciara. One where they
did not know of Marian Robertson, the Harlot. One
where she might find some measure of happiness. One
where her own dreams of a husband and more children
might happen.

First, though, she must face this battle and tie

herself to a man who did not want her. Then she must live a year under his control. Only then could she be free of her past. Taking a deep breath, she walked into the keep, where she had not been in more than five years and faced the man her brother had bribed into marrying her.

Chapter Seven

Duncan stood by the dais and waited for her arrival. Word passed through the keep some time ago that she'd arrived, but he'd still not seen her. His men stood at his side, all except Tavis who readied their supplies and horses for traveling on the morrow. The pain in his head lessened to a bearable level and he'd ordered his men to watch their drink this night. Although this was akin to hobbling a horse after it had escaped, his warning was clear.

A few servants came and went, each one staring at him as they passed, but still no Marian. Finally he saw her standing at the stairway that led to the solar. He was about to go to her when Iain appeared at her side and escorted her forward. The laird had ordered the hall to be cleared, wanting the ceremony to be no spectacle, though Duncan suspected the reports of last night had proved spectacle enough.

He nodded and his men stood with him waiting and watching her approach. Each time he saw her, he noticed something different about her and this time she wore a new tunic and gown, one befitting the daughter and sister of the laird. Her long hair was braided back off her face, revealing high cheekbones and pale cheeks. Her appearance today reminded him that she was above his station and he'd only gained an heiress because her brother needed it to be so.

Did she ken that? Did she know the wealth that was hers by inheritance from her mother and father? She could not have and still have lived such a meager life in the village as she did. Marian would probably be shocked to find out the extent of her value. But would she feel resentful when she learned of his lack of it? Iain drew her to a stop and Duncan bowed before her.

"Lady Marian, how do you fare?" he asked, but she did not reply. He repeated his question with no more success than the first time. Iain shook her hand and she finally met his gaze.

"He is speaking to you, Marian." Iain motioned to Duncan.

"I am well, Sir Duncan," she answered in a soft voice, sounding not the least bit well. "And you?" she asked back.

Duncan could not play this game with her. He needed to speak to her, speak bluntly to her and set things aright before the ceremony and certainly before they shared the bed already prepared above for them. But things needed to be done first.

"Lady, may I make known my men to you?" he asked as he took her hand from Iain's and turned her to face them.

Duncan took his time introducing each of them to her, for they would be her escorts and protection on their journey back across Scotland to Lairig Dubh. And they were the first of the MacLeries she would meet. Iain stepped forward once he'd finished, but Duncan held her hand.

"I would speak to Marian before the ceremony, Iain," he said. It was not a request.

"You may use Struan's chamber there," he said, pointing at a door off to the side of the hall.

He led Marian away from the group and into the small room, closing the door behind him before speaking. He offered her the stool that sat next to Struan's table, but she shook her head. Having never faced this situation, he was at a loss as to where to begin until he looked at her face.

"Truly, Marian, how do you feel? You injured your head last night?" He remembered seeing her touch it several times while talking with Iain.

"It hurts," she answered plainly.

"As does mine," he replied.

"He drugged you last night."

He'd suspected but now had the truth of it. "And I remember nothing, except that we were found together on the ground." Other bits and pieces involving his attack on her were creeping back into place, but he did not want to concentrate on those now.

"Did I…?" The words tumbled out before he could stop them. He watched her now and waited on word of how bad his behavior had been to her.

"You did not…." she began. Then her face filled with a blush as though such talk embarrassed her. After taking in a deep breath, she shook her head at him.

"'Twas as though you were in your cups. Your words

slurred and then you stumbled and fell on me. 'Twas how we ended up as we were found, I think."

"You do not know?" he asked.

"I hit my head as we fell. If there was anything else, I slept through it."

She had not meant to be humorous but he took it that way. God help him if a woman could sleep as he swived her. Duncan smiled at her then and shrugged. "That has not been a complaint of women in the past." He walked to the far wall of the room and stood watching her reaction.

"I did not know what he planned, Sir Duncan. Truly," she said.

"But I have dishonored you and this is the right outcome of such an act." The correct words flowed smoothly, but they both knew them for the lie they were.

"One of your men had the right of it—you cannot dishonor a wh…" He was at her side, covering her mouth to stop the rest of it before she could finish.

"Is that why you did not demand marriage as any woman in your situation would have? The daughter and sister to a laird such as you should demand more than a simple handfasting." He felt anger on her behalf. Even if this was convenient to her brother's or to her own plans, she should demand marriage.

"You did nothing last night, Sir Duncan. Other than being clumsy and I dare not think that deserves to be punished by being forced into an unwanted marriage." She slid her hands down her gown, smoothing some unseen wrinkles as she said it.

"I am not being forced into this union, Lady Marian," he asserted. There were ways of being forced and then there were ways.

She laughed then for only a moment or two and then peered at him. "I appreciate your chivalry and I am trying to return the favor to you by not binding you to me for the rest of your life or mine. A handfasting accomplishes what my brother and your honor demand, but with an end in sight."

"And at the end of our year together?" he asked, wanting to know what she thought of what was to come between them.

"If either of us wants an end to it, it ends. If there is a child or children, you have the right to decide their fates."

The words were spoken with a complete lack of passion, but that lack made them all the more tense. Duncan pressed on, so that there would be no surprises between them.

"So you will share my bed then?"

She blushed then and Duncan was glad of it. Harlot she might have been, but she did not seem to cast her favors about freely. "If you wish it," she whispered.

Better to make his wishes clear now. "Mine is the only bed I wish you to share during our year together." If the words seemed harsh, so be it. A fool he might have been for not seeing the plot going on around him, but the horns of a cuckold he would not wear for any woman.

"I would never dishonor you so, sir."

"Then we are agreed. But one thing plagues me from last night." Short glimpses of their encounter raced through his mind and he thought he remembered the taste of her mouth and the heat of her skin under his touch. "Did not anything of a…personal nature happen between us? I would like to know if it did."

"A few kisses. A caress here and there," she answered as the red blush spread up higher and deeper on her cheeks. "Nothing more," she added, unable to meet his gaze.

Suddenly images of a woman shot through his mind, one trembling beneath his touch, touching her mouth to his as they kissed, his tongue moving deeply in her mouth, imitating the joining he wanted to happen. Heat pulsed through him as he remembered a kiss and then another and then the feel of her breasts, heavy in his hands as he thrust his hardness against her hip.

Did he dare to kiss her and discover if the images matched the truth of her?

Leaning in closer, he touched his mouth to hers gently. 'Twas like the scene in his memories, for she opened her mouth to his and he swept his tongue in to taste her once more. He did not touch her elsewhere, only their mouths were joined as he sampled her softness and thought on the coming night.

When the door opened, it startled both from their thoughts, from their guilty thoughts if their reactions were any indications and from the kiss that they shared. Iain held out his hand to her and said that the priest waited outside to perform the ceremony.

Well, the good thing was that she did not seem hesitant about sharing his bed. And she'd placed no demands on him. He should feel good about that, but it bothered him that she expected so little of him. He grabbed her hand and pulled her back to him before they reached the door.

"And what do you expect from me during this bonding, lady? Surely you have some demand or request of me?"

Her expression emptied as though she'd not thought on it even in passing. Then she nodded and whispered her answer to him so that her brother could not hear it.

"I would ask that you not beat me or my daughter, sir."

Such a simple statement, he could not take it in, for it spoke so much about her life these last years. He'd been correct in his assessment of her and in what he'd told Hamish. She knew not of her value having lived with the humiliation of her sins for so long that nothing else mattered in her mind.

But when she could, she asked for nothing more than the consideration a man would give the beasts that labored for him in his fields. She asked not for happiness, nor the comforts her wealth could afford, nor anything personal to ease her way or her life…nor for love or tenderness a new bride might expect or hope for. She asked only not to be beaten.

Duncan had been feeling sorry for himself, being lured or manipulated into this union for the purposes of others and had never actually thought about what she wanted. And now, now that she had spoken of her needs, he felt like the meanest bastard and offered her what she needed to hear this moment.

"You have my word, Marian. I will never raise my hand against you or Ciara."

Reassured, she met his gaze and gifted him with a smile then and he followed them into the hall.

Marian signed the documents when they were placed before her, not reading them though she could read Latin. She admired the way her brother accomplished things when he set his mind to a task. The contracts drawn up in just a day, bags of gold and deeds to various lands exchanged, a completed treaty establishing an alliance between their two clans, a priest called to witness the handfasting (though none was needed to do so), and even a new gown and tunic for her to wear.

If only he'd been this efficient on that night so long ago, all of this would be unnecessary now.

Now she sat naked under the sheets of a freshly made bed, waiting for the man she would live with and be wife to for the next year-and-a-day. There would be no actual bedding ceremony, but the priest would come to bless the bed and pronounce that any child conceived here or in the coming days was part of a legal union. Marian shivered, partly from the chill in the room and partly from what she knew was about to happen between them.

When the door opened and Duncan walked in, followed by his man Hamish and her brother, she slid down farther under the blankets. Duncan tugged his shirt off over his head and then loosened his belt, allowing the length of plaid he wore to drop to the floor. He did not hurry as he climbed into the bed, allowing her a glimpse of his muscular back and legs before sliding under the sheets and touching her bare leg with his.

'Twas a reminder of the intimacy yet to happen between them. Once he sat next to her, the priest entered carrying the strips of tartan wool that had marked their joining before the witnesses in the hall. Instead of reaching across her to join hands as he had before, he placed his arm around her shoulder and held her hand. His heat surrounded her, made even more complete by the way he tucked her closer to him, his naked skin touching hers from her shoulders down to her feet.

"You have declared yourselves husband and wife before witnesses," he said as he tied the strips of wool around their wrists. "And you shall live as man and wife before God and his Church."

He dipped his fingers into a bowl carried by her brother and sprinkled it on them and on the bed around them. "May you be fruitful in this the Lord's work and in this union." Another dip into the holy water and this time he marked their heads and their hearts and their hands with a sign of the cross. "May this union bring forth children for the Lord's honor and glory. May He bless you as He blesses all his faithful…."

Marian lost track of the blessings and the holy water, but soon it was over and she sat alone, naked with her husband in a bed. Looking down at their hands, fingers entwined and wrists tied together with the plaid patterns of their clans, she waited. The heat grew between them and she would have shimmied away to give him more room but their wrists remained tied together and his arm held her close.

"Should we take these off?" he asked before untying the plaids. He tossed them aside and then let her hand drop to the covers.

Marian thought that the less she tried to say, the better things would be. She was certain he thought her a brainless fool when she asked him not to beat her, but it truly was smarter than saying anything else to him just then. The rest of the truth behind their union had yet to be revealed and his promise not to raise his hand to her might be his one regret.

"Can we put out the candles?" she asked.

He nodded wordlessly and turned over to blow out

the one on the table next to the bed. Climbing out, he continued moving around the room until all the lights had been extinguished. But, the moonlight that lit the cloudless sky outside and poured in through the large glazed window in the chamber, illuminated his very masculine form before her. Marian knew some of him by feel after last night's encounter, but her mouth went dry when faced with the raw power of his naked body.

Surely now that they both understood their places in this arrangement, their joining would simply be to mark their promise and nothing more complex. Certain that he had the experience and knowledge to make it so, she waited for his approach.

Duncan slid back next to her and slipped one of his arms around her again, gathering her close to him. He entwined the fingers of their right hands together, joining them more assuredly than the wool ever had. A tremble or shiver passed through her at his heat, but her body responded as it did the night before…when she never got out the word she wanted to say. But, it remembered and it prepared for his possession, even as she tried to convince herself that this joining would be nothing more than to mark their vows.

Lifting her chin so that he could touch his mouth to hers, Duncan kissed her again, much like the two earlier kisses, simply exploring her mouth with his, readying her for more. She let him lead, opening when he teased, touching when he offered his tongue to hers, tasting and breathing in his taste and his scent.

"Now that I remember from last night. Your mouth was hot when I kissed you then, too," he whispered to her.

When his other hand began to explore her skin and

touched the sides of her breasts, she could not help arching toward him and his touch. His mouth became insistent, his kisses deeper and longer, making her breathless but anxious for the next one and the next one and the next. His fingers teased the tips of her breasts, rolling and squeezing them on one then the other, until they tightened into sensitive peaks that ached for more. Then he soothed them with a touch of his tongue.

Every part of her, whether touched yet or not, ached for him. She felt a wetness gather between her legs and a throbbing deep within. 'Twas when his mouth moved from hers and took one of those taut peaks between his lips and then suckled it that the scream tore free from her.

"Ah, Marian. Softly now," he pleaded, but thankfully he did not stop his actions. "'Twould be unsettling to have your brother seek the reason for your cry now."

She promised him something, what she knew not for all pretenses of wanting or carrying out a sensible joining had fled from her. What words she spoke were the right thing, for he moved back to lick and suckle her breasts again. Although he still held her right hand in his, she reached up and, with her fingers sliding through his hair, held his head close and gave him no choice but to continue his caresses and kisses.

She would have said yes last night. She knew now she would have said yes and, if given the chance to have him touch and tease like this, she would have begged for him to take her, there on the ground next to her cottage. She did not say it last night, but she said it now, begging for something more and he laughed and obeyed her command.

Still using only one hand, Duncan slid it over her sweat-slicked skin on a path that led down under the sheets. Marian could not see her legs or the place between them, but she could feel it. Something like a craving grew there and as his hand moved closer, her thighs fell open for his touch. Just before his finger entered the nest of curls there, he took her mouth once more.

Sliding one finger then two into the wet crevice there, he opened her even more and then rubbed between the folds, creating such a lovely friction and soothing it with each stroke until she thought her breath was gone from her body.

Arching against his fingers, her body trembled until he slid one leg over her thighs trapping her legs under his so that he could continue his arousing assault there. Finally he released her hand and she slid it into his hair and pulled his mouth even closer, breathing in his own breath, sucking on his tongue when he teased hers.

The tension within her grew with every touch, every stroke, and every kiss until she could feel the power of it begin to unfurl deep inside. When he found that small bud between her engorged folds, she keened out as her release crashed over her. With his hand still stroking her, he climbed over her, spread her legs even wider and then he positioned the head of his erection at the opening to her core.

She watched as though outside herself as he filled her woman's core even to her womb with one thrust.

One thrust that pierced her maidenhead.

One thrust that brought on his release.

One thrust that made everything different.

Marian watched through the fog of passion as the truth hit him and prayed he would remember his promise.

Chapter Eight

The sounds of the keep coming to life, though softened high up in the tower as this chamber was, wakened her and Marian pushed the hair from her face and slid back against the pillows of the bed. She could not remember sleeping so deeply before, but it had been years since she'd spent the night in such a comfortable bed as this. The events of the night before came flooding back and she looked around the chamber for any sign of Duncan.

He was gone.

Sunlight streamed in through her brother's expensive glazed window, warming and invigorating her, but nothing would remove the chill in her heart from the last expression on her new husband's face as he realized she'd come to his bed a maid and not the harlot he thought. Indeed, most men would be thankful for such a revelation. Duncan the Peacemaker was not most men.

Marian stretched her arms and legs and thought about getting dressed, but she had no gowns here in this chamber. Only a dressing robe that lay at the foot of the bed. Duncan would be leaving this morn, her brother told her. The treaty successfully negotiated and signed, Duncan could return to his laird with the glad tidings of another peace made.

She began to slide her legs out from under the covers when the burning in that place between them reminded her of the other bargain made and the yet uncertain outcome from it. Did she remain here, a woman joined yet not quite married? Did she go with him? Had he gone to repudiate the arrangements with her brother? If he'd bargained for the Harlot as wife, did her being a maid change it all?

She could not abide this uncertainty, so Marian decided to find some clothing, seek out Duncan or her brother and discover what the nature of their union was to be now that he knew he'd been deceived. He'd kept his word and not struck her when he found out the truth, indeed, his reaction had been surprising.

He'd knelt over her, staring wildly at her face as he realized that he had pushed through her maidenhead with his thrust. Withdrawing even while his seed still poured forth, he climbed off her and the bed and walked to the table. A basin and some washing cloths lay there and he used one to clean the blood and seed off himself. Turning back to her, he had approached with another cloth for her use. Confused and embarrassed at her exposure before him, she quickly wiped herself and handed him back the cloth.

Marian had pulled the sheets back over her and watched as he grabbed his shirt off the floor and pulled it over his head. Then he sat down on the chair in the corner, next to the hearth and simply stared into the darkened chamber. Marian had watched him, wary of his reaction to the truth of her condition, until she'd fallen asleep an hour or two later.

Neither had spoken a word and she had no idea of how things stood between them. But, 'twas time to find out. With her robe wrapped tightly around her, Marian stepped from the chamber and sought out the servants. They would know where she could find her bag.

And found herself facing her husband.

"Come, I have clothing for you," he said as he reached past her and opened the chamber door. Once inside, he closed it and dropped the latch. "I only just realized that you were trapped here since your bag was packed away."

He strived for sounding practical and wondered if he'd been successful, for the sight of her wearing only that robe made it near impossible not to think about how she looked like and felt like beneath it. He inhaled her scent as he passed her and in that instant he could once more smell the musky aroma of her arousal as she'd fallen to pieces in his arms.

He'd been a fool not to recognize that she was a virgin. But, truth be told, the sights and sounds of the night before when he was drunk and drugged had flooded his mind and all he wanted to was hear the wonderful sighs she made as he touched her again…and kissed her again…and… 'Twas no wonder he'd spilled his seed with barely one thrust into her heat.

Shaking himself free of the stimulating images pouring through his thoughts and focusing on the gown and tunic and stockings found in her bag, he moved across the room and placed them on the bed. If he examined his state of mind, he would confess to still being in shock over the events of these last three days and nights, but there were things to be done, and traveling to begin, so he had little time to dwell on them.

In spite of a whole night spent sitting and trying to think this through, he found himself no closer to understanding this and all his turning and twisting of the situation in his head had yielded him nothing except more questions. The woman he thought to be a pawn in her brother's game turned out to be a more valuable piece than anyone knew or could admit. And though he could believe she had no part in drugging him or guiding his feet to her cottage, the thin maidenhead he'd pierced so carelessly and without warning spoke of her involvement on so many other levels.

"There is time before we leave to break your fast in the hall or I can have a tray sent up to you if you would prefer," he offered.

Now she wore the shocked expression, stopping with her hand out between them as she reached for her garments.

"I was not certain of your plans," she said in a shaky voice. "After…" She glanced at the bed, her meaning extremely clear.

"Nothing has changed," he answered abruptly, for what could he say? "The treaty has been signed, the requirements met on all levels and my task here is done. 'Tis time to return to my clan."

"And me?" she asked without meeting his eyes. "What about me?"

He would rather have this sorted out sooner than later, so he motioned for her to dress and he gave her his back for privacy. "I have spent most of the night trying to figure out your role in your brother's endeavors and have gotten nowhere. Are you his pawn or his queen?" he asked, almost rhetorically.

"More likely his bishop, guarding his queen," she answered.

Not expecting an answer, and not an answer that revealed more than she probably wished to, he turned at her words. "You play the game, then? And understand the moves?" Duncan averted his eyes as she finished pulling on the chemise, gown and tunic over her head.

"I play chess, sir, if that is what you are speaking of. Though I have not for years, I expect that I could regain my skills with some measure of practice."

Another surprise, but then she was the daughter of a powerful Scottish laird who would have seen to her education—an education that would have included reading, writing, languages, even some amount of mathematics and the skills needed to run a large keep or castle and its people.

"And his other game, lady? What part do you play in that?"

She grew silent at that question, not answering him immediately. "If you speak to him about what you discovered, I am certain he will make arrangements for me elsewhere," she offered in a whispered voice. Defeat filled it and he wondered at the reasons why she was her brother's accomplice.

"Am I simply your means of escape then?" he asked, trying to understand the players and the game.

"Nay, you misunderstand," she said softly. "I knew not of his plans to draw you into this…." She seemed to search for a word, but could not find the correct one.

He reached out and took her by the shoulders to make her face him. "Did your brother know I would find you a maid when I took you to my bed?"

A frown flitted over her features, darkening her eyes for a moment and then she shrugged under his hands. "He had to expect it. I have lived under scrutiny for more than five years and he knows of any possible transgressions or the lack of them."

"So, whether I married you to remedy the publicly staged dishonor after the feast or now that I have claimed the maidenhead of a clearly virtuous woman, the result is still the same—I have you to wife. Something your brother plainly desires. The question plaguing me is why."

The question that truly plagued him was another and yet unspoken, but it could not remain so. 'Twas so obvious and such an integral part of this whole scenario he thought that she might be honest with him over it.

"Who is Ciara?" he said softly while observing her face for any changes.

And change it did, taking on a defensive expression that hardened her eyes and pressed her lips into a tight line instead of the full ones he kissed so ravenously just a few hours earlier.

"She is my daughter." She pulled from his hold and stepped away to finish dressing, apparently of the belief that her answer was enough.

"Since I was the first man inside you, pardon my vulgarity for pointing it out, my lady, there is no doubt that you did not give birth to Ciara."

Marian crossed her arms over her chest and lowered her chin, into a fighting position whether she realized it or not, and repeated her answer. "She is my daughter."

Hearing noises outside the chamber that indicated they would have to share the corridors and hall with servants and others as the keep stirred to life, he needed to finish this. Leaning in close, he spoke quietly so only she could hear his words.

"Tell me how she became your daughter, Marian. Tell me the truth."

The tension filled the small space between them and he grew aware of her anxious breathing and the beads of sweat that trickled from her hairline, down the edge of her face to her neck. The minute stretched on and on until 'twas clear she would favor him not with an answer. He let out his breath with a sigh.

"So be it then. You trust me not and I trust you not. At least I know the situation between us."

He reached past her for the two strips of wool that had bound their hands and their lives together and took his sgian-dubh from its place on his leg. Slicing the inside of his lower arm, he let the blood trickle out and splashed it on the blanket, the sheets and even the floor, in a path that led to the table. It completely covered the small shadow hers had left in the center of the bed.

She gasped at his actions and reached out to stop him. He waved her off and wiped the blade clean with one of the pieces of wool, before sliding it back in its scabbard. Then he wound one piece around his arm, over the cut, and then followed it with the other which he tied tightly to bind the wound.

"I apologized to your brother for the blood already. A clumsy accident with my dagger that splattered it on the bed and the floor."

Now it was her turn to ask the questions. "Why?"

"I am the Peacemaker," he said, as he crossed his arms and his eyes took on a chilling expression. "I will do whatever is necessary to protect the interests of my clan and my laird. If it was shown that you were brought to my bed a virgin, it would call your father's and even your brother's honor into question. The agreements would fall as would the alliance, all because of my need to proclaim the truth that I had been wronged. And that is something I will not do."

"All for your clan?" she asked.

"Aye. And for that reason, I will discover the truth that you are all working so hard to keep hidden. I will not let you endanger this alliance or endanger my clan in any way because of whatever you hold close and speak not of. And, until you speak the truth of this to me, I will not trust you."

Marian could not help the shiver that ran through her at his cold pronouncement, nor could she tell him what he asked. Too many lives had been lost, too precious a price had already been paid to keep the past behind them. And if it took one more year of her life before she could slip away and live unnoticed with her daughter, well then, so be it. She'd survived worse.

He had no way of kenning that she, too, was a peacemaker. Her mother had depended on her to act as mediator and go-between in all the family battles. Her father expected more—he'd expected her to bear the cost of the sins of others in order to keep the peace and, in respect for the promise given to her mother as she died, she did so.

A call from the corridor broke into the tense moment between them and interrupted their uncomfortable stalemate. Duncan stepped away to open the door and Marian found herself with nothing to do or say. Truly, all she wanted to do was to go to Ciara and hold her close. There was too much swirling around them here, too much of the past still walked these corridors, and she wanted to be away from here as soon as possible.

"Come," he said. "The men are ready in the yard and we have many miles to cover this day."

Marian found her stomach clenching with each step down the stairs toward the hall and the rest of her family. Other than a tense meal with them after the ceremony, she'd not spoken to any of them in years. Her brothers were grown into men with their own lives, even Padruig was betrothed and she'd heard mention that Iain was in search of a new wife. Her father dead and buried more than two years now, and her mother before that.

Another farewell now would simply tear open old wounds and would do no good to any of them. He must have sensed her turmoil, for Duncan drew to a stop just before they entered the hall.

"Have you changed your mind? Would you rather stay here?" he asked, meeting her gaze directly as though prepared for a repudiation.

"Nay," she said, shaking her head. "I just cannot face them and say farewell…when I know I will not see them again."

Did he understand? Could he? Could anyone? She

felt his perusal and then he nodded at her. Calling to one of his men, he asked Hamish to escort her to the horses while he went to take their leave of the laird and the rest of the Robertsons.

She began to understand how he had the successes he did as a negotiator—he could discern people's motives and needs and concerns with only a look. He evaluated a situation and kenned what needed to be done. He did it without seeming to judge and without calling a person's motives into question, or at least he had not with her.

If this was how he would treat her as his wife, if he extended the loyalty he showed them to her, how could she ever think to keep the truth from him?

Climbing up on the back of the horse that stood waiting for her, she peered through those who stood watching and nodded her head to a few of them. Some had been kind to her. Some remembered her from her childhood. Some had not been so kind. But now, as she rode through the gates toward her daughter and then toward a new life, she tried to leave them and all the other ghosts who still lived here behind her.

Chapter Nine

❦

The first day quickly became an adventure. Leaving the village behind in the morning, seeing the falls from the distance as they trekked into the surrounding hills, pointing out animals and birds, learning each of the men's names—each step kept Ciara's interest in the journey. For certain, the presence of so many different horses helped as well. Although her daughter was more outgoing than she'd ever witnessed, Marian did notice that she rode only with herself or with Duncan.

By the second day, Ciara had quieted and then the third and fourth days found her nearly sullen and withdrawn. Thinking back on their journey to Dunalastair, Marian realized that she'd only been a bairn and probably did not remember much of it at all. And most of that was accomplished in the back of a cart. Now, from the back of one horse or another, it became boring and repetitive no matter how much Marian tried to make a game of it.

If not for Duncan… If not for his inordinate patience

and attention to Ciara, Marian knew that the days would seem much longer than they already did. Although (as she learned from Tavis) he had no close siblings or children of his own, and although (as she learned from Hamish) he was not used to this slow a pace when traveling on the laird's business, and although (this from Farlen) she was lucky that he did the right thing and handfasted with her, she truly was grateful beyond words for the manner in which he made the journey as easy as possible for her daughter. And if he did not converse with her along the way, keeping his attentions on the safety and the roads ahead and even on his own business and if he spent every night only-God-knew-where, then she was fine with it. Truly she was fine with it.

For, other than asking her in a hushed voice after a half-day's travel if she were well, he had said nothing to her at all. All messages and orders were passed on to her by others, even Ciara, or called out to everyone.

This marriage did not begin on solid ground, but Marian hoped that they would be able to live peaceably for their year and then go their separate ways. He was an indispensable man to his clan who traveled much for his laird, so some of the time he would be gone from Lairig Dubh. He was a virile, handsome man who probably had a leman or mistress even though he'd had no wife yet, so that would keep him busy for some of the nights. All she would have to do was keep her promise not to dishonor him and she would be free.

They stopped for a short rest by the side of a large loch and the pleasure of walking made her sigh. Ciara ran around the group as the men prepared a meal for them. 'Twas obvious that they were accustomed to traveling together, for they worked together with a remarkable efficiency whenever they stopped along the road. Whether it be preparing a camp for the night or like this, a short break with a meal, Marian found she got in their way rather than being of assistance.

Searching around the lochside, she noticed that the trees began some distance from the edge. At such a distance, Duncan would insist on escorting them off to handle their personal needs, and giving the men time to see to theirs, but he was deep in conversation with two of the men. Taking Ciara's hand in hers, she stood waiting for him to finish. To keep her daughter busy, she guided her in bigger circles where they stood, which also helped to work out any stiffness in their limbs. A few minutes later, after Farlen returned to his duties and Donald mounted and rode off down the road at a fast pace, Duncan walked to where they waited.

"My pardon for the delay, my ladies," he began. "A moment or two of privacy is probably needed?"

Ciara giggled each time he called them "ladies," but she dropped Marian's hand and ran up to Duncan to allow him to guide her. She guiltily admitted that her daughter's quick acceptance of this man bothered her, yet she would never say it aloud. For these last five years, Marian had been everything to her daughter, but now Duncan stepped into their lives and, truth be told, ruled it. Whether 'twas with the permission of the laws and contracts that bound them or by Ciara's own behavior, he now mattered.

They walked up a hill, through the first line of trees and deeper into the forest, far enough from the loch and the men that they could not be seen or heard easily.

Then, Duncan left them and walked several paces back until they were alone. They finished quickly and walked back to the loch, where she helped Ciara wash her hands and face and where she enjoyed the cool freshness of the water. Duncan spoke not a word until Hamish called to Ciara and she ran off to eat. Then she faced her husband alone for the first time in days.

"In the haste of things, I did not have time to make new arrangements for traveling with you and…your daughter," he said, glancing over to where Ciara stood eating with the men. She noticed the slight hesitation, even if he did not, but chose not to speak of it.

"You and your men are a well-trained team," she said. "I try to stay out of the way."

"We have done this for several years." He stopped and looked at her now. "Riding is not so pleasurable now?"

"I have not ridden in years, so this is a bit too much in such a short time." She stretched then, trying to soothe the ache in her back and her legs before she would need to climb atop her horse again.

"We stop for the night at the MacCallum's keep," he said. "If you would prefer, you could travel by cart from there."

"The MacCallums?" she asked.

"Allies to the MacLeries. Connor's wife, Jocelyn, is a MacCallum."

She nodded her head, now recognizing the name. "You negotiated their marriage agreements."

"Aye, and escorted the bride to her husband," he said. Then the most appealing smile covered his face and he laughed aloud. "Though I am lucky to be alive after that journey."

Another laugh escaped as he remembered something else, but the deep rumble of his laughter eased
something in her own heart. "It does sound as though
you were not in any true danger."

"I will share my side of that story before Jocelyn tells
you hers," he said, holding out his arm to her. "For
now, let us eat and get back on the road, so we can get
there before dark."

She accepted his escort and thought about meeting
his clan's allies this night. Was that where Donald had
gone? To take word of their approach and need for
shelter for the night? Just before they reached the gathering of men and Ciara, he spoke again.

"I am certain that the MacCallum can offer you a hot
bath and a soft bed. Real cooked food and other
comforts, to be sure."

So that was why he was enthusiastic about stopping
this night. A bed…a bedding, too? Well, this was to be
her life for the next year, so Marian tried to resign
herself to his presence in her life. The first part of what
they'd done on their wedding night was nice, more than
nice. She would not mind doing that part again.

And since the last part did not look so enjoyable to
either of them, mayhap Duncan would be content with
only the first part? She could admit in the deepest part
of her soul that she enjoyed his kisses and would like to
touch him in places she'd only seen briefly that night
before passion took control. Would he allow her to do
that? Did men let their wives touch them for the pleasure
of it? Her mouth went dry at the thought of such caresses.

She met his gaze then and 'twas almost as though
he could read her thoughts again. Marian said the only

thing she could, even knowing it would draw his attention from the very thing she wished to avoid.

"Will you make arrangements for Ciara then?"

"Ciara? What arrangements?" he asked in a deep voice. He must be thinking of the bedding also. She knew that men's voices changed when filled with passion. She wondered if his body reacted to this talk of swiving as well and glanced down at his sporran to see if any changes happened.

"I…" She cleared her throat and looked away from him. "I would prefer that we not tup in the same chamber where Ciara sleeps."

Proud that she had gotten the words out, her courage now failed her and she let go of his arm and walked over to her daughter. Before she'd gone two paces from his side, the foul curse he spoke under his breath reached her and she shuddered.

If he did not abide by her wishes, there was little she could do about it. However, she hoped that he would go slowly in forcing Ciara to adapt to his ways. Hamish held out a small wooden bowl with some porridge in it and a chunk of cheese. She only wondered how she would get this food down her dry throat.

Duncan had watched every move she made during those first days on the journey, not quite certain of how he could approach her. There were things he needed to know before they arrived in Lairig Dubh, things about what her and Ciara's needs were, things about…her. Iain had spoken of her upbringing and her abilities, such as chess and languages, but said little of her life over these last five years. Mostly he wanted her to tell him the truth of Ciara's parentage and why she'd not warned him of her...condition.

The only words he'd gotten out that first day when he chanced to speak to her with a measure of privacy was to ask if she fared well. He had a need to apologize for his blundering actions in their first bedding, but he could simply not find a way to explain. How did a man tell his virgin bride that he should have recognized the signs of her inexperience when she most likely had no idea that there were signs? How did a man tell her that relations did not usually end in such a manner? And that he would have more care the next time?

The next time? He had bumbled so badly when the evidence of her purity lay on his erection, withdrawing and getting away from her and the bed as soon as he could that the next time would be a long time in coming. Then after scurrying away from her and his own mistake, he, a man of so many words, the man able to persuade and negotiate, the man able to get opposing sides together, could think of nothing to say to her. She'd sat on the bed, leaning against the headboard covered only in a sheet, and stared at him with eyes filled with confusion and pain and humiliation, only to have him stare off into the darkness.

Now, he'd just done it again, bumbling his way through another situation involving Marian and a bed. Would he never be able to deal with her as he did any other person? And how had she so misinterpreted his words and intentions? By Great Thor's Ballocks! As his friend Rurik would say.

Duncan had never had the easy manner with women that Rurik had. In spite of his abilities to talk rational and irrational men into most anything, his mind and his words seemed to break apart when dealing with women over personal things.

Like tupping, er…bedding…sleeping arrangements!

He reached the group and was handed a bowl of porridge and a spoon. Without ever looking at her, he asked a few questions of his men to make certain they knew the plans for the rest of the day. He would speak to them privately about the night. Soon, they were on the road and would arrive at the MacCallum's keep in a few hours. The day was clear and the road dry and good for travel, so they kept a faster pace than they had through the hills a few miles back.

As they rode, he tried to focus his thoughts as he usually did on the tasks at hand and those still ahead. He would need to send word ahead to Connor to inform his laird of the changes in the agreement with the Robertsons and why such favorable terms were offered for nothing in return. Duncan did not want Connor to hear of the terms nor the new wife Duncan brought back with him from someone else…like the MacCallum. He'd made certain not to send news of their arrival on too early or the wily old man would then order a messenger to Lairig Dubh.

What would Connor's reaction be to this development? How much could Duncan share with his laird? By all rights, he should tell him the whole of it, for Duncan had acted on his behalf in the negotiations, but Marian had changed everything. And would the fact that she could not be Ciara's natural mother bring so much trouble with it that Duncan should reveal such personal matters to his laird?

Once he thought of it, he realized that he did not think her complicit in her brother's plot. Aye, she lied about the child. Nay, she could not be the whore that the gossip said she was. Aye, she would not tell her truths to him. The most likely reason for Iain's manipulation of them both was his own marriage plans.

His sister's presence, with the reputation she had and the apparent proof of her sinful past living with her, would not enhance marriage talks between the Robertsons and any other clan. Since Iain's first marriage had ended in disaster with his wife's death and that of their unborn heir in childbirth, he'd taken more than five years before searching out another wife. Now that he'd assumed his father's chair and the leadership of the clan, he would want to marry and have an heir to follow him.

The laird's whore sister and her bastard daughter was simply a complication that could be costly if a potential match was found and had objections to her living there. Which most noble-born women would have... 'Twas probably easier to marry her off as part of another bargain and have her out of the way before proceeding with negotiations for a wife. In thinking on it, 'twas what he would have recommended to Iain—if he'd been asked.

Better to bargain her away than to answer all the questions that surrounded her and the daughter she claimed as her own. Better to pay off her husband with concessions and property than to question the honor of his dead father. Better to quickly get her out of the village and settled far away once an opportunity presented itself so she would not be a part of or obstacle to his new marriage contract.

He heard her soft laugh behind him and turned to see her exchanging words with one of the men. Farlen had been clear in his feelings about Duncan's forced marriage to the Robertson Harlot, but with some persuasion he'd seen reason about not mentioning it to her. Now, it looked as though there was a truce of sorts between the two, for their conversation grew animated with Farlen describing something or someone with his hands and Marian's eyes growing wider with each gesture.

Ciara rode now with Tavis, who had become her newest admirer and who, he knew, was in the process of carving more animals for her collection. Seeing the exhaustion growing in both Marian's and Ciara's posture and expressions, he thought on staying an extra day with Jocelyn's family. First, though, he decided to speak to Marian about it. Nodding to Hamish to take the lead, Duncan waited for him to come forward before pulling his horse out to the side of the group and waiting for her to catch up with him.

"Farlen, ride on," he ordered as he pulled in next to Marian in the group. Farlen nodded to both of them and dropped back to take a position at the end of their group. He allowed a space to form between them and the nearest riders before broaching the first subject with her.

"I would apologize to you for my behavior, Marian," he said in a low voice. "If I had known you were…you were…"

Damn, but he stumbled over words again with her! His horse sensed his agitation and shifted beneath him until he gathered the reins tighter in his grasp. Finally he thought on the way in which she had spoken plainly to him and realized that it was the manner in which he should address his concerns to her.

"If I had known that you were inexperienced in the ways a man and woman join, I could have done things differently."

Her blue eyes widened in astonishment and her mouth dropped open and she appeared ready to fall off her horse. This was not proceeding as well as he'd hoped. The silence around them drew his attention and Duncan saw that his men were all trying, inconspicuously or openly, to listen to their conversation. He leaned over, took Marian's reins from her hands and led her horse off the road to a small copse of trees. Ordering the rest on with a wave, and a smile at Ciara to ease her way, he waited until they were a distance away that made hearing them impossible. If he'd been surprised by her reaction to his words, he never considered what her words would do to him.

"Which things could you have done differently, Sir Duncan?"

Now it was his turn to shake his head and be surprised. "Do you wish a specific answer or something less so?" he asked.

"I should have told you," she said softly. "I planned to tell you, but then…"

She stopped and he noticed her breathing changed. As he watched the rise and fall of her chest, something of his began to rise as well and he caught her gaze resting there while it did. Although there seemed room enough, his tented plaid made his arou al obvious to anyone looking.

As she still did.

If he did not change the path of their thoughts and conversation, Duncan feared he would pull her from her horse and take her right there on the ground. Not a way to clear up the misunderstandings between them and certainly not a way to make his new wife believe he was no ravening beast who would have her even in the presence of her daughter. He handed her reins back to her and turned his horse to face hers. A bit of distance between them was a good thing.

"Aye, if I had known you were a virgin, I would not have… I would not have…" He stopped and cleared his throat, wondering if this was a good idea after all. "Marian, I will just say it—I would not have thrust into you so carelessly if I had known. There are ways to ease a woman's first time and I could have done that."

"And the next time?" she asked.

This would be the death of him. He was trying to speak candidly about what had happened, but in his mind all he could hear were the sounds she'd made as he touched her and the way that she writhed in his arms as he brought her pleasure. And that part of him that had not the full measure of gratification it wanted also responded. Drawing himself back from the swirling state of arousal that was taking hold, Duncan brought himself to the task he'd set and finished explaining.

"There will not be pain the next time. And I will try to make certain that you receive the same pleasure that I do from our joining."

She shivered then, in the middle of the day, in the midst of the bright sunshine and warm breezes off the loch, and he smiled at her body's reaction. Supremely proud that he had not bungled the entire experience for her, he felt some hope for them.

"I cannot allow that if Ciara is sleeping in our chambers," she said in a grave voice. "I worry that she would be frightened."

"Marian," he said. Shaking his head, he moved closer. "I have no intention of having anyone else in our chambers when we sleep or tup. When we join, when we share pleasure, it will be our private time."

"But Ciara sleeps with me," she said, not demanding, simply explaining if her tone was true. "She has always done so."

"We live as man and wife now, Marian. Some things must change." Her expression grew worried and all the lightness and amusement left as the truth of his words sank in. "There is time for deciding the way of things between us. Once we settle in at Lairig Dubh, we will work all of these matters out between us."

He looked down the road and saw that the rest had traveled on over a short rise and were several furlongs away from them. Thinking to end the tension between them, he nodded at the rest of the group. "Should we catch up with them?"

She seemed to catch his meaning and smiled. "A race then?" She took the reins and readied them around her hands and wrists.

"And the winner?" he asked, enjoying the way her face now lit with enthusiasm at a challenge. "Should there be a prize for the winner?"

"The loser must kiss the winner whenever they are asked to."

He was still staring at the gleam in her eyes as she

left him in the dust. Not certain if she would ask him or not if she won, Duncan decided not to be chivalrous at all. He wanted to win now that she'd set the prize and so he urged his mount on, overtaking and passing her just before they caught up with the others. The laughter that bubbled out of him felt good, a welcome change to the seriousness and dread that had filled him for days. And the matching laughter from Marian, made his heart tighten in a way he never expected.

Most of all it felt good to be a winner.

Now he need only decide when to collect the prize.

Chapter Ten

He was watching her again.

The worst part is that he only watched. Well, Marian admitted that to herself and she would freely admit that she anticipated rather than dreaded the kisses he would demand from her. His mouth had done wondrous things to hers and to many places on her body and she hoped they would do that again. 'Twas just the other part she could do without. Marian handed Ciara the cup again so she could drink and tried to ignore the heat that built within her.

He licked his lips, a movement innocent of any other meaning during a meal, but she sensed it did now. Her body reacted even if she did not, with a shiver that made her remember his every heated touch. She glanced away, not certain of how far he would take this game he now played and not wanting to embarrass herself or him by revealing the wanton side she was coming to know truly did exist within her.

If he honored his promise, he would not take her this

night for they all shared one chamber in Laird MacCallum's keep. He'd stood behind her as they were shown to it and she felt the disappointment as his shoulders slumped, for only a moment's time, and he let out a sigh. He did not press for another chamber or for her to place Ciara somewhere else. He only watched her, focusing his gaze on her mouth and then followed the steward as he gave a report to the MacLerie's man.

Now, the meal was nearly done, night was full on them and the day's travel pushed exhaustion down hard. And, other than a few tense moments when Duncan said her name to the laird and his son and they exchanged glances that spoke of recognition, the evening had been a good one. Ciara, though she should be asleep by now, continued to chatter to anyone who would listen about Duncan's men and their horses and their journey and her new home. Marian had seen this before and knew that soon her daughter would collapse in a heap where she sat.

She turned back to the table and finished the food he'd placed before her. So many years had passed since she last sat at a table like this, being treated as an honored guest, that she'd nearly forgotten the way of it. Duncan had insisted that she sit next to him and that Ciara be permitted at table this night, and the laird's steward made the arrangements. Only a hint of a disdain touched his face as he moved some stools and benches to accommodate the request of the MacLerie's man. Apparently the fear of disappointing Connor's emissary was stronger than any personal disgust over allowing a fallen woman such as her to enter their hall and sup with them.

Tired now, of the miles on horseback, of putting up the pretense of civility that being Duncan's wife meant, of worrying about what was to come in their new life, Marian could not stifle the yawns any longer. Ciara quieted at her side and Marian felt the pull of sleep on her. Duncan's hand on her shoulder startled her awake.

"Come, let me see you both to our chamber. I can finish my business with the laird after you are settled in," he said as he helped her to her feet. As she'd expected, Ciara drowsed close to sleep, leaning heavily on her side.

He did not wait for the request. He scooped Ciara up in his arms and carried her from the table, through the hall, to their chamber. She opened the door and watched as he placed her daughter with infinite care on the bed in the corner and arranged a blanket over her. As he turned to leave, Marian walked over to put another on top of Ciara, but he stopped her by taking her wrist and tugging her to him.

"Kiss me, wife," he said in a gruff voice. He wrapped his arm around her waist, drawing their bodies together and then he stopped and waited for her response.

The room around them grew silent, but for the sounds of their breathing. His heat warmed her and the intimacy of the embrace surprised her. He moved not, only watching with those intense eyes that seemed to change from brown to golden and back in the flickering of the candles' light.

Marian reached up and smoothed the hair from his face. He'd worn it loose at dinner and, although it softened the masculine angles of his face, it gave him a mischievous look. Then, rising on her toes, she kissed his cheek. 'Twas like tempting a wild beast instead of soothing one, for she'd barely begun to stand down when he slid his free hand into her hair and held her there. Then his mouth possessed hers as it had in so many other kisses they'd share.

Thoughts and feelings tumbled in her mind and in her heart. Would he remember his promise? Would he stop before…? Would he keep kissing her this way? How did the heat pour from him so? How did a simple kiss go this far? Did she want him to stop?

He pulled back from her first, drawing in a ragged breath and then another as she did the same. Her breasts ached, the core of her throbbed with need and her mouth hungered for the touch of his. Marian discovered that, at some time during the kiss, she'd grabbed his shirt and tugged it open to reveal the golden skin of his chest. Mortified at not even realizing what she'd done and that she still clutched it, she let her hands drop and waited for him to release her.

Duncan let her go, but 'twas a near thing. The only reason he did was to show her that when he gave his word, he stood by it. He would not take her to bed when her child lay sleeping there. His erection, standing large and hard between their bodies, proclaimed that he wanted to, and surely she felt it there, however, he could control this insane desire that had sprung to life within him.

Mayhap 'twas having a woman close at hand after months of celibacy and even longer since he'd been closely involved with one. Mayhap 'twas his mind telling him to accept that which he could not change… for now. Mayhap 'twas simply the natural course of things between a wanting man and a warm and willing woman?

From the way she'd accepted his kiss and melted in his arms, opening her mouth to his and touching his chest, oh aye, she was willing. 'Twould just be about the timing of such a thing. And now was not the time, for dark smudges appeared beneath her eyes, telling of her exhaustion from these last days.

"Get some rest now, Marian," he said, hearing the thickness of his voice from the desire that yet surged through him.

"When do we leave?"

Duncan realized that he'd never discussed staying on an additional day with her as he'd planned to. Desire had gotten in the way then, too. "Not until the day after the morrow."

"Not at dawn then?" she asked, stepping out of his arms.

"I thought it best to give you a day to linger here and recover a bit. I do not want to explain to my laird how my wife arrived at Lairig Dubh in worse condition than his own did." He smiled at the thought of that journey, but 'twas only now, years after, that he could look back in humor.

"I cannot wait to hear Lady MacLerie's explanation of that journey," Marian said softly. "I do appreciate your patience, sir. With Ciara and with the difficulties of the journey as well."

In spite of the silence between them during their days of travel, she had noticed his efforts. Something in his heart softened at her words. A questionable beginning, even a bad turn or two between them, but she was intelligent enough to understand that things could improve for them. He nodded at her thanks and turned to the door before remembering the question he did want to ask of her.

"Marian, what did you tell Ciara about…?"

"I told her the truth—that we would be traveling with you to your home and live there with you."

"As husband and wife?" Duncan did not ken why, but it was important to hear her say the words. Through each introduction here, to the MacCallum and his son and others in his clan, he'd presented her as his wife, though she'd never yet said the words about him.

She blushed then before answering. "Aye, sir, I told her we were husband and wife."

"Good," he said. "'Tis good for her to ken how it stands between us, Marian."

Although his body wanted very much to show her exactly how it stood between them, he still had business to discuss with the laird who sat waiting on his return to the table.

"I will return after I finish speaking to the laird," he said as he turned, nearly missing the confused expression on her face. "I said I would not bed you in the same room as your daughter," he offered. "But I will be sleeping here."

Before she could argue, he closed the door and walked back to the hall. Hamish caught him before he got too far.

"Ye have a settled look aboot ye. Is all well?" Hamish asked.

"I think it will be well, Hamish. I need to sort this all with Connor and hear his opinion on the contracts."

He'd not shared the personal details about his wedding night with anyone, not even Hamish, and he would not until he had the opportunity to figure out where the pieces of this puzzle fit. But, by his word and especially by his deed, she was his wife and, by the wording of the contracts, Ciara his daughter and that was how he planned to treat them.

The other side of that argument, to treat her with less respect than he would if he had chosen her to wife, would be a grave insult—to her brother, to his laird and to his honor. An insult that could end the treaty and bring dishonor to everyone involved. An insult that would end in war. An insult he would not offer.

So, though Marian did not realize yet that he took his responsibilities seriously, she would learn.

Soon.

This very night.

Some hours had passed since dinner and she'd found it difficult to sleep. Oh, aye, exhaustion claimed her, but then she awoke with every noise. And in a keep the size of this one, with the number of people who lived here, it seemed they never settled down for the night.

She heard the door open then. Lying still next to Ciara, she waited to see what he would do. His steps were light and quick and, after some rustling of clothing, she felt the blankets lift and tried to prepare herself. Without a sound, he slipped in next to her and lay on his side at her back.

He still wore his long shirt.

She still wore her chemise.

When Marian began to shift over toward Ciara to give him more room, he slid his arm around her and held her there. As more of his body spooned behind hers, she felt his warmth seep through the thin layers of cloth between them.

She also felt the growing hardness there and held her breath at both the disappointment and the anticipation in her heart. 'Twas his right to take her whenever and wherever, but he'd given his word to her and he was about to break it. Just when she was about to remind him, he leaned his head to hers and whispered in her ear.

"Hush, now. Sleep."

Which, if his snoring was any proof, he did within moments, leaving her wide-awake and surrounded by his heat, his masculine smell and his body.

Trapped effectively between him behind her and Ciara in front, Marian tried to let go of the nervousness that filled her and listened to his rhythmic breathing. Soon, as the warmth soothed her aching bones and the strangeness of lying in a man's arms eased, Marian could feel the pull of sleep on her and she gave up the fight.

This was not so bad a way to spend the night.

This was a hell of a way to spend the night.

Unable to move without waking her because he held her so close and unable to sleep, well, because he held her so close, Duncan lay there, forcing his breathing to a steady pace and trying not to notice the enticing breast under his hand nor the welcoming place between her legs where his hardness now rested. He knew the moment she gave up the fight and slept deeply in his embrace.

If only they were alone.

If only they were naked.

If only he hadn't given his word to calm her damn fears!

And that was the true reason behind any hesitation on his part. He would fight the temptation she was in this moment because he was, above else, a man of his word.

Although it only seemed like moments since he'd closed his eyes, the sun streaming in through the slat in the shuttered windows spoke of a day fully dawned. Duncan could move now, and he did, turning on his back and lifting his head. Marian now lay on the other side of the bed and she curled into a ball so that he almost could not see her face. Realizing that Ciara was not there, he began to sit up and found her standing at the bedside staring at him.

"Good morn, Ciara," he whispered, pointing to her sleeping mother and then touching his finger to his lips to warn her off making too much noise.

"Dinna worry, Duncan," she said. "When Mama falls to sleep, nothing wakes her."

Looking past her, Duncan saw her toys spread around the floor and realized she'd been playing quietly there without waking either of them. Pulling the edge of his shirt down onto his thighs, he sat up and then got out of bed. With no wish to expose himself to the child, he did not avail himself of the chamber pot sitting beneath the wooden table there.

"What game do you play?" he asked, wrapping his plaid back in place around his hips and over his shoulders. He would have to relieve himself soon.

"The black horse chases the others," she answered, showing him how one followed the other. "Tavis promised he would make me more."

The innocent smile rewarded him ten times over for having his man carve the small wooden animal. "Only horses? Or do you not wish for some other animal? Mayhap a goat or pig?" Duncan swallowed against the growing tightness in his throat.

How and why had Iain allowed this child, his niece, to grow up in such poverty when he had the means to make her life much more comfortable? Even if he had not known their circumstances while his father still ruled the clan, he could have made a difference once he'd allowed her back. Or he could have paid to make their life better somewhere other than Dunalastair if Duncan was correct about his suspicions.

Then, why had he not done so?

Watching the child play on the floor, he worried more over the tingling in the back of his head, the one that came to warn him when something was amiss. Granted, having his sister with her terrible reputation in the keep would be untenable, but other arrangements could have, and should have, been made for her.

So, why had he not?

"...Duncan?" The soft voice followed by a sharp tug on his hand. "Duncan?" Ciara whispered.

"Oh, aye?" He shook off his own thoughts and looked down at the girl.

"Could Tavis make a pig?"

Duncan smiled. "Pigs are his favorite animals. Mayhap he could show you the laird's pigs?"

She jumped up and gathered all her toys together, throwing them quickly in the sack she used to carry them. "Can we go now?" Ciara crossed the distance to the door and looked at him. "I am ready."

Not certain that sending her daughter off at dawn to see the laird's pigs would be acceptable, Duncan thought of waking Marian to ask permission. Remembering the dark bruises of exhaustion beneath her blue eyes, he decided not. Standing and securing his belt, he then tugged on his boots and slid his dagger back into its scabbard. Although the MacLerie's diplomat now, he spent too many years training and fighting to ever be without a weapon. Expecting no trouble, he could leave his broadsword in the keep.

Accepting Ciara's hand, they sneaked quietly from the chamber and went to find Tavis. Duncan had other plans for the morn that did not involve MacCallum pigs, so he led Ciara to where his men broke their fast in the hall. After ordering a bath for Marian, he explained the situation to Tavis who, in good humor and with much experience handling bairns and children, agreed to serve as the lass's escort for a few hours.

Sitting at the table with the rest of his men, he spoke to Hamish and the steward about using a cart for the rest of the journey for Marian and Ciara. After a bowl of thick, steaming porridge and a cup of watered ale, he asked for another bowl and cup to take to Marian.

"A well-married mon, are ye then?" asked Hamish.

"A small courtesy, that is all," he answered.

"I think more than courtesy is involved," said Farlen. "Now wi' the lass gone, I think we ken the reasons."

The chuckling made its way through his men, but he did not join them. Hamish who'd begun this then made it worse.

"We dinna expect ye to pass up the benefits of having a wife simply because ye didna choose her," he said. "She is a comely lass, though no' what we expected."

Duncan waved them back to their food, unwilling to discuss Marian where they could be overheard. He stood, taking the porridge and ale with him and motioned for Hamish to walk with him. The servants should have the bath ready in their chamber by now.

"The stories have been exaggerated," Duncan finally answered, revealing some, but not all of it. For all they knew, he spoke of her appearance.

"Aye and nay, Duncan. Some see the face she wears, but some would see past that," Hamish offered. "Can ye?"

They stopped just outside the door and he peered at the man he called friend. Hamish had been married for a dozen years to Connor's half sister and had served as overseer of the village and farms, so he had many years of dealing with people, especially women. And mayhap understanding them?

Duncan shrugged. "There is more at risk here, Hamish, than simply my kenning the truth of my new wife." He paused, trying to decide whether or not to say more. "There may be things at work behind this that are dangerous to the clan."

"I dinna doubt it, but she is yer wife now and ye need to stand by her," Hamish whispered furiously.

"I hope it will not come to that, Hamish. But, for now, she does not trust me to tell me the truth and without that, I do not see a way out of this."

"And ye? Do ye trust her?" There was a gleam in Hamish's eyes that gave the answer they both knew. "Weel, then. Now ye ken what ye must do."

"Trust her? 'Tis more easily said than done, I fear."

"Teach her that ye are a mon she can trust."

Hamish kenned his ways. In any negotiations, first

trust had to be established, then work could begin. His main objective in sending out men to gather information before proceeding with any talks was to discover some common ground between the two sides, the two opponents. The more knowledge he had in hand when discussions began, the sooner he could find that which both of those involved held to be important.

They'd reached the door and he stood there holding the bowl and cup and realized that he was doing exactly that with Marian—making small promises and keeping them, each one a small step in giving her a way to trust him. And when the time came for her to trust him with that larger truth, the one that ruled their lives in so many ways, he hoped she would finally have enough faith to share it with him.

He gave the bowl to Hamish while he lifted the latch of the door and then took it back before entering. His plan was underway and he'd already chosen the common ground on which he believed they could proceed. Marian's frank acceptance and even interest in it guided him in the choice. And, with Ciara occupied outside with Tavis and his men sent off on tasks that would keep their attentions elsewhere, now was the time to begin exploring and advancing toward trust.

"'Tis exactly what I plan to do," he said as he closed the door behind him and turned to find Marian climbing out of her bath.

Chapter Eleven

If she was surprised to see him, his shock over her naked appearance was more than that. He'd interrupted her as she stood in the wooden tub, reaching for a drying cloth on the floor. And, since their wedding night took place mostly in the dark and in a hasty manner, her body now presented to him in the light of day stunned him.

And that randy part of him took notice.

Creamy white skin, the shade that blushes to a mouthwatering pale pink, generous rose-tipped breasts and long, shapely limbs enticed him. Duncan noticed that hair between her legs did not match that on her head, but before he could ask, she'd grabbed the cloth and held its meager length and width in front of herself.

"Ah, your pardon, Marian," he stuttered out, in no way the confident man he thought to enter the room as. "I brought you some porridge and ale."

Duncan put the bowl and cup down on the table and turned back to her. She'd not moved an inch from her spot, but he recognized the panicked glint in her eyes. Panic he did not want to see there.

"Here now, let me help you." He held out his hand to her in a slow manner as he took only one step toward her. "There is water splashed on the floor and you could slip." She hesitated for only a second before taking it.

Good. Not so startled or frightened of him, he thought.

He found the larger cloth folded on a stool, shook it open and draped it over her shoulders. He did not want her covered, nay if he was successful only his body would cover hers shortly, but he did want her comfortable in his presence. If the cloth barrier accomplished that, he would use it…for now.

"Do you mind if I use the water?" he asked once she'd dropped the small cloth in favor of the larger one.

Her gaze moved from his face to the tub and back to him, this time looking up and down his body as though determining his size. The intensity and frank curiosity of her examination only helped to inflame his body, sending waves of heat and anticipation through his blood and into…

Marian turned away then and reached for the bowl of thick porridge. He'd trapped her between the bed and the tub with her clean clothes sitting on the other side of the chambers from her. Nowhere to go, nothing to do but to eat the food or to watch him or both.

"You may not fit in that tub," she said when her eyes met his once more.

He thought of several replies and let each one go until a touch of mischief crossed his mind. She was correct in her assessment—he would never fit in such a tub—however that did not mean he could not use it. He released his belt, dropped his woolen tartan on the floor and leaned down to loosen and remove his boots.

Marian's gaze still rested on his face as he found another bucket of steaming water and added it to that already in the tub. He tugged his shirt over his head and stepped into the tub, standing and not even trying to hide his erection from her view. She'd managed to lift a spoonful of porridge to her mouth, all the farther it got, as she stared at him.

This was more difficult than he thought it would be, teasing her into his bed. It loosened his own lust and he dreaded the possibility that he would simply take her again. He shifted in the tub, turning his body until he did not face her, and washed his shoulders and arms and chest with the cloth and soft soap.

Marian took advantage of his turning away to retrieve her clothes. After a sip of ale to wash down the porridge that had nearly blocked her throat at the sight of his tall, muscular, very-naked, very-aroused male body, she put down the bowl and cup, lifted the bottom of the drying cloth that she'd circled around her body and walked past him to find her chemise and gown. She'd gotten halfway when he said her name. Looking at him, she saw the cloth in his hand and realized what he wanted.

Her mouth went dry at the thought of washing him, even his back, but the rest of her surged with heat as she stepped closer. From the expression in his eyes, they both knew where this would lead. Did she want this?

From the way he'd held her through the night, his hardness against her bottom, Marian accepted that he could control his lust when he needed to, and since he'd given his word, he needed to. Now, though, there was no such restraint for him. 'Twas no surprise to her that he wanted to bed her, but now, gazing into his eyes as he held out what was simply and clearly an invitation, she also knew that she could refuse.

She wanted this.

All the talk that women passed around about the whole bedding experience, all of the claims men made about tupping a woman, all the comments thrown at her over the years about what a harlot could do and did to a man, all of that, played into her decision. Then there was his own promise and her own curiosity about the way it could be between a man and a woman. All of that convinced her 'twas past time to learn if it could be as good or as bad as all the talk.

She wanted Duncan.

The pleasure he'd given her with his mouth and hands spoke of so much more and she wanted it to be him that gave it to her. Her body ached now with the memories of how he'd touched her and rubbed her… and, yes, how he'd even tasted and licked her.

She wanted it all and she wanted it now.

Marian took the cloth and dipped it into the water that only reached as high as his knees. When she tucked the edge of the drying cloth in so she could use both hands, the tenderness of her breasts surprised her. They pressed against the cloth, tightened by the rubbing of the cloth and the desire that now raced through her at the thought of touching Duncan's body. She lifted her gaze to his and the smile that tilted the corners of his mouth most attractively made any last remnants of resistance or hesitation melt away.

Once assured that she was a willing participant in this, Duncan turned his back to her and waited for her first touch. His breath grew ragged and tight as he heard her step closer.

Would it be his back? Or would she first touch his shoulders or his arms? Or his arse? Just when he was about to turn to discover why she delayed, he felt the lightest touch between his shoulders. She squeezed the cloth to release some of the lather and then spread it over his skin, in widening circles.

He could not believe that he stood naked before her, allowing her, nay nearly begging her, to touch him. And she did. It aroused him even more, if that were possible, and he fought not to turn, take her in his arms and to the bed. This needed to go well between them for many reasons, not the least of which was to help her to begin to trust him. The greatest of which was to find out if she brought danger to his clan.

Right at this moment, though, those benefits counted for naught and were rapidly losing ground to the pure sexual wanting that she caused within him. Still, he clenched his fists and his jaw, trying to endure the sweet torture of her touch on his skin. Closing his eyes made it worse so he tried to keep his gaze on the rim of the tub.

His skin was hot beneath her fingers—she could feel it right through the cloth—as she moved it over the strong muscles of his back. Because of his height and the additional inches added by the depth of the tub, he towered over her and she had to reach high to get even to his shoulders. That movement loosened the cloth around her with every stroke, but she continued to wash him.

Marian kenned that this was not about the bath, this was a prelude—a plain and simple one—to them tupping. And at this moment, she did not mind the thought. When her hands reached his lower back she paused before moving down over his well and tightly muscled buttocks. In considering what to do next, she dropped the cloth into the water. Leaning over to reach it, the drying cloth around her shifted, releasing and baring her breasts even as he shifted, placing his maleness directly in front of her face.

His very large and hard maleness.

Time seemed to slow just then, with her bent over in front of him and him watching her be revealed by the slowly slipping cloth around her. Neither moved and the chamber was filled with silence as even their breathing seemed to stop. When she dared to look up at him, his eyes gazed back with an intensity that sent shivers down her spine.

Marian glanced back down and his hardness pulsed and moved before her. *It* startled her, she had not the thought that *it* could move on its own, yet *it* did. Without considering the danger of her next move, she reached out and touched the tip of it with a finger. He gasped at her touch and when she would have drawn her hand away, he did not allow it. Entwining his fingers and hers, he pulled her hand back to him and wrapped it around the length of his hardness, guiding her fingers around until she held him in his hand.

"Will it hurt?"

"You or me, lass?" he answered, his voice ragged with desire.

"Me." The whispered word floated up to him.

"Nay, lass. I will no' hurt you," he promised.

His head swam, his thoughts scattered and his body bucked beneath her touch, but he would not allow himself to pull away from her grasp. He helped her slide her soapy hand along his length, feeling the exquisite torture of it as he watched her do it. He knew that her continued caress there would bring things to a finish much more quickly than he'd like, so he held his hand over hers to stop her movements.

He needed to do this right to show her that she could trust him. He needed to do this right to make up for his rough handling of her their first time. And he needed to do this right because, regardless of what had happened before they said the words, she was truly his wife now.

Duncan stepped from the tub and took her by the shoulders, drawing her rose-tipped breasts to his bare skin. The heat of it seared through him and he allowed their soapy skin to slide over each other's until she panted from arousal as he did. Then he leaned down and captured her mouth with his, tasting her and touching his tongue to hers while she opened completely to him, giving him the signal he waited on before moving forward. A quiet sigh and a shift in her body said aye.

With an arm around her shoulders, he held her steady while ridding them of the cloth that stood between them. He pushed it down on her hips and then tugged it free, tossing it to the floor next to them. A few steps—him forward and her back—and he moved them to the side of the bed. He eased away from her mouth and saw the passion-glazed expression in her eyes and the way her lips looked well-kissed already. As he began to ease them down onto the bed, she stopped them.

"The mattress, Duncan. We will ruin it," she whispered.

As quickly as he could, he stepped away and pulled all the bedcovers off the mattress and onto the floor, forming a makeshift pallet there. As he turned back to her, he realized that the door was not secured. Lifting the bar from its place next to the door, he lifted it into one loop and then leaned it against the door, more for a warning than a true deterrence to anyone trying to enter.

He turned to find her watching every movement he made. He felt his erection grow stronger as her eyes moved over his skin and he could not wait to bury himself in the wet tightness that waited for him. As he reached her, she shook her head. He recognized the glimmer in her eyes now and waited for the name.

"Ciara?"

"Tavis is showing her the pigs and will no' return for at least another hour," he assured her.

Duncan stood before her and then took her in his embrace. Wrapping his arms around her, he held her close, rubbing his hardness against the slick skin of her belly and enjoying the feel of it. With the soap and water still glistening on their skin, he slid down to his knees savoring every inch of his journey there. With their differences in height, he reached to her shoulders and with a tilt of her head, he could kiss her mouth... and he did. When she began to melt against him, he held her against him.

"It willna hurt," he whispered as he followed the

curve of her chin with his tongue, kissing, licking and nipping his way along.

"Ciara is well-cared for and willna return for a wee bit." He trailed kisses down her neck and onto her shoulder, stopping there to tease the sensitive spot he'd found with his teeth, too.

"The mattress willna be ruined." Now he felt her knees weaken, so he held her up as he suckled on her breasts, waiting for that breathy moan from her before moving to the other one.

"The door is barred and we are alone." Now he slipped his hand between their bodies and touched the damp, red curls that covered the entrance to her heat. He could feel that she wanted to sink to the floor, but he held her up. With one finger then two, he moved into her wetness, teasing and rubbing the folds and finding his way in deeper to the path that led to her woman's core.

Her hands rested on his shoulders now and instead of pulling away from his touch, she pushed against his hand, forcing his fingers in deeper. Duncan allowed her to sink to the floor, guiding her onto the sheets and never stopping his caressing of her most private places. Once she lay next to him, he pulled her to face him and positioned her leg up on his thigh, opening her to his touch even more.

When she gasped and moaned at every fondling touch, he kenned she was ready. Sliding his length between her legs, he stroked her now with the length of him. Then with his hardness positioned at the opening to her core, he paused.

"Can I have ye now, wife?" He eased himself into her tightness and stopped, a scant inch inside of her. "Can I?"

"Aye, husband," she whispered in a breathy moan. "Aye."

If Marian could have breathed, it would have been forced from her as he quickly pulled her under him and filled her with every inch of his thick maleness. That which she'd held in her grasp now thrust deep inside until he could go no farther. And still she could not breathe from the intensity of his motion and the stretching of her body from deep inside.

'Twas at that moment that she realized there was no pain. Fullness, aye. Stretching and some nigh to burning, aye. But the pain did not happen. He lay still within her for a few seconds and then he moved. Just a small bit back and then deeper than before. This was a new feeling and she waited for more.

"Wrap yer legs around me, lass," he ordered gruffly and she did so, never dreaming that a simple thing like that would make it possible for him to go deeper still.

Now, he withdrew until she could feel only the very end of his hardness within her and then he plunged back in. Gasping at each thrust, Marian shifted her hips and allowed him to move even farther into her until she thought he must be touching her womb. As the sensations moved through her, from inside out and from the intense stretching there, he reached down and slid his finger along her cleft, searching for something there.

Her body screamed as he found what he sought, his touch on some spot inside the folds of skin made her ache and throb and ache more with each touch. He was relentless in his attention there, taking it between his finger and rubbing it until she thrust herself against him. Marian felt the tightness growing within her, from her skin to the deepest part of her, until he tugged and squeezed the bud and forced her toward the edge of a full measure of passion.

Just as he watched her find her pleasure, Duncan thrust forward, pushing his whole length into her tightness. With a hand under her bottom, he pumped inside her, pushing in deep and then back away, then in deeper until he felt her wet channel tighten around his erection like nothing he'd felt before. She clutched at his shoulders as he filled her again and again, her release exploding around him in waves and waves of contractions over his length.

He felt his seed gathering and it took only a few more thrusts before he came, withdrawing from her depths just in time. He allowed his seed to flow under her onto the sheets. Trying to catch his breath, he leaned back on his knees and glanced at her. She lay there, eyes closed, breathing deeply, recovering from the satisfaction he'd given her. Her body shuddered as more waves of pleasure moved through her. But, only her inexperience kept the truth of his actions from her.

No matter that they were joined. No matter that they were man and wife before her clan and his. He would not spend his seed inside of her before he discovered the truth she hid. He could not. Pleasuring her and bringing them both to release was one thing, but taking the chance of conceiving a child with her was another.

Duncan lay down at her side, gathering her close, enjoying the nearness of her during these last quiet moments. Glancing down, he noticed the color of the curls there between her legs and remembered he wanted to ask about it. Much lighter than the hair on her head, a different color even, it was pale, reddish-gold, while that above was a dark, muddy brown. Startled at the difference, he realized she was now watching him.

"'Tis a different color," he said. "You dye your hair?"

"Aye," she replied, moving away from him and gaining her feet. She moved around the chamber, gathering her clothes and his and returning to where he now sat in the nest of bedcovers.

"Why? Why do you change your appearance?"

He guessed the answer even as he asked the question. And she had changed her appearance—from hiding her true form within baggy, loose gowns and tunics, to changing the color of her hair. "Tell me why, Marian."

"I want no attention drawn to me, and especially not because of my appearance."

She turned then and began pulling on her chemise and gown and tunic. Each one he'd seen her wear was the same dark brown gown with green or brown tunic. Each one would blend into the trees and into her garden, the colors were so dark and dreary. Even her hair would do so.

All part of her plan. And a painful penance to pay from some past transgression that she would not admit to him.

"You were not a whore, Marian. We both know the falsehood of that story. So why would you, the daughter of a nobleman and sister to the laird, allow such a falsehood to be told?"

"Think you I had a choice?" Her words came out filled with anger and pain.

He took her by the shoulders and brought her to face

him. "Then tell me your truth. Let me help you," he urged.

The burst of anger fled and he could tell the moment it did. She shrugged off his hold and gathered her stockings and shoes together and put them on. He waited, hoping she would say more, but the silence in the room and between them grew. He finished dressing and watched as she placed the sheets and blankets back on the bed, keeping out the one he'd soiled and tossing it into the tub. Their eyes met for only a moment, but he read that truth within hers.

Aye, she had noticed. And now she would wash away the evidence that he'd withheld his seed from her body before the servants could gossip about it to anyone who would listen. They would snicker behind their hands as she passed by about her husband needing to see her monthly cloths and seeing proof that she did not carry another bastard within her, before he would take the chance of not knowing if 'twas his or another's.

Even if not the truth of what was between them or his reasons for not planting his seed within her, it would become the truth on the retelling as stories did. Her entire reputation was based on nothing more than ill-spoken words.

She scrubbed the sheet wordlessly and twisted it out before hanging it over a stool to dry out. One of the servants could hang it out with other laundry later.

A wife, but not truly married. A whore, but still a virgin. A mother who had never given birth. Was there anything that she truly was besides a liar and a fake? If she thought she had a chance for a new life with this man, she'd been mistaken. 'Twas just as well that she not carry a child while her future was so uncertain.

A commotion in the hall outside their chambers grabbed her attention and Duncan walked over and removed the bar from the door. Ciara came running across the hall and Marian could see another carved toy in her hands.

"A pig, Mama! Tavis made a pig just for me! And it looks just like the mama pig in Laird MacCallum's yards."

The young soldier blushed at Ciara's words, but Marian accepted the kindness he offered her daughter with a smile.

"And have you thanked Tavis for his gift?"

Ciara stopped then and curtsied in front of Tavis, which only made him blush more. "My thanks for your gift," she said. Her tone was so serious that Marian nearly did not recognize the voice as her wee bairn's. Ciara tugged her closer and whispered, "I am going to marry Tavis, Mama."

Startled by the words, spoken as an oath rather than the whimsical wish of a young child, Marian could only smile in reply. Duncan stood behind her through the exchange, not saying a word. Once Ciara noticed him, she ran to his side and showed him the newest toy of her collection. Not for a moment did he seem impatient with her daughter's demonstration of a pig's gait or sounds. Only when his men gathered near, did he turn to face her.

"I must go," he began quietly. "I must make arrangements for the rest of our journey."

She would not meet his gaze. Her body still hummed

with the last remnants of pleasure he'd given her, but his final act of rejection left her spirit cold and bruised. Mayhap she should be grateful that he was being practical and not allowing something to happen by accident that she, and he most especially, would regret later?

Somehow, though, it all just hurt. And it hurt more deeply and in a way that none of the slurs or insults ever had. She'd known them for the lies they were, but this was so much about the truth between them that it made her want to return to her quiet cottage in the woods and not have to face his censure again, particularly after such a personal and private experience as they'd shared.

She nodded without looking up and took Ciara by the hand, waiting for them to leave so she could collect her thoughts and regain some measure of control. Knowing the day to be clear and sunny, she decided to take a walk. But was she permitted such a thing here?

"Sir Duncan?" she called out to him. "Am I permitted to walk out to the village?"

He walked back to her so quickly and with such a furious expression on his face that she backed away from him, fearing his anger. "My name is Duncan," he said in a low voice. "You do not call me 'sir.'"

His rage even startled Ciara, who clutched Marian's hand tighter and whose lower lip began to tremble. Marian tucked her behind her skirts, blocking her from his sight or reach. He took a deep breath then and regained his usual calm demeanor.

"You are the laird's guest here and my wife, Marian, and permitted any walk you wish." He noticed then that even his men were staring. "Do you wish an escort?" he asked as he stepped back away from her.

The laird's guest or not, the MacLerie's man's wife or not, she was still the Robertson Harlot and would still be taunted wherever her reputation had spread. From the curious stares of those around the large open hall, they had heard. Part of her wanted to simply turn back into her chamber and never leave it. Part of her wanted to scream out the truth that Duncan kenned. But, the calmer, more rational part of her understood the cost of such an admission and would never speak of it.

"Nay, we can find our own way about," she said, leading Ciara across the hall toward the main doors of the keep.

"Marian," he said from behind her.

She turned to face him, but he said nothing, he only gazed at her with some indecipherable expression in those dark, piercing eyes of his, and at this moment, she was too tired and sore and hurt to try to make sense of it. She would rather face the reproach of strangers than the scorn of this man, who'd made her feel such glorious sensations with his attentions one minute and then the pain of his rejection the next.

Even worse, he made her begin to question everything she'd done more than five years ago and made her wish for some different outcome than the one she kenned would be hers. Marian clearly understood that Duncan presented a danger to herself and to Ciara, but she thought it was simply that her life was now tangled up in his. Until today, she had not realized the worst of it—she wanted to tell him everything.

Chapter Twelve

Marian, he discovered, did not sulk when she was angry. She did not complain if she believed she was ill-treated. She did not draw attention to herself if she was uncomfortable. Indeed, he did not hear a cross or angry word from her for the rest of that day nor the rest of the journey.

Indeed, he heard not a word at all from her.

Oh, aye, she spoke to her daughter, to his men, to the MacCallum warriors who joined their traveling party, to the laird on taking leave of him, to his son when agreeing to bring his greetings to his sister and on and on. What she did not do was speak to him.

She'd spent the rest of that day walking the village paths and the grounds of the keep. She said she needed no escort, but fearing what could happen once word of her identity got out, and it would, he'd sent along a guard to follow them. If the laird's feast to honor their marriage surprised her, she did not show it. Marian simply took her place at his side and spoke to everyone at table...except him.

That did not stop anyone else from speaking on her behalf, and speak they did. Hamish's words nearly blistered his ears after witnessing his angry outburst at her and without even kenning what had happened. Tavis spoke to him as though he were a child, like his siblings or Ciara, about the correct way of treating those who we take into our care. Even Farlen, who he'd had to threaten with bodily injury in order to treat Marian civilly, now told him with his own measure of certainty every mistake he'd made in dealing with his wife.

The laird turned their farewells into a private sermon about how a man should treat his wife and even Athdar, too young to ken anything about women other than their value in his bed, lectured him on the tender feelings of the fairer sex. When he ended it with a suggestion that Duncan should speak to Rurik for more guidance, Duncan kenned that Marian had won this fray.

The worst of this was that Duncan could not explain how they'd come to this. 'Twas not his sharp outburst in the hall, although that had made Ciara nervous around him for days. It happened when he bedded Marian and did not remain within her when his seed was released. He'd not truly planned to do that; 'twas more a simple decision in the moment when he realized that he could not trust her and did not want to add another child into their problems. And seeing how devoted she was to Ciara, though the child could not be her own, he worried that she would become as attached to any child she bore, making the end of their handfasting a terrible thing to face.

Although he knew these precautions were in no way

completely reliable, they were at least an attempt to prevent her from carrying his child. If he did not trust her, if she planned on leaving him behind in a year's time, if she would not share herself with him, then a child born in such uncertain circumstances was not a desirable thing. And yet, part of him pushed for him to take her, make her his in all ways and bind her to him through a bairn.

All of these things, this indecision, were swirling in his thoughts, as well as what he could and must tell Connor on their arrival. 'Twas Connor's place to have the whole of it, but Duncan planned not to share the more personal parts of it with his laird.

And, before the week was out, he planned on sending men back to the Robertsons to find out more about Iain's first marriage and the details of Marian's "disgrace." That seemed the logical place to begin his search. Once he gathered the information he needed, then he could deal with Marian, her brother and the truth behind her daughter's seeming virgin conception and birth.

A few hours before they would reach Lairig Dubh, an arrival timed so that a huge welcoming and feast was not possible, he only knew that he had much to discuss with his wife before their arrival. He gave instructions to Hamish and then guided his horse over to the cart where she rode with Ciara for the final part of the journey.

"I would speak to you, Marian," he said when she ignored his presence. Ciara lay sleeping, clasping a small wooden horse and pig in her hands and cocooned in a mass of blankets on a thick pallet next to Marian in the cart.

The silence grew around them as he realized that every single one of his men and the MacCallum's, too, strained to pick up any word they spoke.

"Alone," he growled, staring them all down. He held out his hand to Marian, and motioned for her to step on his foot and sit before him on his horse. She carefully slid out from next to her sleeping child and stood holding onto the side, ready to take his hand. At the last moment, she dropped it and spoke.

"May we walk instead?" she asked quietly. "My back is sore from riding in the cart."

He nodded, climbing from his horse's back and helping her down from the still-moving cart. They waited for a break in the line of horses and carts and, leading his horse along beside them, stepped into it. Her first steps were stiff, but soon she was moving more smoothly and did not appear to be in pain.

"I thought that we should speak about what to expect when we arrive in Lairig Dubh," he began. "If 'tis acceptable to you, I would have us stay in the keep." When she started to speak, he shook his head. "I think we should stay there until I can have a cottage built for us in the village."

"A cottage? Do you not need to be near your laird for your work?" she asked. He noticed that she did not raise her head to meet his gaze, but only followed the ruts and lines of the road.

"I thought that it might be easier on the lass to adjust to this new life if she lived in somewhat similar circumstances to what you did in Dunalastair. Well, with a few changes."

"Changes?" She did raise her eyes then, only for a

moment but then she lowered them and her voice. "What changes do you mean?"

"Me, for one. I have need of more space than your cottage had, so ours will have several chambers as well as more land around it for your garden and for my…"

He stopped speaking before he revealed his own dreams to her. If she had her way, she would be gone in a year and she would take the child with her. He could stop her, of course, the contracts gave him complete control over both of them, but that matter was for another day. And his dreams would remain private. "…workroom."

"My gardens?"

"I ken of your success in growing herbs and plants. Indeed, Iain plans on sending you cuttings of many of the plants you left behind in our hasty departure. Jocelyn has been lamenting over her lack of those skills and would be glad of someone to oversee that for her or to maintain gardens large enough for the clan's needs."

Her eyes lit up for the first time in days and she seemed pleased by this news. There was more, but he wondered how she would react to it. Well, better to have it out between them now than to wait and surprise her with anything in front of his clan…and his laird and the laird's wife.

"I suspect that this will be something you do not wish to hear, but I will provide clothes and food and even any servants that you have need of, Marian. My wife and child will not live as poor peasants," he said in one breath.

Then he added the worst part of it, "I do not pretend

to understand the reasons or actions of your father and other kin in their treatment of you and an innocent bairn, and I ken you will not speak of it to me, but I will not stand by and allow my wife and child to live as you did in Dunalastair." He found that his fists were clenched in anger at the thought of how she'd lived. "At least while you are my wife."

Marian tripped at his words, but regained her balance before he could reach out to help steady her. First, his arrangements that she and Ciara would be at ease in Lairig Dubh. Then his railing against the way she'd been treated. And then his admission that he knew she looked at this as only a temporary situation.

Another man trapped in these circumstances would not think about her needs at all, and not those of a small child now in his care. In spite of the hurt he'd caused her that day, he still considered her life in his home.

He was a confusing, complicated man—one who deserved better than to be dragged into the middle of this family debacle and one who it would take years to know fully. Years she did not want and did not have. She felt the burn of gathering tears in her eyes as she felt his outrage on her behalf and she had no words to offer. The loose ties of their handfasting were the only things she could give him. Finally, after she wiped at her eyes and swallowed several times to clear her throat, she could speak.

"My thanks for your consideration in this, Duncan. I will do what I can to keep myself and Ciara out of your way."

"That is not what I want, Marian," he said. His face grew red and she could tell his anger grew. "I want...I want…" He let out his breath and whispered fiercely, "I dinna ken what I want!"

She'd only just noticed that his burr grew deeper and more obvious when he was angry or when he was… aroused. It made him even more appealing. Marian was certain he would have no problem finding a good wife once she left.

He dragged his fingers through his long hair, loosened around his shoulders now and then cursed under his breath. This was not the calm man known as the Peacemaker. This was a different man unfamiliar with turmoil in his life. Turmoil brought by her and her child. Truly, no matter the rest of it, he did not deserve this.

He took her hand and pulled her from the rest, stopping on the edge of the well-worn path and waiting for the others to pass. When they had, he turned to her.

"We must have an understanding of things between us, Marian, or they will meddle. Connor, Jocelyn, Rurik and his wife, even Hamish, will be as old women in our affairs."

"But the earl must have many important things to see to," she offered, frowning over this. "If I stay out of his way and yours, he will have no reason to meddle."

"That will simply gain their attention. You do not ken these people, Marian. If they sense that something is not right between us, they will nose around and seek out the reasons. There is little privacy in Lairig Dubh."

What he described to her sounded like heaven— people concerned about each other, meddling even, to help each other along. The least she could do was be the wife he needed her to be in front of his people while she was with him.

"There is nothing amiss between us for them to seek out, Duncan. I ken what you need of me and I will not disappoint you. I have already promised not to dishonor your name. I also promise not to embarrass or disappoint you before your clan."

He searched her face for some sign of anger or dread or anything that could tell him what she was thinking or feeling and he found nothing. Her offer seemed genuine, but what would it mean between them?

Duncan could only nod, accepting her offer and praying it would be good enough to avoid many of the problems he could foresee. Many marriages had less solid ground beneath them than this one. Many began as handfasts and found substance or children or even love that bound them past the year-and-a-day. But a few had ended and each had gone their own way.

At this moment they had no way of knowing which way his and Marian's bond would end or what he would discover about her past and yet she offered to stand at his side through it all. Now, his only battle would be with himself as he must keep the facts of her true condition on their wedding night a secret while he uncovered that which lay hidden. He nodded and tugged the reins of his horse, drawing him closer.

"So, we stay in the keep until a cottage can be readied for us?" she asked, drawing them back onto the common things they must discuss. They walked side by side toward the last of the men in their group, neither rushing nor lagging behind.

"Mayhap Ciara might be more comfortable in the nursery with the other bairns?" he asked.

He could see the panic in her eyes, but she did not

refuse immediately. Instead she walked a short distance in silence before turning to face him.

"Duncan, I…"

"I ken…you want to say nay."

"Aye! She is so young."

"She is a strong, intelligent and resilient child, Marian, and I think she will flourish in the presence of the others and with the attention and guidance of their caregivers and attendants."

He thought she would argue now, but instead she asked, "And you think that the earl and countess will allow such a thing? She is but a bastard…."

"They will allow it if I ask it of them. I only wait on your word to ask." He paused then to give her a chance to answer, but saw by the dark look in her eyes that she could not give the word. "And there is time to decide."

He thought she would not speak at all, but when she did, her words surprised him.

"Do you negotiate every aspect of your life, Peacemaker? Even with women?"

He'd not realized that he was doing that at all, when she had seen it clearly. Patterns in life were hard to break, so that he carried the important work he did for his clan over into his way of living should not be remarkable. One of her talents had been seeing those patterns and knowing how to use them within her family.

Her father's pattern of favoring and protecting his eldest son at any cost was not much different than any other nobleman's now that the English and Norman custom of all lands, wealth and titles going to only that son prevailed over much of their kingdom. The clan way of finding the best man, be he eldest or not, be he son or nephew or brother, declined now in the Highlands in favor of the king's custom and so Stout Duncan turned a blind eye to his other sons while pushing Iain into his role as firstborn son.

Her brother's pattern was action, then guilt and remorse, then reaction. She'd watched him grow to manhood and make the same mistakes again and again because of his inability to think before taking a reckless or ill-considered move that would have far-reaching consequences.

Her own pattern? She'd come to recognize that she was a watcher—she watched those around her and then tried to guide them along their path. And when guiding did not work, unfortunately, she stepped in and meddled where she should not. 'Twas her interference that brought Beitris to Dunalastair as Iain's wife and then her interference that…

She shook her head. She could not allow herself to think on all the repercussions of her matchmaking now. Marian lifted her head and looked at Duncan. He was staring at her as though she'd delivered some revelation instead of a simple observation that anyone could have made.

"How could you ken that?" he asked. He stopped walking and she stayed at his side.

"'Tis your way, when other men would take what is theirs, answer to no one, ask no one, you try to reason things out and bring acceptance of the unacceptable by logical means and practical arguments. I have watched you, even now you do it with me."

"You think you ken my ways after our few encounters?"

How could she explain her ability to him? Should she even try? Aye, he deserved at least that truth.

"I can see how you think and how you act, Duncan. 'Tis something I can do," she said, not certain that she was explaining it as she'd like to. "You take nothing on first glance, you investigate, you question, you search. Then you consider all the facts you have gathered and act. 'Tis why you married me and did not fight your way out of the situation as most men would have when faced with what you faced."

His mouth dropped open and she knew her words had shocked him.

"I may have only known you for a matter of days but even now, when you have the right to do what you will, to me, to my daughter, you wait and learn. Only when you ken all of it will you act, either for or against us, depending on whether what you discover will hurt or help your clan."

"How? How do you ken so much about me?"

"Your reputation precedes you as well, Peacemaker."

He accepted the humor in her words and was about to reply when he heard an order to halt called out. This would be their last stop before they'd reach Lairig Dubh. He had more questions for her, her insight was accurate and frightening in a way, but they would have to wait for a later time. For now, he needed to return her to her daughter, see to their comfort and give her that last opportunity to change her clothes that every woman seemed to need when meeting new people.

Marian was, after all, a woman first, and then…? Well, it would take him some time to discover everything else she was, but he would discover who she was.

Chapter Thirteen

The dark stones of Broch Dubh loomed ahead, at the top of the steep path. The road from the village climbed through the hills and led to the gate of the formidable castle. In spite of its name, it was not simply a tower, it was a castle with four towers and what Duncan had described as several acres of yards surrounded by high, thick protective walls.

'Twas almost as forbidding as its laird, the Earl of Douran, by reputation the Beast of the Highlands, Connor MacLerie. Marian remembered his name being discussed when she approached a marriageable age and the reactions of her mother and other women to it. Her mother trembled in fear as she recounted the story.

When his wife could not or did not produce a son and heir for him, her mother said in a hushed whisper, he threw her down the stairs of the tower, killing her. The woman's screams, damning him, were heard by everyone in the castle, as was her terror as she fell nigh to fifty feet to her death. And when she lay broken and dying on the cold stone floor, he'd fled, refusing to even have a mass said for her eternal soul.

Pray God, her mother had urged as she made the sign of the cross on herself, that he never comes calling here about you.

Marian found herself shivering now, from her own terror at the story of the Beast. Even as someone who kenned the inaccuracies that a reputation could contain, she found it difficult not to fret over meeting a man who carried such a one as that.

"Are you chilled, Marian? Do you need a cloak?" Duncan asked from his place at their side. He rode his horse next to the cart where she and Ciara rode.

"Nay," she said. "'Twas just an odd thought passing."

"He is not a beast."

Marian turned and looked at him, surprised by his guess. "How did you ken?"

"When you have been faced with it for years, you can see the change in someone's eyes and their face when they think of it. The story has been told so many times, and details are added to make it more horrifying than it was."

That it mirrored her own situation seemed to elude him when he said the words, but then she saw the recognition of it in his own expression. She tried to remember how many details had been added to her own story and not hold the ones she'd heard about the earl against him.

"When you meet Jocelyn," he added. "You will see the untruth of it in her eyes. Although she believed I was bringing her to her death, she would never leave his side now."

Marian watched as the first of their escorts passed through Broch Dubh's massive portcullis and into the main yard. Regardless of the late hour and the darkness of the night, many waited there for their arrival. Ciara climbed up on her lap and Marian felt the nervous shivering of her little body. Between all the horses and the late timing and all the other sights to see and hear, her daughter shook with excitement. When they reached the steps leading to the doors of the keep, Duncan helped them down from the cart and led them forward.

Two torches threw light on the landing, but did not illuminate the faces of the two giants standing there. With their huge bodies outlined by the flickering glow and being unable to see their faces, 'twas not difficult to shiver a bit herself. Duncan took her hand and brought her before them.

The nearest one stood nearly a full hand taller than Duncan and was fair in coloring. His crossed arms revealed the muscles and powerful arms of a warrior. The other one, standing back in the shadows, was darker in his coloring, taller than Duncan but not the other man, and his form looked as deadly and dangerous as the other. Which was laird? Who was the other? Marian felt Ciara step closer to her, a sure sign of her fear.

"Here now, Connor. You are frightening them," the taller one said as he moved into the light.

She nearly gasped at his appearance, for he had to be the handsomest man she'd ever beheld. His pale blond hair, worn long and pulled away from his face in no way lessened his fierce appearance or diminished his masculinity. The ancient runes marked on his arms, where the muscles were at their widest, spoke of a heritage not of the Highlands, but the plaid he wore around his waist and over his massive shoulders said otherwise.

"Lady," he said softly, holding one of his large hands out to her, "I am called Rurik Erengislsson. Welcome to Lairig Dubh." In a move she would have thought unlikely, his next action was even more welcoming. "And welcome to you, little lass," he said, while crouching down to meet Ciara's gaze. He held out his hand to Ciara who smiled shyly, still clutching at Marian's skirts.

"Rurik."

'Twas only one word, but Duncan's tone carried with it some warning to this man. Rurik smiled then, presenting the very image of an innocent man, but it was that smile that made Marian realize how this man could win over most any woman he met. The stories about his appeal to women, from cradle to grave, were most likely true and it was something tangible, a quality she could almost touch. She pitied the woman who he turned his formidable attentions on…or mayhap she envied her.

"Connor," Duncan said now, not waiting for Rurik to leave. "May I make my wife known to you? Marian Robertson, this is Connor MacLerie, the MacLerie, and the Earl of Douran. My laird."

Marian understood what was expected when meeting nobility. She dropped down to a deep curtsy and bowed her head before him, taking Ciara with her. Rurik stumbled back at her movements while the other man stepped forward out of the shadows where he'd been watching everything. Rurik, consummate warrior and quick on his feet, regained his footing and moved out of the laird's way. When Marian lifted her head and glanced at Duncan's laird, she understood how his reputation had grown from rumors to what it was. His gaze was more intense than Duncan's, if such a thing were even possible, and she waited for his words, not daring to even breathe.

"Welcome to our clan, Marian Robertson."

"My lord." Marian drew Ciara in front of her. "May I make my daughter known to you, my lord? This is Ciara."

The laird followed Rurik's example and crouched down so that he was face-to-face with her daughter. Then Marian realized why they did it—they were both fathers with wee bairns. Their attempts to make her daughter welcome were touching, truly, for it was such a small gesture but so significant.

"Welcome to you both. Now," he said, standing to his full height and reaching over to clasp Duncan's arm in his. "Jocelyn will be very upset if we dawdle out here since she awaits us in the hall. She made us wait dinner for your arrival and I ken she is fretting over it at this moment." He turned to motion Rurik to go ahead of them and then he held out his arm to Marian.

"Come, lady. I am certain that you must be ready for something to eat and then a warm bed to ease the discomforts of the road."

With Rurik as their leader, the laird as her escort and Duncan at their backs, they made their way into the keep, up another set of stairs to reach the main floor and then into the great hall where many sat at table eating their dinner. A petite woman, great with child, paced along the table that sat on the dais at the far end of the hall. Marian managed to keep up with the long-legged men who walked with her, but 'twas a near thing.

When they reached the dais, Rurik was pulled aside by a woman and Jocelyn stood before them. Marian began to sink into a curtsy, but the laird's strong hand on hers kept her standing.

"This is Duncan's wife, Marian Robertson. I hurried them along as much as I could, Jocelyn."

Marian watched in amazement as this man practically groveled before his wife! The lady stepped closer and Marian could see that the laird's wife was not much older than she herself and that she was far along in her pregnancy. The lady threw her arms around Marian and hugged her strongly.

"The daft man!" she whispered into Marian's ear. "He worries so when I am carrying and he forbid me to come out into the cool night air to wait for you." Lady Jocelyn leaned back and said louder, "Welcome to our home, Marian, now yours as well. Come, I can only imagine what more than a fortnight on the road with *men* was like for you." She shuddered then, as though thinking on the sheer horror of the situation.

The men frowned at her words and looked one to the other as though one of them could explain the problem, but none dared contradict the lady's words. Within minutes, Marian found herself eating a steaming bowl of tasty stew and drinking watered ale. Freshly baked bread and creamy butter and cheeses finished out the plain but filling fare. Duncan, she noticed, had not yet spoken to his laird, which she thought he must need to do. Just as they finished eating, Jocelyn motioned to one of the maidservants.

"Would your daughter like to see the nursery, Marian? She is welcome to sleep there while you stay here in the keep."

Marian felt Duncan's gaze on her and took a deep breath. So long on her own, making her own decisions and taking care of herself and her daughter, left her out of practice with trusting in others for such things. Now, it appeared that she had not only a husband who believed 'twas his right to interfere, and it was, but also his kin and clan. This was simply the first of many such choices to make and it terrified her.

"Connor's son and daughter as well as Rurik's daughter are there. Ciara will be in good company," Duncan whispered so only she would hear. "'Tis not a prison, only a chamber, Marian."

'Twould not do to appear to insult his laird's wife by refusing such an invitation. He tried to smooth over her fears and she felt a measure of gratitude for his calm and easy manner at such a tense and fearful time.

"Aye," she said, letting out her held-in breath and standing. "Ciara would love to meet the other children, lady."

"Marian, we are both the daughters of lairds. There is no need to call me by some title and bow and curtsy every time we encounter each other. I am Jocelyn. And this is," she said, placing her hand on the laird's shoulder, "this is simply Connor."

It must have been the long day's travel or the presence of so many people after being unaccustomed to it for so many years, but the tears in her eyes came as a surprise she did not want to think on. She blinked them away and, with a nod at…Jocelyn and Connor, Marian took Ciara's hand and began to follow the maidservant off the dais. She would see her to the nursery and try very hard to leave her there for the night.

The maidservant chattered to Ciara as they walked along the long corridor and up one flight of stairs to a tower room. Opening the door for them, the girl waved them inside. With another deep breath to fortify herself, Marian entered.

The chamber was larger than her cottage and was filled with small beds, even a cradle, toys, chairs, a table, storage trunks…and children. Two girls and one boy, him about Ciara's age, were being cared for by an assortment of servants. A large hearth built in the wall warmed the room of any chill and the remnants of a meal still on the table spoke of their care.

"This is Duncan's wife and her daughter, Ciara," the girl said to the other woman. "I am Glenna, lady, and this is Peigi, and we see to the bairns."

"I am no bairn," the boy said, crossing his arms over his chest and lifting his nose in the air. From his coloring and arrogance, she kenned this was Connor's get.

"Of course no', Aidan," Glenna said, going to his side. "Ye are the oldest one here and the laird's son. No bairn ye be."

Marian smiled as Glenna smoothed the ruffled male feathers and continued with the introductions until she and Ciara had met all the children. With a skill Marian admired, Glenna drew her daughter into the group and had her playing with Rurik's daughter.

"Ciara, you may stay here for the night if you wish," Marian said with more confidence than she felt. "Glenna and Peigi ken where I will be if there is need."

Part of her wanted Ciara to refuse. Part of her wanted her bairn to need no one but her. A larger part, though understood this was a good thing and tried to tell her heart 'twas so.

Luckily her daughter accepted the invitation and Marian left the nursery as Ciara and the others were sharing sweet cakes with Glenna and Peigi.

She lingered for a few minutes outside the chamber, listening with her ear pressed against the door, in case Ciara changed her mind. Instead she heard only the laughter of children and the soft voices of the women inside. Wiping the tears from her eyes, she forced one foot in front of the other and walked down the steps that would lead her back to the hall and away from her daughter.

Caught up in the anxiety of their parting, the first of many like it she feared, Marian paused at the bottom of the stairway. Several small groups of men and women passed her in the alcove, not knowing she watched and listened as they made their way to the hall…to see the Robertson Harlot.

"Hurry! Hurry! The Robertson Harlot is here at table with the laird."

"She doesna look much like a whore."

"I'd heard she has the largest titties!"

"Nay! Nay! Quite a disappointment for a whore."

"I canna see Duncan keeping her. They handfasted, did ye ken? She's no' good enough as wife to a man such as he."

Each word and laugh was like a blow to her, stinging

and cutting her deeply. She leaned back into the shadows, willing them all to pass without seeing her there.

It was all lies, all of it, yet bound by the past, she could offer no retort, no argument to clear her name or her daughter's. The pain of it seared her heart and she felt the tears flowing down her cheeks.

'Twas why she'd sought refuge in the anonymity offered by Iain. Returning to Dunalastair as a widowed cousin, she changed her appearance, used another name and lived quietly. No one there mentioned her disgrace or the events of that bygone night for fear of the laird's displeasure or wrath.

Now, though, with her identity laid out before the MacLeries, these reactions were what she'd come to expect. Marian was certain that, just as the Beast's story was used to frighten daughters into compliance, so too was the Harlot's. The story was too large and too widespread and, with the laird's negotiations with the Robertsons just concluded, too interesting for the clan not to tell…and to retell.

Marian waited to be certain they'd all gone past and thought about her promise to Duncan. How much more dishonor could be suffered than to have your wife called a whore? How much more shame than to ken others think you unworthy of a man such as he?

Not ready to face more of it this evening, Marian decided to find a servant who knew where Duncan's chambers were and go there without returning to the hall and facing such humiliation. Stepping out of the alcove, she turned and found him standing across the corridor, staring at her.

She'd been gone too long from the table and Duncan wondered if she'd changed her mind. He'd expected the difficulty she had in letting Ciara stay somewhere else for the night and he'd been pleased when it appeared she'd decided so. Then after staving off Jocelyn's attempts to pull more details from him and after ignoring Connor's glare since he'd bear his wife's displeasure at not being able to glean it from him, Duncan excused himself to find her.

Somehow, he'd managed to avoid thinking about some of the more personal repercussions of Marian's reputation through this whole series of events. Oh, aye, his men knew the story as did most anyone who lived in the Highlands. Before meeting her and finding out just how untrue it was, it had not bothered him in the least—'twas simply gossip about a woman. Now, though, it involved his wife and he knew it for the lie it was.

Worse, looking at her after she'd heard the mean, crude comments, he realized that somehow she was as trapped in the lies as he. Her eyes lost their sparkle and swelled with tears both shed and unshed and her face lost its color as she stood and heard these strangers' judgments of her.

And they were all lies.

Before he knew what he could say, he walked to her side. He thought to reach out and hold her, but he did not think she would accept his touch at this moment. Truth be told, the only time he'd touched her, other than helping her on or off of her horse or the cart, was when they'd tupped.

"I promised not to dishonor or embarrass you, Duncan, yet my very name has done that."

"Have you been whoring in this hallway since you left my side, Marian?"

She gasped at his both ludicrous and vulgar question.

"Of course not!" she answered. "I have never been a whore."

"Then you have not dishonored me or embarrassed me. You did promise not to disappoint me, though, and your silent skulking off into the shadows as though guilty of the gossip they monger, would do that."

"I cannot face them," she said softly. "'Tis too much to ask of me." She twisted her hands nervously in front of her, reminding him that she had just relinquished her daughter's care to a stranger. "I cannot." Marian met his gaze for only a second, showing him the terror there then dropped it to the floor.

"Then you will allow them to rule your existence here, and your daughter's," he argued. "Is that what you want?"

"If we go back into the hall, do you plan to announce that you spilled a virgin's blood on our wedding night? Duncan, will you proclaim that you were the first man to enter the Robertson Harlot?" Her words should have sounded bold, now though they pleaded with him. "Will you?"

She'd neatly nailed him to the wall with her question. He could not or his arrangements, agreements, contracts and negotiations all fell to the floor, scattering all the good they'd achieved for his clan and hers. But, he must do something and do it now.

He held out his hand to her and waited. "Come."

Marian glanced at him and then up the stairs where her daughter remained, clearly undecided between the choices that faced her, clearly not ready for either one. He watched as she wiped the tears from her eyes and face with the edge of her sleeve. Taking a deep breath in and letting it go, she took his hand.

Neither said a word as they entered the hall, but their presence was noted and the gathering there fell silent as he led her back up onto the dais. He guided her behind the table to where Connor sat and whispered a few words to Connor. Connor nodded and stood at their sides, motioning for Rurik to join them. As he expected, they did so without a question. Once those in the hall had quieted, he held up their joint hands and spoke.

"This is my wife, Marian Robertson. No matter what came before the day we joined ourselves each to the other, she is mine now and I am hers. If anyone speaks ill of her or calls her whore, they attack me as well and will answer for it."

Duncan paused and waited for the words to echo around the room. Then Connor reached over and placed his hand on theirs.

"She is mine and I protect my own," Duncan called out louder, using their clan's motto as his own.

Connor added his voice and his blessing as laird as he repeated the words. "I protect my own," he shouted, lifting their hands so all could see.

Rurik joined then, calling it out once more. "I protect my own! A MacLerie! A MacLerie!"

When the battle cry was called, no one in the clan hesitated. The men stood first and answered the call, and then the women, until the entire hall shook from the sound of it. As they quieted once more, Connor released his hold, but Duncan held on to her hand. He nodded his thanks to Connor and Rurik, he would speak with them in the morn, and leaned his head down so Marian could hear him.

"Come, I will show you to our chamber."

Shock filled her gaze and she looked a ghostly pale white, so he put his arm around her waist and guided her to the north tower and his room. Once there, he sat her on the chair nearest the window and poured a cup of wine for her, a courtesy arranged by Jocelyn. She was so unresponsive he nearly had to pour it down her throat to get her to drink, but after a sip or two, she drank it on her own.

He'd not noticed the sparsity of his room and its lack of comfortable furnishings or decoration until just now. This was simply a place to sleep when he was here in Lairig Dubh, a place to keep his few belongings and a private place to bring a woman if need drove him to it. Now as he looked around it, he saw he had only a small trunk of clothing, another that held the books and parchments of his work and…nothing else.

Well, a wife.

She'd not moved, other than to lift the cup to her mouth and back down again. Had he pushed her too far too soon? He'd only realized, when saying the words to Jocelyn, that Marian had been on her own, and making her own decisions, for the last five years. Bringing her back into a clan, and one she kenned not and wanted not, and forcing her to live among so many when her custom was to live alone would be a hard adjustment to her.

Duncan needed to get her into bed, so he turned and walked over to it, stopping first to lift off the extra blankets that Jocelyn must have had sent there. Tugging on the top layers, he pulled the bedcovers down. If she watched him, she did not react. Going to her side, he knelt down next to her, tilted the cup and told her to drink the rest. Then he began to loosen the ties of her gown.

Still no reaction.

"Come, lass, you need to stand," he said softly, drawing her to her feet so he could get her tunic and gown off.

He accomplished it far easier than he expected because she did not resist him, a fact he feared more than anything. Soon, he lifted her into the bed, took off his own clothes, put out the candles and climbed in next to her. Shifting her onto her side, he slid one arm beneath her head, around her body and held her close.

The tears should not have surprised him, for she'd been much stronger and for much longer a time than he would have thought possible before she let go of it all in his arms. But these tears seemed to rip her apart as she sobbed so deeply he thought she would lose her breath. Listening to her cries and thinking on all that had happened to her in these last weeks made him realize how desperately unhappy she was.

Oh, there was an attraction between them, one that with enough time and left on its own could have developed into something more. Instead it had been used, she had been used, most foully to trap them both in this handfasted marriage. After the changes in her life since his arrival in Dunalastair, 'twas no wonder at all why she cried.

The tempest calmed after a short time and he held her until he felt her body go limp. He smoothed the hair back from her face, adjusted her covers and let her sleep. Just as he felt the pull of sleep on his thoughts, a soft knock came at the door. Slipping carefully from her side, Duncan tugged his shirt over his head and opened the door.

"'Tis the lass, Duncan. She is crying so," Glenna said.

"I will come."

"We tried to soothe her, since 'twas her first night here and all, but nothing works."

"I ken what she needs."

He followed Glenna back through the keep and up to the nursery. He heard the soft weeping that nearly imitated her mother's before he entered the rooms. Ciara sat in Peigi's arms, crying even as the woman rocked her gently to and fro and whispered soft words to her. She lifted her head and stopped crying when she spied him.

"Duncan," she said, holding out her little arms to him. He lifted her from Peigi's lap and held her against his chest.

"Hush, now, sweet," he whispered, rubbing her back as he spoke. "What is the matter?"

"I dinna like it here, Duncan. I want my mama," she whispered back, causing him to smile.

"Come then, I will take you to her, Ciara."

He nodded to the women and carried her through the now dark keep to his rooms. Marian had not moved, so he lifted the girl over and laid her next to her mother. Ciara squirmed her way into Marian's arms and he heard her say her daughter's name, though still asleep.

Once convinced they were settled for the night, Duncan left his room and climbed the stairs leading to the top of the tower and out onto the battlements.

Making his way around the outside of the tower and then the keep, he met up with the soldiers on duty and spent some time catching up on the news of the clan while he'd been away. Several bairns had been born, one of the oldest of the villagers had died and Father Micheil had witnessed the exchange of wedding vows between two couples.

Apprised of all of the goings-on he'd missed, Duncan continued walking the battlements for a long time before walking the rest of the grounds around the keep and outbuildings. He was too wound-up for sleeping so he spent most of the night thinking on the words he would use to explain the situation to Connor. After supporting him and Marian without question this night, Duncan owed him at least an honest accounting of how he'd come to this point and what he planned to do to keep the clan safe and unharmed by whatever machinations. He spent the night walking and thinking, turning ideas and words over in his mind, seeking the right thing to do.

When the sun rose brightly the next morning, promising a clear and sunny day, he was still walking.

Chapter Fourteen

A soft knock dragged her from sleep and Marian found herself surprised by two things—the sun was high in the sky, and her daughter lay sleeping at her side and her husband did not. Climbing carefully out of the bed, she wrapped a blanket around her shoulders and opened the door a crack to see who knocked.

"Good morrow," the cheerful young woman said. "I am Cora, Lady Jocelyn's maid, and she sent me to invite you and your daughter to break your fast in the solar."

"What time is it?" Marian asked, embarrassed to be caught abed as the day must be nigh on three or four hours past dawn.

"Lady Jocelyn said not to fret over the time, just to come to the solar when you and your lass are ready."

Marian made sure the woman told her the location of the solar and accepted the invitation. Closing the door, she discovered that someone had taken out her gowns and tunics and laid them over a trunk. With not many to choose from, Marian brushed the dirt of traveling from the best one and got dressed. 'Twas when the thought of how she'd come to be in bed undressed struck her.

Looking around, she saw no signs of Duncan. His clothing she discovered in the other trunk, but nothing was disturbed in it. His cloak was gone as was the sword she remembered seeing ever at his side. Had he not slept here? How had Ciara gotten into her bed?

She thought she remembered him bringing her here and giving her wine. And when she thought back to last evening, she remembered crying in his arms. Marian felt the flush of embarrassment in her cheeks as she remembered his arm around her, holding her close as she sobbed out her misery. 'Twas only the second time ever she'd let her feelings loose and both times had happened since the Peacemaker walked into her life just over a month ago.

Marian climbed onto that bed and slowly roused her daughter from sleep. After their journey, sleeping in such a large and comfortable bed such as this was seductive. Ciara finally rubbed her eyes, sat up in the bed and looked around the room.

"Where is Duncan?" she asked.

"I ken not, sweet," Marian answered.

"That is what he called me, Mama," she said as she scooted off the edge of the bed and went searching for her sack of toys.

"Ciara, when did you see Duncan? This morn?"

"Nay, Mama. He came in the night when I cried. I wanted to see you, but Glenna said I should stay with her and the bairns."

She left Ciara in the nursery after their evening meal and had not gone back. But Duncan had. In the night.

"What did Duncan do?"

"He held me and whispered to me and then he carried me here to sleep in the big bed with you."

"He did?" she asked. He would never cease to surprise her, and nothing did more than this.

"And then he covered us up and told me to sleep. And I did."

"Come, Ciara. Lady Jocelyn is waiting for us to visit her."

Marian found her brush and arranged their hair into long braids. With the dye wearing out of her hair each time she washed it, she needed to find more of the plant root she used for the brown color. Tempted to wear a kerchief, she decided that it would bring more attention to her since none of the women in the keep seemed to be wearing them. So, she wrapped her braid around her head, covering the hair that was losing its brown shade.

If only her hair had not been cut, she could have covered her whole head with it and not worried for several more weeks. But that, like so much of her past could not be changed now. She finished arranging and took Ciara to the lady's solar. Greeted with friendly words, she was introduced to Rurik's wife, Margriet, who by the looks of it, was also carrying.

The signs were mostly Rurik kneeling in front of her with his large hands rubbing over her abdomen, clearly outlining the bairn growing inside her.

Was every woman here as fruitful as this?

Her expression must have spoken for her, for Jocelyn began laughing and told Rurik to leave. He did not immediately react, apparently enjoying the feel of his babe moving under his hands, but when Connor bellowed his name out from several floors below, he moved. But before he left her side, he kissed his wife senseless right in front of them!

With Rurik gone it took several minutes for everyone, including the lovely Margriet, to recover from his enthusiastic display of affection. A wonderful, hot, thick porridge sat warming near the hearth, and soon both she and Ciara were eating large bowls of it, sweetened with honey and creamed with fresh milk and butter. Noticing that only the two of them ate, she asked about it.

"My husband prefers to break our fast in our chambers, so we have already eaten," Jocelyn explained, but she did not explain the blush that filled her cheeks as she did so.

"As does Rurik," Margriet added, as a blush crept up her cheeks as well.

Then the two women looked at each other and burst out laughing. Finally Margriet leaned in closer to Marian and whispered so that Ciara did not hear.

"Our husbands find our blossoming bodies arousing, Marian," she explained, to Marian's complete confusion. "'Tis a struggle to get rid of them most morns."

Whatever could they mean? Surely Connor and Jocelyn did not…? Still? But she was carrying. And not Rurik and Margriet as well? None of this made sense to Marian.

Men such as these usually kept lemans for their pleasure, so that their wives were not burdened by such things, and especially at times like this when they were…breeding. And men such as the laird and his valued warrior, with their status, their power and with their nearly breathtaking appearance, should have no difficulty finding any number of willing women to warm their beds. Coming up with no way to ask strangers about such things, Marian simply shrugged and turned her attentions back to her food.

"Marian, I need your help," Jocelyn began. "Duncan tells me of your talents with plants and herbs. Is that correct?"

"Aye, lady…Jocelyn." She nodded, giving the bowl to a waiting servant and wiping her hands on a linen cloth. "I kept a garden back in Dunalastair. My brother promised to send me cuttings so that I would not lose everything."

Ciara finished her porridge and Margriet called her over to play with her own daughter in one of the corners of the large chamber. As she watched Ciara took out her carved animals and offered one to the younger child. Content that she was playing, Marian turned her attention back to Jocelyn's request.

"I tend to the one here, but these last few months have been difficult and now the daft man will not let me work there. 'Tis hard to explain to someone who knows not how to break up the soil with their fingers to avoid damage to the roots the importance of such a thing."

Marian smiled, understanding her exact concern. Some were too heavy of hand. Some trampled tender plants underfoot. Some could not see the difference between one plant or vine and another. Very few could care for plants correctly.

"With our harvest quickly approaching, the men

will be busy seeing to that, but I thought that mayhap you might take the garden into your care and prepare it for winter?"

"Oh, Jocelyn, I would like that!" she answered. "When can you show it to me?"

"Since the day is a fair one, we could go now," Jocelyn said. "Bring your daughter, if you would like and I can show you both the keep and grounds."

"I would like that." Marian called out to Ciara and held out her hand. "Come, sweet. Lady MacLerie will show us around the keep. We will have gardens to work in."

But, the displeasure at being asked to leave her toys and her playmate lay clear on her face. Margriet smiled and looked from one to the other.

"Ciara may stay with us and play, if you would like, Marian. 'Twould be no trouble."

"Mama! May I?" Ciara jumped to her feet and ran over to her, tugging on her skirts and whispering. "May I?"

"Only if you promise to do as the lady tells you." Marian rubbed Ciara's head, smoothing her hair back.

Ciara jumped up and promised to do so. "I will, Mama. I promise." Then, with the ability that children seem to have, she ran back and lost herself in the play.

"I can find you if there is a problem, Marian. Worry not about her," Margriet said, answering Marian's unspoken fears.

With a nod, she turned to follow Jocelyn out of the solar, down to the main floor and out through the kitchens. If everyone quieted a moment when she entered or when she passed, she tried not to notice since she was, after all, a newcomer to the clan, the keep and the village and would have sparked an interest even if her name was not known. Even if…

Jocelyn continued pointing out things and places and people that Marian should learn, so Marian paid close attention as they walked. She promised the cook to come back and speak about which herbs he favored and the steward about which ones were needed by the household. Just as she was beginning to believe that this undertaking might be bigger than her abilities, Jocelyn reassured her that others in the village also tended their own plots and provided other plants to meet the clan's needs.

They entered a gated plot of land and Marian took note of the size and layout of the garden. Many sections were overgrown, some looked well-tended, others not. Walking around the perimeter of it and then up and down its lanes, she evaluated the good and the bad…and the worst of it. Her assessment must have shown on her face, for she looked up to find Jocelyn frowning back at her.

"'Tis truly that bad, Marian? If you had come at summer's start, you would have found it in much better shape, as I was at that time." Jocelyn laid a hand on the swell of her belly and laughed. "Where do we begin?"

"Where do *I* begin," she repeated. "I suspect your husband would not be pleased to find you working when he has told you to cease."

"Daft man that he is," Jocelyn muttered. "Come, show me where you would begin."

They walked up one path until Marian came to the worst of it. "I need to clean this out to see where the new growth begins and what I can remove."

Jocelyn provided a small trowel and Marian was soon on her knees, digging happily into the rich soil of the garden. Marian lost herself in the work, following Jocelyn's instructions and directions and at sometime later Jocelyn joined her in the work. She never realized it until Jocelyn's startled cry as Connor lifted his wife bodily, yet with an unmistakable care, to her feet. Sitting back on her heels, Marian watched as the laird held his wife until she regained her balance. Even then, his arms stayed around her.

"Jocelyn, you are not to do this work," Connor growled.

Marian climbed to her feet and started to bow to Connor, thinking of some way to explain away or at least mitigate his ire at his wife. He shook his head before she spoke her first word.

"Nay, Marian. Think not to interfere in this matter," he said, frowning at both of them. When she thought she might have already made herself the unwelcomed guest, he shook his head again. "You must stop this bowing to me. The only time you need do that is when the king's man is here or some other outsider."

"Aye, my…" She caught the words. "Aye, Connor."

Jocelyn wiped her hands of the dark soil and glanced at her husband's angry face. "I was simply helping Marian learn the garden," she explained.

Once he let her go, she looked around for the person who usually reported her behavior, and especially her bad behavior, to her husband. Rurik was nowhere to be seen, but she could be certain he'd told Connor of her activity here. "Connor, it feels good to move and to stretch, even as the bairn grows bigger within."

She smiled when she saw him understand the reference she made to their earlier private time this morn. He would not allow her to take on more physical tasks with the bairn expected in another two months, but that did not stop him from enjoying her body as he would. They had bent and stretched together just this morn, and she now enjoyed his discomfort and the blush that moved up his face.

"Jocelyn…" he began and then stopped, looking from her to Marian and then back. Finally, wise man that he was growing to be, he realized he could not win and stepped away.

Jocelyn enjoyed his discomfort for a moment and then she reached up and touched his cheek. "I thank you for your concern, Connor. I promise I will not do anything more than is safe for me and the bairn."

He covered her hand with his and turned into it, kissing her palm. She enjoyed his touch for another minute and then stepped away. Marian was studying the soil intently, but Jocelyn did not miss the flush of embarrassment in Duncan's wife's cheeks. Hardly what she would have expected from a harlot.

"Husband, if you would but bring that bench here, I could sit and talk with Marian while she works." She waited as he did just that and as she settled on it, she asked, "So, how did you ken of my working here? Rurik as usual?"

"Nay, do not lay the blame on him this time, wife," Connor said. "I was on my way to speak with Duncan when I spied your disobedience from yon window in the tower." He nodded above and behind them at the window, where Rurik now stood waving. He sighed as she raised her brows to him. "Mayhap Rurik pointed you out to me…."

Whether Connor detected it, she knew not, but she caught Marian's hesitation and pause in her work at the mention of Duncan's name. Well, 'twas a usual thing for a newly married woman to take notice of her husband.

"I have delayed you from your work long enough, Connor," she said, itching now to learn more from Marian about how their handfasting had come about and knowing she would learn nothing with Connor's presence. "I will see you at the noon meal?"

Connor leaned down now and kissed her fiercely, as was his custom. Before he let her go, he whispered to her.

"Tread lightly, wife."

Jocelyn understood the warning and 'twas not about her behavior, but about her intention to seek out more information from Marian. Connor did ken her ways, as she did his—Jocelyn waited for his words.

"Marian. Would you join me after the noon meal? I would like to speak with you about Dunalastair. I visited there long ago and would be pleased to talk with you about it."

"Aye," Marian replied, though no enthusiasm entered her tone, something Jocelyn could understand from her own arrival here at the home of the Beast of the Highlands.

Now, she knew him as husband, protector, lover, friend, father of her children and even as laird, but 'twas a difficult thing to get past his reputation on first meeting. Mayhap, with Marian's own experience with a sordid reputation, her fear of Connor would go away quickly?

"Until the meal then, ladies," Connor said, with a polite bow of his own.

Jocelyn watched him leave, enjoying the way his legs and hips moved and the outline of his broad shoulders and strong arms. Aye, she loved the man and she loved watching him and touching him and being loved by him. A few minutes of silence and she realized that Marian must think her a lovesick fool to be gawking at her husband in the middle of the morning in front of strangers.

The fear in Marian's eyes removed all worries that the woman even thought on the trivial matters of Jocelyn's attraction to her husband, unseemly as it could be at times. Was she afraid of Connor? Or of the questions she knew he'd asked her?

"Duncan told us that your marriage was done in haste and you were forced to leave without your plants…or many clothes." Bringing their discussion to something menial might help. "I have some gowns that I cannot wear now, because of my increased girth…and breadth…and width." She let out a frustrated breath at all the changes her body seemed to make on its own. "I think you and I might be a size, though not now, but I would rather have them worn than sitting in some trunk." Jocelyn slid her hands around her body, considering the added inches on her hips and breasts. "Did you gain like this while you were carrying your daughter?"

If she had not looked quickly, Jocelyn would have missed the puzzled expression on Marian's face at her question. Marian stood and wiped her hands clean of the loose soil.

"Nay," she said, shaking her head now and not

meeting Jocelyn's gaze. "I thank you for your offer, Jocelyn, but I cannot accept them."

"Truly, they sit in a chest, probably gathering mold. And who knows if I will ever fit back into them once I have this bairn. Come," she said, standing. "Let us see if any fit you before making any decisions."

Marian had the sense, it seemed, to give into the inevitable, for she nodded and followed her back to the solar. If Marian felt like a peasant, that was how she would act, but Jocelyn knew better—her guess was Marian was a noblewoman wearing this other life as some sort of penance. Until she could discover the truth, she would, as her husband warned, tread lightly.

But that did not mean she could not try to find the reasons behind the other emotion that she read in Marian's eyes…loneliness.

Duncan paced along the corridor in front of the tower that led to Connor's chambers. When he could no longer delay, he climbed the curving stairway up to the top floor. The documents of the treaty as well as those of his handfasted contract were in the leather case in his hand and bags of gold and other gifts for Connor lay inside the small, locked chest he carried. He stared at the door to his laird's, and friend's, room.

'Twas where he was to meet and review the outcome of his negotiations and the tangible results and successes of those talks. Never in all of his life did he expect to be bringing back news of his own errors in judgment and how they'd caused the problems they had.

When he went to see the MacCallum laird to negotiate for a bride for Connor, no such thing had occurred. When he went north to the MacDougalls in Lorne to gain space on ships to Flanders and the continent for MacLerie goods, no unexpected twists or turns happened. When he'd met with the king's men to work out the agreement that made Connor the Earl of Douran, nothing untoward came of it.

But this simple task to shore up support to the east and to agree to mutual defense in case of need, and he ends up in a public disgrace that can only be redeemed by a hasty wedding, and a handfasted one at that. What would be Connor's reaction to all of this?

The sound of Connor coming up the stairs, along with Rurik from the sound of the bickering, forced Duncan to collect his final thoughts and steel himself for this encounter. The dread that curled in his gut was something new and different for him. Never had he faced Connor with such a feeling before. If negotiations did not go as planned, if the results were not everything the clan elders and laird had hoped for, so be it. So long as Duncan gave it his best efforts, in preparation and execution, he could present his work to his laird with a clean conscience.

This time, though…this time 'twas something completely unlike anything he'd ever experienced. Mayhap Connor could have some insight about the situation once they'd spoken? When he'd faced failure in the past, he learned from the errors he'd made. This time, he had no idea where his lapse in judgment or preparation had been, so 'twas hard to give it an adequate evaluation. Lost in his thoughts, he did not realize that Connor and Rurik now stood before him.

"Duncan?" 'Twas not Connor's voice, but the laird's rough shake of his shoulder, that brought Duncan out of his stupor.

"You look unwell," said Rurik. Connor opened the door to his chambers and led them both inside. "Marian looked well enough, so I dinna think it's something catching."

Duncan walked in, put the wooden chest and his leather satchel on the table near the window and shook his head. "I am not ill, Rurik. And when did you see Marian?" He did not bother to explain that his sleepless night caused his rough appearance, for that would only bring more questions.

No matter that he was married. No matter that he was about to be a father for the second time. No matter that he would never stray from Margriet's side or her heart, Rurik had some power over women that could turn them to addle-brained idiots in his presence. Duncan had seen it more times than he could keep count of and thought he'd seen a glimmer of it last evening when he was introduced to Marian.

Her eyes had taken on that strange, soft look when she first saw him in the light of the torches, the same expression that happened to most every woman on meeting his half-Scots, half-Norse cousin who could be the heir to the Earl of the Orkneys if he'd chosen to be. The danger with Rurik, though, was that he loved women in a way that they could feel. Even though he would die before betraying Margriet, he had a manner of talking to them as though they were the only females left on earth.

The worst part was the sharp burn of jealousy at the

thought that she might prefer Rurik's light, affable way to his own, confused, somewhat distant one.

"Just a few minutes ago," Connor answered instead. "She was working in the garden with Jocelyn."

"That should accomplish two things then," he said. At Connor's raised brow, he continued, "Keeping Jocelyn from working too hard. Against your orders, if I remember correctly from the last time she was carrying?" Connor answered with a slight tilt of his head. "And improving the cook's temper over the lack of his favorite herbs since you stopped allowing Jocelyn to work in the garden."

Rurik laughed out loud at his comment. He'd long been complaining over the changes to the quality and tastiness of the food in Lairig Dubh since Connor had ordered his wife to ease from her duties as her pregnancy progressed. "I for one would be pleased to have the cook happy once more."

After Connor poured them some ale and sat in his chair, Duncan opened his satchel first and handed the parchments that outlined the treaty to Connor. The laird perused the words there, but would save a thorough reading for later. Although Connor was skilled in several languages himself, Duncan kenned he would wait for Jocelyn to read it first. He trusted her that much.

Another stab of jealousy pierced him.

Mayhap living among happily married men was a bad example for him? Duncan guessed that he'd expected, when he married, his marriage would be like those of his friends. He'd delayed marrying in the hopes of finding a woman who could be his helpmate and his friend, much like Connor's and Rurik's wives were to them. Instead he was handfasted to a stranger, one with a child who could not be hers, other yet-undisclosed secrets and plans to leave after their year-and-a-day had passed by.

Connor asked several questions and Duncan answered them, outlining the basic agreements and what they received and what they gave away. Since Rurik oversaw the clan's warriors and fighting strength, his questions centered on that aspect of the treaty. When Connor had a firm understanding of the agreements, Duncan handed him the wooden chest.

"From Iain Robertson to you," he explained. "And, on my word, this chest has not been opened since he locked it in my presence and gave me the key."

Duncan held out the key to Connor. He hoped Connor would allow him to stay when he opened it, for an intense curiosity built within him over the contents.

"I would expect nothing less than that, Duncan." Connor stared at him for a moment before continuing, "I ken that some things did not turn out the way you planned them, but you still have my faith."

Another stab—this time guilt, for he had decided not to reveal everything to Connor about Marian and her past. The laird's expression of faith may have been well-intentioned but was ill-timed.

"Now, sit and tell me how you came to be a married man."

The words, balanced in tone and volume, sounded like a request, but the order lay inherent within them. Duncan sat down opposite of Connor, drank the rest of his ale and thought on how to begin.

"As I am certain Hamish already explained," he said, kenning that Connor's brother-by-marriage would have spoken to him after the scene in hall, "I was drugged, and dishonored the laird's sister. Marriage seemed the right remedy to the situation."

"'Twas no' as simple as that," Rurik offered. "'Tis a bit difficult to dishonor a wh…" Rurik wisely stopped before saying the word.

"Not marrying her would have been understandable as well, Duncan. If you think the laird was behind this and you knew that all along, why agree to it? You ken you would have my support, regardless of your choice." Connor stared him in the eyes. "Was there something between you and the lass?"

"An attraction, aye," he admitted. "I met her by accident and stopped to see her and her daughter once or twice while at Dunalastair Keep." He would admit to that as well. "I think Marian was a burden Iain wanted to rid himself of. There's talk of a new marriage and his disgraced sister living in the village would have been an impediment to most noble families in marriage negotiations."

"Hamish said no one knew the woman was the Robertson Harlot." So, Hamish had given an accounting to Connor first.

"Even better then, get her out of the way before people began recognizing her."

"I imagine that the laird's man knew your ways and used it against you?" Rurik asked.

"My ways?" His comment was reminiscent of Marian's.

"Aye, your ways. Peace at any cost. A man of honor,

of his word. The Robertson knew you would not try to weasel out of the situation and he would have his sister gone before she could become a true problem. Neatly done." Rurik obviously approved of the handy little deal. Or at least how it was accomplished.

"Think you he planned this from the start?" Connor asked.

Duncan shook his head. "Nay. I suspect from some of his comments that he took advantage of an opportunity presented to him."

Connor stood then, signaling that this questioning was done. "You should feel honored that he believes you man enough to put his sister into your care. With all that entails."

"More like dumping his problems into my hands," Duncan muttered.

The backhand from Rurik was unexpected. He leaned over and slapped Duncan across the face and then rose to his full height, crossed his arms over his chest and waited for Duncan's answer.

"You do not ken…" he began.

"It does not signify," Rurik answered. "You claimed her as wife before her people and yours. Now you must honor that vow even as you demanded the clan to."

"She does not want to be my wife."

The words slipped out before he could stop them. In spite of the rest of it, in spite of the circumstances that brought them together, in spite of every problem caused by this joining, Duncan was devastated by the fact that Marian did not want him as her husband.

Oh, aye, he could understand that she wanted no marriage, content to live quietly and out of sight in the village where she grew up. He could even understand not wanting to be part of a forced marriage, especially to a man who was not noble born and would not be worthy of the wealth and power she would bring to him. But, the part that ripped into his soul was that she did not want him as her husband and seemed to be counting down the days until she was free of him.

"Many marriages start out that way, Duncan. You were witness to my own debacle. Jocelyn—" Connor stopped and lowered his voice "—Jocelyn called me by another man's name when I bedded her the first time. The name of the man who was her first love, who she'd planned to marry."

Duncan had to fight to keep his mouth closed at this shocking disclosure and dared not look over at Rurik for his reaction. Considering Connor's temperament at that time, 'twas a wonder that Jocelyn survived the night...or that the man involved was still alive.

"I tell you this only to show you that even with a rocky start, a true marriage can grow." Connor paused and added, "And if you tell anyone I spoke of that incident, *anyone,* I will cut off your ballocks." Rurik choked and coughed at the threat, but nodded in acceptance of the warning.

"Connor, I offered her marriage. She would not accept it and instead demanded a handfasting in its place." Duncan ran his hands through his hair and then rested his head against his hands. "This would seem to be the escape she has been wanting, a way to get away from her family and her disgrace and then a way to get out from me."

Connor nodded his agreement. "Could you blame

her for that? To live her life hiding in plain sight and having no chance for much more?" Connor shrugged. "Have you seen what is in that box?"

Duncan looked up, curious now. "Nay. 'Twas closed when I arrived and he only locked it in front of me. From the sound and weight of it, some gold. What else?"

Connor lifted out several sacks. Tossing one on the table, he read from a small piece of parchment attached to it. *"My sister's dowry—to be administered by the MacLerie."* The next one was the same size as the first. *"Matching my sister's dowry—as a gift to Duncan MacLerie."* A third, smaller sack landed next to the others two. *"For Ciara Robertson's care and well-being."* The last one was about that same size. *"To the MacLerie for his assistance in all matters regarding my sister."*

The silence grew around them, broken only when Rurik let out a sharp whistle. "You are a rich man now, Duncan."

True, according to the contracts signed by her brother, all of the gold that named Marian or Ciara as the recipient, whether sent with other instructions or not, belonged to him to do with as he saw fit. The niggling feeling moved down his spine, from his head to his legs, warning him of something bigger here, some yet unseen part of the puzzle. Connor recognized it, as well, for his dark, intense expression spoke of his suspicions.

"Rurik. I would speak to Duncan alone."

Chapter Fifteen

With a nod, Rurik accepted the dismissal. "I will be in the yard, if you are up to it, Connor." With a hearty laugh, knowing that such a challenge would be met, he left, pulling the door closed tightly behind him. Duncan felt Connor's scrutiny, but said nothing.

He'd never doubted his cousin's loyalty and would never, for there was nothing that would make Duncan betray him or his clan. Indeed, Duncan stood ready to lead the clan if anything happened to Connor before Aidan was of age. But something was making him lie to his laird and Connor must discover what reason lay behind his deceit.

"I trust you and your abilities no less because of this, Duncan. You made no mistakes that endangered our clan or its aims in this treaty."

Connor watched Duncan's eyes for any sign of subterfuge and found none there. There was more, much more, to the story of his marriage to the Robertson Harlot, but Connor was having no success drawing it out of him.

"So, other than to smooth ruffled feathers, very ruffled if the amount of gold is any indication, what reason would Iain of Dunalastair have to pay you off?"

His cousin and heir to the high seat stared back at him. Would he share his concerns with his laird or would he keep some secret that the Robertson was paying a high price for? Connor could accept that Duncan would keep some personal issues and concerns to himself, as laird he should expect a man to have some measure of privacy.

"I fear there is more to this, Connor. I was so surprised by the simple audacity of it that I was caught off my guard and in a situation that had only one way out of it."

Connor stood and walked to the table. He filled their cups once more and handed it to Duncan. "What do you suspect?"

The plain question caused a myriad of emotions to flit across his cousin's face. Duncan started to speak and stopped, shrugging. "I ken not. I am looking into the matter. I have sent some men back to find information I may have missed."

Connor asked the one question that would settle whether or not he became involved or whether he waited on Duncan to do as he said. "Is she a danger to your clan, tanist?"

"I will never allow her to be a danger to my clan. On my honor."

Connor held out his hand to his tanist and gave him the formal acceptance due him in this oath of honor. This was not the explanation he'd hoped for, but Connor would never doubt Duncan's loyalty.

"I asked to speak to her after the noon meal. Would you prefer to be present?"

"Prefer?" Duncan asked.

"You are her husband. 'Tis your right."

He thought on it for a moment and then nodded. "I would let you become acquainted with her alone."

"And your gold?" This much gold could spin even the soundest of heads. "What should I do with this?"

"I told Iain, I have told Marian and I will tell you, Connor. I can provide for my wife and her child without that." He nodded at the bags still sitting on the table. "Hold it until the matter is settled one way or another."

"Duncan," Connor said, waiting for him to meet his gaze. When he did, Connor smiled. "You could make her want to stay married to you if you set your mind to it."

Unfortunately the expression staring back at him did nothing to reassure him that keeping her was what Duncan wanted to do. This did not bode well at all. Not for Duncan. Not for Marian or her daughter. But especially not for him, for it would be practically impossible to keep Jocelyn from meddling in this situation once she came to realize that they needed meddling.

And he'd never seen a couple who needed meddling more than this one.

"First I will find out if she presents a danger to this clan, then I can decide about the rest of it," he said with the sound of great confidence of a man who rarely had to deal with women.

If there was one thing that Connor knew now, it was that things were never as simple as one and then the other. And the heart had a way of jumbling everything out of order. He suspected that there was more than an attraction between Duncan and Marian. He also supposed that neither of them realized it.

Damn it! Now he was thinking in the same manner that softhearted Jocelyn did and that could only lead to trouble. Connor needed to stay away from such things and allow Duncan and Marian to find their own course. If a true marriage was destined for them, he had no doubt it would happen.

"Use whatever you need to settle your doubts."

"On another matter…" Connor nodded for him to continue. "With your permission, I would like to build a cottage in the village for Marian and Ciara."

Connor walked to the window and looked out over the yard and the walls, down to the village at the river's edge. The adage "keep your friends close, but your enemies closer" ran through his mind and he shook his head.

"Can it wait until spring, Duncan? I would rather have you close and I ken that Jocelyn would appreciate the presence of another mother, another woman who has given birth that is, in the keep when her labor begins."

He tried to cover his surprise when an instant of sheer panic filled Duncan's eyes, turning his gaze back to the activities below them. Then, his cousin said, "I will tell Marian."

"Now, I have to beat Rurik senseless. Will you come and watch?"

Duncan laughed then, sounding very much like the friend he kenned and he began gathering up the treaty and contracts from the table. But Connor had other plans for them.

"Leave them for now. I will have Murdoch arrange for their storage later."

They walked toward the chamber's door when he stopped them. Something else had occurred to him, mayhap another bit of Jocelyn's meddling rubbing off on him.

"Speak to Murdoch about moving to that larger chamber in the south tower. With the lass's child, you need something to give you and Marian a bit of privacy." He pulled open the door and let Duncan walk out first. "Aye, I heard about last night in the nursery. And next time you find yourself needful of a place to sleep, there is a small room off the stables that goes unused."

He left Duncan standing behind him and began the trek down the stairs to find Rurik and then a meal and then to speak to Marian and unravel part of her mystery. Aye, the guards had reported Duncan's sleepless and restless night to him. Very little went unnoticed here in Lairig Dubh and little went unreported to him by one or another. All in a day's work as laird.

Marian stared and stared, but still could not accept that the woman staring back at her from the looking glass was herself. In the few short hours since she and Jocelyn returned from the gardens with the intention of examining Jocelyn's gowns for any that might fit her, she'd been washed, her hair scrubbed and cleaned of the brown stain she wore in it, dressed, adjusted and fixed some more! The woman staring back looked so much like the girl she'd been those five years before, even on the night of her fall from grace.

She turned and let Jocelyn and Margriet and Cora have another look at the back of her. Wearing a gown that fit as it was meant to, her womanly curves were outlined and accentuated. Her hair, closer to its true reddish-blond color, now hung down her back loose, but for a circlet on her head to keep the curls from her face and to hold up the small gauzy veil.

The women sighed and smiled, content with the changes they'd wrought, but Marian was fearful of what was to come. She'd seen it before, the reputation combined with her appearance led to men behaving stupidly and usually she was the one to pay the price.

"You must remember to hold your shoulders back when you walk, Marian. Slumping forward only…" Jocelyn began to instruct her and then just stopped and smiled again.

"Your husband will be surprised by this change in your appearance?" Margriet asked.

"Most likely, he will swallow his tongue!" Jocelyn exclaimed before Marian could answer. "Just look at her, Margriet. If Rurik were not married to you…" She let her words drift off.

"This was a bad idea, Jocelyn. I am a married woman now, my hair should be covered," she said reaching up to remove the lovely circlet and veil.

"Do not touch that," Jocelyn ordered. The tone of her voice warned Marian of her seriousness. But the soft touch as she took her hand and patted it lessened the harshness of it.

"I ken, we…" She nodded to Margriet and back. "Ken that this is all so much a change from your life. A new village, new people to meet, living here in the keep after living on your own for so many years. All of it and more yet to come."

Jocelyn tugged her over to a bench and pulled her down to sit, never letting go of her hand. "I can only imagine the terrible things people said or did to you that made you hide yourself away under those clothes—" Jocelyn pointed to the pile of discarded gowns and tunics "—and under that hair."

"This is done now, Marian," Margriet added. "You are part of this clan now and your husband has made it clear that any transgressions are to be left behind you. So, this is a good way to start anew."

Marian rubbed the soft gown and tunic and felt the new linen chemise beneath them against her skin. She felt five years younger in these clothes, with her hair loose around her shoulders. For a moment she let all the years and all the changes and hardships fall away. Closing her eyes, she fought against letting loose the memories of being the laird's only daughter, a cherished one she thought, and of having her whole life waiting ahead of her.

"I do not ken if I can do that, Jocelyn."

She looked at both women, both so completely re-assured of their places in life, surrounded by loving husbands, respected by their kith and kin. Afraid to accept the friendship and concern they offered and knowing that she would not be here long enough to become part of the clan, she shook her head.

And yet, she could not tell them that part of it. She could not admit that she did not wish to stay married to their cousin, a man who was honored by this clan for his work on their behalf. A man who deserved a better wife than she could ever be to him. A man who should be married to a woman of his choosing and not one he was forced to.

"Margriet, why do you not braid Marian's hair while I search for something she can wear over it?"

Jocelyn rose and walked toward the door and Marian caught sight of some furtive hand movements over her head and saw Margriet shaking her head against whatever Jocelyn planned. Margriet put her needlework down and went over to Jocelyn and the two exchanged words for a brief time. Then Jocelyn left and Margriet directed her back to the stool in front of the looking glass. Then, standing behind her, she lifted the circlet and veil from her head and gathered her hair into her hands preparing to arrange it in a braid.

Margriet took the brush and began to run it in long, slow strokes through Marian's hair. The feel of it soothed her as it always had and soon Marian closed her eyes and let her thoughts drift as the motion of the brush continued. Soon, how much time had passed she knew not, the door opened and Margriet stopped brushing her hair.

"Marian."

She opened her eyes to discover Duncan standing at the doorway staring at her reflection in the looking glass. Uncertain if he was pleased or displeased by the change in her appearance, she sat unmoving, waiting for some sign. For so long she'd avoided this kind of dealings with others, and especially men, and now she had no experience at understanding them.

Then, and though only for a brief moment, his eyes took on that glint that men's did when they found out she was the Robertson Harlot. He seemed to conquer it, for it disappeared and something more appreciative and less threatening entered his eyes then.

"Hamish tried to tell me that there was a beautiful woman hidden beneath the baggy gowns and muddy-brown hair, but I could not see it."

She turned and faced him then. "He said that?"

"Aye, and he had the right of it." Duncan walked up behind her and stood there for a moment. She watched as he raised his hands as though he would touch her hair and then dropped them at his sides. "Jocelyn said you were uncertain of this change."

"I saw the look in your eyes, Duncan. The others will get it as well and I just do not want to hear what they will say. And neither will you."

He touched her then, placing his hands on her shoulders and squeezing gently. "You saw the appreciation that this man has for his beautiful wife. And if you see anything in other men's gazes, it will be their jealousy that you are mine and not theirs."

She met his eyes in the looking glass and offered a warning, one he seemed uninterested in abiding. "They will see the Harlot, Duncan. The flaming-red hair, the womanly curves and expect something that is not here."

"That was never there, Marian," he said softly. "Come with me now. Enjoy a meal among these good people." He guided her to her feet and she stood before him. "Give yourself a chance to adjust to this place before condemning them."

She would have argued and told him of the last three villages where she lived before returning to Dunalastair. She would have spoken of the way men acted once they learned that the well-known whore lived in their midst. She would have, but she could feel his concern and she kenned he believed the MacLeries would be different.

She had not the heart to disabuse him of his mistaken ideas.

"Please do not make me eat at the laird's table." The thought of sitting up on the dais, where everyone could see her and watch her unnerved her now.

"Come. Worry not, for Connor and Jocelyn eat with the rest of us during the noon meal. I saw Hamish with Margaret. Mayhap you would like to meet her now?"

He held out his hand to her and she took a breath before placing hers in it. His smile, warm and pleased, was almost reward enough.

"Ah, before you ask your next question, Ciara is in the nursery sharing a meal and her newest carved sheep with Lilidh and Isobel."

"Tavis made her another one?"

"He's quite taken with the lass. No one else has appreciated his talent with carving like Ciara does." He stopped and looked at her then. "Ready to go then?"

"Aye" was such a simple word to say, but one that would put an entirely unknown series of events into motion and change her world forever.

Marian felt the danger in it—the danger that she would grow to like this place, these people, this man, too much to let it and him go when she must. The danger in the attraction to a place she could call home. The danger in giving control of her life and her daughter's over to this man forever. If she found acceptance here and buried her past, how could she look elsewhere for a future?

So much to think on and so many possibilities to consider! For now, she decided to look on this as a simple invitation to a meal and that made the saying of it much easier.

"Aye."

They walked hand in hand along the corridor and then turned into the hall where many of the clan gathered for the noon meal. 'Twas not a festive event, like the meal last evening seemed to be, but a simple break in the day during which they shared a meal before returning to their daily tasks and duties. Duncan led her to one of the tables and stopped in front of Hamish. The woman at Hamish's side stood when he did.

"Marian, this is Margaret, Hamish's wife and Connor's sister," Duncan said as he introduced them. Margaret bowed her head in greeting. Having never heard of the MacLerie having a sister, Marian was puzzled.

"Connor and I shared a father, lady, but no' a mother."

Hamish broke in before the pause was apparent. "Did I no' tell ye, Duncan, that she was hiding her true looks from us?"

"The puir woman!" Margaret said, reaching out and guiding Marian to sit at her side. "How ye survived nigh on a fortnight on the road with these brutes? Mine alone," she said, laying her hand on Hamish's arm, "would try the very patience of the good saints in heaven."

"Here now," Hamish argued. "We saw to her comfort, Margaret. Lest ye think her roughly treated, ask her how Duncan ordered a respite for two days at the Mac-Callum's so that she and the little lass could rest."

Margaret looked at her husband and then at Duncan and back again. Marian got the strong feeling that such stopping on a journey home was not the normal course of things for them.

"The men were quite kind, Margaret. Truly," she said at the woman's expression of disbelief. "Even when I was cross or my daughter tired of the road, they never lost their good manners or behaved badly."

"Well, that was a first then for them," Margaret muttered, though her eyes were filled with love for the one she called husband.

Reaching over to a platter of some kind of fowl, Margaret lifted some slices off and placed them on their wooden trenchers. She did the same with other foods—cheeses, bread, stewed turnips and more—until their plates were filled to overflow. Marian could not have eaten it all if she had the whole day to do it.

"Tell me of your daughter," Margaret said once everyone was eating. "Hamish tells me she is a sweet lass. How many years has she?"

Marian answered the woman's questions about Ciara and, as the meal progressed, the topics moved from family to clan to king and country and back again. Marian sat quietly most of the time, listening and eating a small portion of the food on her plate and answering questions when they were directed at her. She learned much about how things were done here in Lairig Dubh, including that they had little use of standing on ceremony or rules that would elsewhere be considered paramount to the order of things.

The laird's bastard half sister ate in his hall. He'd taken the village overseer and made him one of the men who represented him to other clans and even to the king's court. He ate among his clan and no one bowed to him or called him laird. Yet, the deep respect for him was unmistakable here. If anyone who'd ever called him "the Beast of the Highlands" saw how his household and clan lived, they would think that the story was told of the wrong man.

As their meal progressed, several people stopped at the table and asked Duncan to introduce them to her. Jocelyn walked by several times beaming a smile at her. Even Margriet's Rurik waved from the other side of the hall. She found herself invited to meet the women of the village and Margaret's children as well as offers of help with the garden.

Murdoch, the old steward, and Gair, his young apprentice, asked if they could speak with her on the morrow about the gardens, and told Duncan they would meet in the south tower after the meal. She puzzled over that until Duncan explained that there was a larger chamber they could make use of instead of his, if she approved.

The meal sped by, and 'twas not until she stood at the bottom of the steps leading up to the laird's chambers that she realized all of that had kept her worrying at bay. Now, though, her dread increased with each step and when she stood before his doorway, she had to take several slow, calming breaths before she had the courage to knock. Before she could, the door opened and Jocelyn stood there. Then Connor stepped around her and apologized to Marian for a delay in their talks.

"Let me escort Jocelyn down the stairs before we talk," he said. "Go in. There is wine or ale on the table. Pour some for us both."

Daft man, Jocelyn mouthed as they walked past.

Transfixed by the sight of this warrior laird, walking his pregnant wife down the stairs because of her ungainly size brought tears to her eyes. Marian entered, as bid, found the pitchers and cups and poured a small amount of wine into each. Sipping it, she let the warmth trickle down her throat.

Walking over to the long table, she recognized the copies of the treaty just entered by their clans and other parchments she did not. Sitting down in the chair, she perused the treaty and laughed when she realized that the MacLeries could have gotten so much more from her brother.

"Something is humorous in there?" Connor asked when he entered and closed the door behind himself. When she started to place the documents back on the table, he stopped her. "Nay, do not stop. Pray continue and tell me what made you laugh."

"My brother artfully dodged giving better concessions about leasing this land and this one," Marian said, pointing out two sections of the language. "And this rate of interest is much too high when you look at the length of time involved."

The laird was looking from her to the parchments before them and back again, his mouth dropped open in surprise. But surprise over what?

"Aye, I can read Latin," she said, sitting back down in the chair.

"And I thought the grants were much too generous," the laird said, shaking his head. "What else?"

"Truly?"

"Aye, read the rest of it and tell me how the MacLeries fared against the Robertsons." The laird sat down, crossed one leg over the other and watched as she read the rest of the document.

Marian did not rush as she read the complex language and all the clauses of the agreement—her brother made certain to keep some of the more valuable land grants to himself, but paid more in gold than she would have expected. She explained this to the laird, who simply grinned at her words.

"I wonder what Duncan would say if he realized these details?"

"Oh, nay, laird…Connor," she said, handing the documents back to him. "I did not mean to disparage his accomplishments in any way with my comments."

"And you did not. I simply meant that if Duncan had spoken to you while these negotiations were going on, he would have been able to bring home an even better treaty…for the MacLeries."

"The Peacemaker was being pressured at the end of his talks. Mayhap these concessions were put in place then?"

"Quite possibly. But Duncan has never been pressured into any agreement he did not want."

Marian shook her head. "Then this was the first, for certainly he would not have agreed to our handfasting without being forced into it. Any generosity on my brother's part was simply to smooth over any insults to Duncan's honor. Iain wanted me gone and Duncan presented him with an opportunity to get it done."

"Iain paid much for your removal from the Clan Robertson, Marian. Why would he do so?"

"Having your whore sister around when you've just taken the high seat of your clan is not something enviable, laird. Mayhap he simply wanted to rid himself of the inevitable questions that would be asked?"

"You are not like any whore I have known, Marian."

"And you are not like the Beast you are called outside these walls."

The words slipped out and were spoken before she could stop herself. He asked too many personal questions and she needed to keep her wits and steer him away from any that would reveal too much. "Laird, I…"

"Oh, fear not. The Beast roars when he needs to, Marian."

She swallowed and then swallowed again, trying to make words come out. "Your pardon, laird, for my boldness." She lowered her eyes and waited.

"Duncan tells me you do not wish this handfasting to be made permanent."

Had Duncan shared every personal detail with his laird? She shook her head. "Nay, laird. 'Tis the only honorable thing I can do for him."

"Honorable? How so?"

"I am certain you ken how it came to take place. My brother drugged him and brought him to my cottage. Truly he was unable to do anything but stumble and fall. He did not dishonor me that night."

Connor met her gaze then, staring intently at her as she spoke. A shiver tore up and down her spine, warning her to have a care for any misstep could prove her downfall.

"He offered you marriage—surely he thought he'd done something wrong?"

"Come now, laird. We both ken the tenuous place in which he found himself—between his orders from you and the possibility that to not accept my brother's offer would cause your talks to fail. The Peacemaker is known by the deals he makes and for his purpose of keeping or bringing the peace at nearly any cost. This time the cost of success was his hand in marriage to me."

"'Tis a different way of looking at the matter. But again I ask you—why did you demand a handfasting instead of a recognized marriage?"

"Your man stepped into a family problem, one he had no hand in creating and I thought he should not be made to carry the cost of fixing. Aye, a year is a long time to put up with a farce of a marriage, but at least, he kens that there is an end and he can then seek a bride of his choosing."

The silence that met her explanation unnerved her more than his previous laughter or sternness. There was more to this than she'd revealed. More even that she could reveal if she wanted to and still not touch on the truth that Duncan discovered in their marriage bed.

"And you will be free as well," he said quietly. "Was that your aim all along? Did you play a part in this that Duncan kens not?" His voice may have been soft, but his intention—to find out potential danger to his kin and handle it—was clear and strong.

"I knew him not before he rode into the village and helped me," she said through clenched teeth. Always accused and never able to defend herself was something she simply could not let go this time. "He was kind to my daughter. When he was trapped, I thought on the best way to get us both out of it."

"I had to ask it, Marian."

"He does not deserve this, laird, and he deserves far better a wife than me. Handfasting will let him have at least that."

She thought he was done with it until he opened the locked wooden chest and lifted out a small packet. Opening it, he took out one sheet, smoothed it flat and pointed to her. "Does this offer speak of who deserves whom? At least in your brother's eyes?"

Why had she not read this before signing it? Marian steeled herself for some shock or surprise in the marriage contracts, but this was not the contract. It was a copy of her father's will and no amount of warning could have prepared her. She knew she was an heiress, both through her mother and father, but she thought that that had all changed when she was sent away in disgrace. Now, though, the words on the parchment explained in great and specific detail how much she was worth…and it was a tremendous amount. Gold, land, even a claim to an ancient title passed to her by her mother's family, were all listed there.

And all of it would be hers and her husband's on the day her handfasting was made permanent. If that did not happen, it could still be her daughter's, a legitimate daughter could inherit in her place.

Oh, what a web of temptation and deceit Iain had woven around the two of them! Paying Duncan a huge amount as a dowry and then dangling the rest in front of his face. What man would not want all of it? What man would not do whatever was necessary to insure that their arrangement became permanent?

An honorable one, her heart whispered.

"Does he ken?" she asked.

"He kens about this gold—" he tilted the chest to reveal several bags within "—but your brother sent this will to me. I have not shown it to him."

Marian stood now, the need to get away grew from deep inside her. "Will you?"

"I know you do not ken the man as I do, Marian, but even all of that would not tempt him to keep you against your will."

She turned to go, but he stopped her with a hand on her shoulder. "I think you should be the one to tell him about this. I will keep it here safe until the day comes when you can trust him enough to tell him."

He released her and she ran from the room. His words called out a warning to have a care on the steps, but she heeded him not. How she made it to the bottom she kenned not, but soon she found herself in the one place where she could find calm and control. Heedless of the damage to the borrowed gown, she knelt down on the damp, pungent soil and began tearing out weeds.

Darkness was falling when she realized she needed to find Ciara and tend to her daughter's needs.

Chapter Sixteen

Duncan opened the door to the chambers and smiled. Jocelyn was truly a formidable force in getting things accomplished, even when she needed to do it out of Connor's sight or knowledge. In the space of a day, she and the other women living in the keep had turned this collection of storage rooms into a chamber that offered both the lass and he and Marian places of privacy. And in the middle was a place they could share.

By the light of several candles, he spied Ciara's collection of wooden animals that seemed to grow now by the day. A deer now joined the sheep, pig and horse in the pile on the small table in the center of the room. The remnants of a barely eaten meal sat there on a wooden tray.

Two doors lay slightly opened and he went first to the one that led to the smaller room. Ciara lay cocooned in blankets and sound asleep on the small raised pallet. Tempted to touch her head, he did not for fear of waking her. Pulling the door back to its nearly closed position, he faced the other one.

Opening it with a care to be quiet, he found Marian in the bed there. But she'd fallen asleep sitting up against the headboard of the bed. Her hair was braided back but some reddish-gold tendrils had loosened and drifted over the edges of her face. The shade of it made her skin look paler than it was but the color also made her look as young as she was instead of much older. The blanket that must have covered her now lay around her hips, exposing her body to him.

She'd done a good job at hiding her fairness from him and anyone who looked on her. The frumpy gowns, both in color and fit, the dark, muddy hair and the way she carried herself when in company all completed the disguise. Now, though, staring at her in the soft glow of candlelight, he wondered how he'd never seen it. She shifted in her sleep and opened her eyes as she did.

"Duncan," she said on a sleepy whisper. "I tried to wait for you."

"No matter," he answered, shaking his head. "You have had a busy and straining day, Marian. Slide down under the blankets and sleep now."

Instead she did the opposite, rubbing her eyes and stretching, and, damn it!, his body reacted as he knew it would. 'Twas bad enough that she was a fetching lass, but now she lay with only the thinnest of linen chemises on to cover her attributes from his sight. But his randy body remembered every inch of it.

And, although they'd not spoken since she'd left Connor's chambers, he suspected that something had happened between his wife and his laird. She passed him in the corridor and never even took note of him being there. Nearly at a full run, she scampered through the hall and kitchens and outside to the gardens without saying a word to anyone. Once there, she sank to her knees and tore at the weeds.

He followed only to make certain she was fine, but he stayed because he was not certain she was. Her movements reminded him of a wild creature trapped within a cage. Her fingers moved at a frantic pace and she did not stop for nigh on half-an-hour's time. When she did, she sat back on her heels and rocked to and fro, with her eyes closed.

This pattern repeated several times until she simply sat back and stopped. Just when he thought to reveal his presence, Jocelyn's voice rang out, calling Marian's name. Connor's wife waved him off and he returned to his duties knowing that Jocelyn would have a care for her.

She was not at the evening meal, requesting a tray be sent to their chambers for her and Ciara. Now, she stared at him across the small space and he swore he could see the part of him that waited only for her word.

"Is this how you pictured it?" she asked, but it took him several seconds to understand that she meant the chambers and their arrangement rather than the sight of her sitting nearly naked in his bed waiting on his arrival.

"Aye," he said in a thick voice. Clearing his throat, he repeated, "Aye." He walked to the corner where his chest of clothing sat and began to take off his belt. His plaid dropped to the floor and then he pulled the long shirt over his head. Walking over to the bed and sitting on the edge of it, his boots were the last thing to come off.

"I have not thanked you for bringing Ciara to me last night," she said.

"You needed each other, Marian. 'Twas clear to me."
He did not turn yet or try to lift the bedcovers.

"You did not sleep…in your chambers."

She wanted some explanation, he could tell. "I did not wish to disturb you, so I took a walk. I did not sleep… anywhere."

"I would understand if you kept a woman in the village, Duncan. I will not make an issue of it," Marian said, never dreaming that it would anger him.

"A woman in the village?" He turned and faced her and she could see the anger rising in his face. "What makes you think I would do something like that?"

"Men of your status frequent other women when they have needs that their wives cannot or will not fulfill. I learned that in my father's house."

He shook his head then and closed his eyes for a moment. When he opened them the anger seemed gone. "I forget that, in spite of your reputation, you are an innocent."

"Not an innocent," she said, but he shook his head again.

"Not experienced in the ways of men and women. Aye, some men do have lemans, but I pledged my faithfulness to you when we spoke our vows. Do you not remember?"

Now it was her turn to shake her head. "I do not remember much of the ceremony. I was too worried over what was to follow."

"I demanded faithfulness from you before the ceremony. I thought it only fair to give my promise to you as well."

He did lift the bedcovers then and climbed in next to her. Holding them up a bit, he said, "Here now, slide down. Let us enjoy the comfort of our first night in our own bed."

Did he mean only to sleep? His body, especially *that* part of him, seemed ready to join with hers, yet he did not touch her except to guide her down next to him. She felt his arm as he shifted them onto their sides and slid it down over her belly and to her waist, drawing her closer to him. His manhood lay nestled against her buttocks, hot and hard, yet still he did not take her.

The next touch was unexpected for he reached up and pulled the leather strip from the end of her braid and loosened it. When her curly hair was freed of restraint, he nuzzled his face in it and inhaled the scent of the soap that now floated around them. Then he rested his chin against her shoulder and she could hear the sound of his breathing there.

After the events of the day—her confrontation with the laird, her complete transformation in appearance, lost hours in the garden then hours spent readying this chamber for him—she should be exhausted. But an awareness filled her body, an anticipation of the pleasure she knew he could give her and the relief and release that his pleasuring brought, and Marian discovered she was disappointed by the thought of only sleeping.

A few minutes later, when he still had not moved to take her, she whispered to him. "I am ready."

That part of him sprang to life, but otherwise her husband did not move. "Lie with me," she said, pressing against his erection.

He spoke not a word, but he reached between them and lifted the edge of her chemise to her waist. Then he moved his hardness down until it slid between her thighs and into that place that already felt moist and throbbed as he rubbed its length there. Duncan kept his arm in place, but moved his hand over to touch that place from the front. She lost her breath as he slipped one and then two fingers deep inside her, bringing the wetness out and making her body tighten with pleasure.

When she tried to turn in his embrace, he held her there, placing his other hand on her breast and teasing the tip of it. She cried out softly as Duncan kissed her neck and then found the sensitive place there with his teeth. The pressure of it, along with his relentless fingers and hands, made Marian ache from the sensations he created in her.

Then he stopped moving his fingers and only pressed against that tender bud deep within her folds. She reacted by moving against them, but instead of beginning again, he filled her from behind, sliding his length easily into her and pushing until he could go no farther. The pleasure of it nearly overwhelmed her and she reached back to grab his hip and keep him close. The deep chuckle echoed against her ear and then he began to move in earnest against her.

Each time he pushed deep inside of her, he stroked between the aching folds there, making her gasp. He moved his manhood faster and faster and his fingers kept pace, until she thought she might scream out her release. His mouth suckled the back of her neck, his teeth scraping and biting lightly, but somehow enough to increase all the pressure building within her.

Finally everything in her tightened and exploded and she fell into all the pleasure waiting there for her.

Duncan thrust again and again until she was spent and then withdrew his hardness from her core and released his seed between their bodies. Out of breath and replete with the satisfaction she'd found in his arms, Marian lay unmoving until he recovered. Feeling the wetness on her gathered chemise between them, she asked the question that had plagued her.

"I ken that men do that with their whores, Duncan. But why do you when you ken I am not?"

"What do you mean?" he asked.

"Spilling your seed like that. Men who worry over whose bairn a whore or loose woman carries do that. Men who think a woman is not worthy to carry a child of theirs do that. The servants who clean this chamber will see it and believe that you have no faith in the wife you have forced them to accept. Word will spread."

Duncan tried to gather his scattered thoughts and wits before answering her. He was still unrecovered from her soft plea that led to their joining. He was still unrecovered from their joining, if truth be told, yet she asked a question that he needed to answer.

A tug at his memory made him realize that he'd done the same thing at the MacCallum's keep and it had caused her bout of anger that lasted days. Now, with her explanation, he could understand why. He climbed from the bed, pulled the soiled chemise over her head and tossed it into the corner. When he turned to face her, he found her lying on her back, raised up on her elbows, staring at him and waiting for an answer. With her breasts naked before him and her hair curling down over her shoulders, a vision too enticing to resist, he avoided looking at her by sitting on the edge of the bed.

"If a child is born to us, I have the right to declare us wed or I have the right to determine the child's fate," he said, repeating the terms of their handfasting.

"Aye, Duncan."

He took a deep breath and let it out. "Marian, after seeing you with Ciara, I could never keep your child from you. It would kill you as quickly as cutting out your heart." He paused, running his hand through his hair and shaking his head. "Yet, I do not think I could give up a child conceived between us."

He heard her indrawn breath at these words, but continued, "So, my other choice would be to force you to stay with me in a legal marriage that you do not want. And that would destroy any happiness between us, for I ken how much you want to leave at the end of our year."

"Duncan…" she whispered, laying her hand on his back.

"So, spilling my seed outside of your womb is a way to try to avoid conceiving a child while we live together as husband and wife. It seemed the best way to insure that we all end this year in the way we have agreed to."

"I did not realize your reasons."

He faced her once more. "And I did not realize your confusion over the practice. I should have explained."

She lifted the bedcovers for him this time and he climbed back in, sliding down to lay at her side. He waited, suspecting she had other things to say and she did.

"I have not had someone in my life who cared about me since my mother died. And, truly, she cared more about what I could do for the clan than she did about what I needed or wanted. 'Tis difficult to accept such kindness from a stranger when family gave me naught of it."

Duncan reached out and took her hand in his. Entwining their fingers and bringing them to his lips, he pressed a kiss on hers. "And I have had so much of it in this clan, that I gladly share it with you and Ciara. Mayhap we can find a way through this year and make a choice at the end?"

In that pause, before she could say anything, Duncan found himself offering a prayer to the Almighty for more than just working this out for a year. Even without her truth, his heart wanted her even as much as his body did.

"I would like that, Duncan."

He pulled her into his arms and sealed their agreement with a kiss. 'Twas only a kiss, a touch of their lips, and then their tongues, but once begun, their passions flared and he soon found himself planted deep within her heat as she moaned out another release. Duncan gave her a full measure of satisfaction before seeking his own and sometime later, after sharing their passion another time in the dark of the night, they fell asleep wrapped around each other.

Chapter Seventeen

Rurik frowned and Connor grimaced, but 'twas Jocelyn's smile that warned of disaster as Duncan reached out to move his pawn. He had no other choice that would not sacrifice his king or queen. Studying the board for several more minutes brought him no other choice but to move the rook…directly into Marian's grasp. Two additional moves and she swept the rest of his pieces into her collection.

"A fine game," Rurik exclaimed, clapping him on the back and nodding at her. "Once he lost both his bishop and his rook, the game was done. Well done, lady."

"When exactly did you become such an expert on how to win against her, Rurik?" he asked, pushing back from the table and the site of his defeat.

Only Connor remained undefeated in this nightly ritual that began with Marian's request to learn the game anew. From her unbroken record of defeating everyone willing to compete, she had not needed to learn much. He also had the distinct feeling that she could have won their earlier games, if she'd had a mind to.

"I ken my limits, Duncan," Rurik answered. "I will gladly keep my wins on the battlefield or in the practice yard and let your wife have hers on the board."

Those in the hall watching, and the gathering grew larger with each match, laughed then. Marian said nothing, for she never gloated over her victories and always seemed more interested in learning something from each game than in the winning of it.

Of course, none knew of their own practice of the loser granting a boon to the winner of their matches or the long nights of pleasure that seemed to result no matter who won or lost. A man did not mind losing when there was so much to gain from it in the privacy of his bedchamber.

Although most were intrigued by her reputation, none held it against her and she was accepted here as any other person would have been—based on their own worth and the merits of their behavior. Connor would allow no other way in his household or clan. But, she always looked to him before accepting a challenge when another man was involved, and many of the young men seemed eager to do so. Not many were so eager to do it a second time.

Their lives settled into a pattern now, with the harvest completed and the laird's wife about to give birth. Marian had worked wonders on the garden, reaping much even while preparing it for its sleep until spring. Duncan helped the men in repairing any cottages that needed it before the season's change was upon them and soon, the village and keep stood ready for the cold, dark winter.

Stores of grain and hay and grass and preserved meats and fowl and fish filled the storage barrels and chambers to overflow. Countless bolts of wool and other fabrics lay waiting in the weavers' room for the idle times and hands of winter and threads were organized and needles and scissors sharpened for their tasks ahead. All lay ready for the vagaries of weather and fortune of the coming winter.

Though much was right between them, so much was not.

Marian accepted his counsel and guidance in most everything she did, from her work in the gardens to decisions about Ciara to trivial matters about her hair and clothes. They discussed his work for the clan at length and he found her suggestions on ways to improve his skills and enhance his talent for negotiating insightful and worth his consideration.

She was turning out to be the perfect wife for a man such as him—learned, gifted in household skills, articulate and intelligent and loving—but still she held back from him.

One recent night as they joined, as he held himself unmoving inside her, he asked her to stay with him. He was growing to learn what his heart had learned at their first meeting and he wanted her at his side forever. A sadness filled her eyes that made it impossible to continue and he simply left her body. They lay in silence for a long time that night before sleep came.

And he waited also, not yet daring to ask her in the light of day what the passion of the night had drawn from him.

The men he'd sent east to uncover the truth of what had happened to Marian had not yet returned and that could mean only one thing—they had discovered something and were following its path to the source. He'd instructed that nothing be committed to writing, for he wanted nothing to fall into the wrong hands before he heard it himself. Only upon their return, or upon Marian's trusting him, would he learn if she was a danger to his clan.

Then when the darkest days of the season lay heavy over the Highlands, Jocelyn was brought to the childbed with her third bairn. Duncan feared Marian attending the birth, since she had never borne a babe, but with a surprise disclosure that she had attended several births, nothing kept her from Jocelyn's side when she was needed.

He and Rurik and Hamish waited in the hall for word of the birth that night. Connor, having been through this before, would not leave Jocelyn's side regardless of the arguments against his presence. Jocelyn labored through the day and into the night before Connor called out the news as he entered the hall.

"My wife has given me another lovely lass," Connor yelled out. "Come, drink with me to their health!"

Everyone present filled their cups and offered their good wishes to their friend and laird on the birth of his second daughter. If Connor wanted a different outcome than the one he'd received, nothing in his words or manner gave it away.

Connor turned to them and smiled. "She is a comely lass, too, with her mother's eyes."

"Felicitations, Connor," he offered.

"I hope," he said, placing a hand on Duncan's shoulder, "that you soon ken the joys of holding your own bairn in your hands for the first time."

Duncan met Rurik's gaze and saw a strange glint

there. "You ken what I speak of, Rurik. Tell Duncan of the joy of it."

Connor seemed almost drunk though he kenned no wine had passed his lips since Jocelyn made known that her labor pains were upon her. It must be the joy of which he spoke.

Like a dagger's sharp blade being twisted in his heart, Duncan felt the sharp pain of knowing it would not happen with Marian. Months had passed and though he never mistreated her and always made her certain of her welcome here, she held herself apart from him.

Marian and Margriet entered the hall and walked toward them. They both looked tired, their hair matted with sweat and their sleeves pushed up and their gowns stained from their work, but the smiles they wore spoke of the success of the laird's wife to safely deliver a child.

"Connor, Ailsa said you may come back now," Marian said.

"Jocelyn and the babe are cleaned and one of them is eating happily," Margriet said. "Your wife and her mother will be down shortly, Hamish."

Connor nodded, happy at this news, but he looked at Duncan and whispered. "See to her." He ran off to return to his wife and new babe, leaving Duncan mystified over his words until he looked at Marian.

Margriet walked into Rurik's arms and he held her tightly. Her own time would be quickly upon them and no doubt 'twas that, and her previous childbirth, that most likely filled her thoughts now.

Marian said nothing and stood watching the other

couple. Her expression was troubled, he could see fear and something else written in her eyes. But mostly he noticed the dark bruising below them telling of her exhaustion from the long day and night.

"Come, there is a fire waiting for you in our chambers," Duncan said, putting his arm around her shoulders and leading her to their rooms. Instead she drew out of his embrace and stepped away.

"I need to go outside, Duncan. I will not be long," she said, already walking away from him.

She did this whenever she was troubled by something. Instead of seeking out others as he did, she sought space and air no matter the time of day or night or the weather outside. And she sought solitude.

"Marian, wait, let me get your cloak," he called out, but she did not stop nor even hesitate in her path toward the main doors of the keep.

Torn between the need to see her safe and the knowledge that trying to cage her inside would make matters worse, Duncan stood there for a moment or two. Then, he called out some orders to one of the servants and, grabbing someone's cloak from a peg next to the door, he followed her outside.

The cold air had settled over their mountains and valley this last week and the ground crunched beneath his feet as he searched for her. Torches were impossible to keep lit in the brisk winds that carried a hint of snow over the walls and through the yard. Luckily, one of the guards on the wall pointed off in one direction and he guessed Marian's destination.

The small chapel sat near the entrance to the kitchens, but could be reached from the yard. Duncan walked past the stables and to the stone building. Father Micheil kept an oil lamp burning on the altar there at all times, and though it flickered from the wind when he opened the wooden door, its light showed him the figure of his wife kneeling there.

He said nothing, only walked to her side, knelt on the cold, hard floor with her and spread the cloak over her shoulders. Duncan fought against the biting cold as he waited with her while she prayed. Soon, his teeth were chattering.

"I will return soon," she whispered. "Go."

"Can you not pray in our chambers, Marian?" he asked. "Surely the Almighty would understand you being there instead of here?"

She faced him then and the desolate expression in her eyes chilled his soul more than the icy winds did his skin. "She nearly died tonight, Duncan. Jocelyn nearly died."

"What happened?" he asked, standing and drawing her to her feet.

"The bairn was stuck and Ailsa did not think she could save her." Tears poured from her eyes now. "They both nearly died."

Duncan knew that Marian had grown close to Jocelyn during her time here, but somehow he also knew that this was about more than just Jocelyn and her babe. All he could do was offer her sympathy and a strong shoulder until she was ready to reveal the rest of it.

"She said…" Marian gasped trying to say the words. "…to save the bairn and not her own life."

After those words, she collapsed against his chest,

sobbing again. Now he did not delay. She needed to get inside, out of this body-numbing cold, and into dry clothes. He lifted her into his arms and carried her back to the keep. He'd arranged for Ciara to stay with the other children in the nursery this night, so he did not have to worry about waking the lass.

Something in one of the other births she'd attended must have gone wrong and cost the mother her life. 'Twas the only explanation he could come up with for her hysteria. He pushed open the door to their rooms and carried her to their bedchamber. As he had called for, a tub of steaming water sat there waiting for her use. Several other buckets stood by the hearth, in which a blazing fire now roared.

He stripped her of the cloak and her own soaked and soiled gown and tunic. Duncan sat her on the bed and took off her stockings and shoes. Then, lifting her once more in his arms, he carried her to the tub and sat her gently into its soothing heat. Using the empty bucket left on the floor, he washed and rinsed her hair and then her body, from head to toes. He hoped that the heat seeping into her flesh would warm her enough to calm her spirits as well as her exhaustion.

In a short while, they lay in their bed, and she'd still not said another word and he had not the heart to press her for more of an explanation. He could discover what had happened from Connor on the morrow.

He held her as she slept, but her sleep was filled with fits and starts. She called out names and, from the sound of it, suffered from night terrors. Some of the names he recognized and others he did not, but he heard the fear in her voice as she spoke with someone in her past.

Someone who'd died giving birth.

It could only be one person and it was something she would never speak about to him—Ciara's mother.

Duncan turned ideas and suspicions over and over in his thoughts throughout the night, but had nothing substantial by morning. Marian looked no more rested when she rose than when he put her in bed the night before.

The same occurrences happened every night for more than a week and he worried for her health. Others noticed, of course, and a few, thinking he had something to do with it, even warned him against ill-treatment of her. Thinking on the times in his life when things he'd dealt with or witnessed ate at his soul, Duncan knew that the only thing that helped him was to talk the matter out with a trusted friend. Connor had been his rock in the dark times of the soul.

Mayhap Jocelyn could serve as Marian's rock if she could not bring herself to trust in him? When another sleepless night found her ghostly pale and he could not risk her withering away before his eyes, he made the suggestion.

"Marian," he said as she pushed away the bowl of porridge. "We must speak about your condition."

"I am well, Duncan," she lied with her words and her eyes.

"Marian, 'tis clear that something has been bothering you since the night of Jocelyn's labor." A slight movement, nervous and furtive, then a blank stare. "Did Ciara's mother die that way?" Sometimes bluntness was the only way. "Have Jocelyn's difficulties made you think on Ciara's birth?"

"Please do not do this, Duncan. I beg you." She stared at him now in desperation. "I cannot speak of it."

He took her by the shoulders and pulled her close. "You must. Look at you! Whatever is stopped up inside you is killing you trying to escape!"

"I cannot." Her voice was faint now and she looked away from him.

"If you will not trust me with the truth, think about speaking with someone you can trust. It is killing you." He softened his voice then. "Jocelyn can be trusted. I would trust her with my life. Be at ease and speak to her."

Duncan remembered the night that he and Jocelyn bore witness to the horrible truth about Connor's first wife's death. Words about it would never pass his lips in this life for they'd both sworn never to speak of it as Connor's life hung in the balance. And he believed Jocelyn's oath.

She did not respond, so Duncan decided to take matters into his own hands. Picking her up, he carried her out of their rooms and to the tower where Connor and Jocelyn's chambers were. Climbing the steps, he stood before their door and knocked. Connor, carrying the new babe, opened it. The joyful expression turned to a frown when he saw Marian's condition and that Duncan was carrying her.

"Come inside," he said, backing into the chambers. "Jocelyn, Marian needs you." Duncan sat Marian in one of the large chairs Connor had and backed away. Jocelyn climbed out of the bed, pulled a shawl over her shoulders and sat down next to Marian.

"Connor, why do you not take the bairn down to the hall and announce the name we have chosen for her?"

Neatly dismissed, Connor nodded for Duncan to follow him. He closed the door behind them praying that Jocelyn could get to the bottom of this.

Chapter Eighteen

Jocelyn sat for a moment wondering how to approach this situation. Then she walked to the table, dropped some dried herbs into the pot of steaming water there and waited for them to steep.

"Sheena," she said aloud. "We are calling her Sheena, which means 'God is gracious.' Appropriate, do you not think, considering how close we came to losing her?"

She dribbled a small amount of honey into two cups, added a sleeping herb into one and poured the brew into both. The smell of the herbs and the honey melting together was delicious. Carrying both over to where Marian sat, she handed her one and then sat down, with a great deal of care and not an insignificant amount of pain.

"You were a great help to me, Marian. There are parts I have no memory of—" Marian met her gaze then before turning away "—but Connor told me how you helped."

"Jocelyn, do not do this."

Jocelyn sipped from her cup and urged Marian to do the same. If nothing else, the concoction would warm Marian and bring some color to her pale face.

"You ken the problem with boils, Marian. They grow and grow, causing pain and disease within, until they are lanced and drained. I think there is something inside that needs to be lanced." Jocelyn sipped from the cup again and then put it down. "I think that you were no whore. I think that you wear that reputation as a disguise in order to hide the sins of others."

Sliding down to her knees in front of Marian, she took the cup and held Marian's icy hands in her own. "I think that you did not give birth to Ciara and that her mother died in childbirth," she said softly.

"Did Duncan tell you that?" Marian gasped.

"Nay, 'twas all a guess on my part after watching you these last months and getting to know you. And if that is something you have told Duncan in confidence, then he will not tell anyone. And I will not share your confidences with anyone, either. Neither him nor even Connor, unless you give me leave to."

Keeping something from her husband or from Duncan would not be the best thing to do, but Jocelyn could see that Marian's was a soul that needed to unburden itself of a troubled and haunted past. Duncan thought she might help and he would understand the need for absolute trust if Marian was to speak about anything. Connor was another question completely.

"Was she your friend then?" Jocelyn asked.

Tears streamed down Marian's cheeks as she

nodded. "She was my best friend. Her name was…" Marian hesitated as though unable to speak the name.

"'Tis not important to tell me her name," she whispered.

"She died giving birth to Ciara. Now she is mine."

Jocelyn felt the burning of tears in her own eyes and swallowed against the tightness of her throat. "You must thank God every day for the gift you were given, Marian. The child is a blessing and you have raised her well."

Against the odds, with a humiliating reputation and no help from her family to speak of, this young woman had taken in the child of a dead friend and raised her to be the happy, intelligent and healthy child Ciara was now. "You were there when she was born then?"

"Aye."

"And I am certain you did all you could to help her?"

"Aye." Marian closed her eyes then and Jocelyn suspected that the terrible event was even now running through her thoughts once more.

She rubbed Marian's hands again. "I do not pretend to ken His mind, but 'tis God's will when one should live and another pass. We can only pray for the living and the dead and for acceptance of His will."

Jocelyn climbed slowly to her feet and sat down once more in the chair. Her curiosity was roused, but this matter, and Marian herself, needed delicate handling. There would be other opportunities to be curious.

"Would you hear my advice on this, Marian?"

Marian nodded and Jocelyn handed the cup back to her with instructions to finish it. Once she'd swallowed the last mouthful of the brew, Jocelyn smiled.

"First, why not ask Father Micheil to pray a mass for the eternal rest of her soul? I will go with you and you need not mention any of the specifics to him that you do not wish to."

She tugged the blanket back up on her shoulders then and took a deep breath. "I think you should tell Duncan what you told me. He can help you carry the burdens inside you."

"You do not understand, Jocelyn. This is not for him to ken. It will make things harder…." She did not finish.

"One of the best things about being married is having another to share the good and the bad with, Marian. Two carrying the same burden lessens its weight on each." Feeling the resistance in the young woman, she added, "I cannot force you to tell him, but anyone who loves you the way he does…"

Marian's gaping mouth and shocked expression stopped her from saying another word. "He loves me not," she began, but Jocelyn interrupted her.

"Anyone with eyes in their head can see the love you share. The way he treats you and the way you look at him. The respect and caring you show each other and your daughter. Is it clear then to everyone in Lairig Dubh except mayhap you?"

"He loves me not," she repeated.

"But do you love him?" Jocelyn asked quietly. At the stricken expression in her eyes, Jocelyn smiled. "And you think to protect him by keeping the truth from him?"

Marian nodded then, but could not say the words.

"Then you have learned little of these MacLerie men. They would rather have a head-on battle to the death than deal in secrets. Connor learned this the most difficult way of all. Give Duncan the weapons he needs to defeat the phantoms of your past and find a future with him."

The sound of her husband returning stopped her from saying anything more. "I am here to listen, Marian. Come anytime."

Connor burst through the door, followed by Jocelyn's other two children, Duncan and Ailsa who looked none too happy at the number of people in the chamber and her being out of bed.

"They love the name. The children, the clan. God *was* gracious to us that night," he said, leaning down to kiss her on the mouth. "Is aught well?"

"This is too soon for ye to be out of bed, lady," Ailsa began. "And too soon for the wee bairn to be in the chilled air of the hall."

"I held her close, Ailsa. She is warm enough," he said, holding out his hand to her.

Jocelyn let him help her from the chair and into bed before she accepted her daughter in her arms. Aidan and Lilidh climbed in next to her to get a better look at their new sibling.

Watching as Marian took Duncan's hand and let him lead her from the room gave Jocelyn some hope. Love was there almost within their grasp, all they need do is reach for it. As she and Connor had done.

Not certain if the short visit to Jocelyn had done any good, he watched Marian walk down the stairs to the main floor. He had duties to see to, but wanted her settled first. Her quiet invitation back to their chambers gave him hope.

Ciara now spent more time with the other children in the nursery and both Peigi and Glenna watched over her closely. She was there now, giving them the privacy they needed. Closing the door behind them, Duncan waited as Marian sat down on one of the benches along the table, pushing Ciara's growing menagerie to one side. Duncan sat at her side and waited for whatever she had to say. He took her hand in his, held it and whispered to her.

"Whatever it is, Marian, your words are safe with me."

"Just over five years ago, I watched my friend die giving birth to Ciara."

It all came out at once, but it cleared up so many things for him. "And seeing Jocelyn so close to death stirred it up?"

"Aye, Duncan," she said, now leaning against him. He put his arm around her and held her close. "The words about choosing were almost the same. The pain, the hours, the bleeding—all that was."

"Do not say that you delivered Ciara?" She was no midwife, and had been just an inexperienced woman of ten-and-eight years or so.

"I was the only one there. He said they would both die without my help, but my friend died anyway." Her voice was filled with desolation as she described the horrific events to him. "She had only enough strength to save her daughter and she begged me to see her safe."

"He?" Duncan raised his head and looked at her. "Who told you that?"

She sighed then. "I pray thee, ask no more of me now."

This was the first time she'd told him anything of her

past. And she'd just revealed enough to give him some idea of what had happened at Dunalastair that night.

Or did he?

All he really knew was that Iain and his father, Stout Duncan, were at the center of it, and with her father being dead, only Iain could answer his questions. And that Marian felt some need to keep their secrets even now. Then, Marian yawned and he felt her body sag against his.

"Jocelyn put a sleeping herb in my cup," she said.

"And you drank it?" he said. "Mayhap it will help you get some rest?"

"She meant well, Duncan. She told me to tell you the truth. I just cannot tell you all of it." Her words were slurring and he wondered if this was what he'd been drugged with at the feast.

"Worry not on this now, Marian. Sleep and then we can speak about it," he said, lifting her to her feet and then carrying her into their bedchamber. "Sleep, love, and I will be back when you wake up."

He did not bother to undress her, he only slipped off her shoes and pulled the blankets up to cover her. Kissing her forehead, he sat on the bed and waited for her to sink into sleep and then waited to see if it was a restful or fitful one before he left. When her breathing became even and deep, he knew Jocelyn's potion had worked.

Sliding quietly from her side, he left the door open a slight bit and tidied up from the morning meal she did not touch. Then, he went back to his duties while Marian slept.

None of this made sense to him, but if he let it turn over in his thoughts for a day or two, he would have a clearer idea of what was at work here. In the meanwhile, he would see to Marian's needs and hoped that sleep would help her recover from this incident.

Much later that morn, Connor summoned him to the solar, the place where he carried out his business since his wife and newborn daughter and several servants and other family members were ensconced in his chambers above stairs. The grim expression that met him warned him that all would not settle quietly as he'd hoped.

Warmth surrounded her and she was loath to find a way out of it. Opening her eyes, she saw that she was in her bed and piled high with all the blankets they had. No wonder she felt warm. Pushing herself back, she leaned against the headboard and looked around the room. Alone, it seemed, for no sounds alerted her to anyone's presence in the other room, either.

The small blocks of glass in the top of the outside walls revealed enough light that she kenned night had not yet fallen. Pushing back the blankets, she discovered that she slept in her gown and stockings. Sliding her feet over the edge of the bed, she stood and let a moment or two of dizziness pass. The effects of the herbs Jocelyn had added to her drink.

She wondered if sharing her heartbreak with Jocelyn and Duncan helped her put that past behind her or not, but one thing had become very clear in the midst of all the shadows of memories and hopes and dreams. In spite of her efforts to keep herself unmoved by his ways and his basic goodness, she'd fallen in love with her husband.

Jocelyn may have said the words first, but Marian's heart recognized the truth of it.

Marian loved Duncan.

This was not a good thing, she thought as she fell back on the bed. This muddied the waters of an already-confused and murky path toward a less-than happy-ever-after ending for them.

It changed nothing. At the end of a year, now just nine months hence, she and Ciara would leave here and start a new life. Her heart would break, but that feeling was nothing new to her. 'Twould take some time, but she could get past it and then he and these times together would remain in her memories forever as a respite from the harshness that was her life.

She loved him and she told herself that the best thing she could do for him was to leave and to remove him from all of the trouble she'd caused in his life. He would curse her for it, and then find the wife he wanted.

She loved him and she could rip her still-beating heart out of her chest and it would hurt less than the thought that she had to leave him behind.

For his kindness to her and her daughter. For his attempts to give them a comfortable life while they lived here. For his efforts to give her the caring family that she'd never had. For those reasons and many more, she loved him and because of that she would leave him when the time came.

Sitting up, she rubbed the unexpected tears from her eyes and went off to find out the time and day and to find her daughter and husband. This life with Duncan was destined to end soon enough and the reminder this last week of how fleeting life could be simply made it clear to her that she had to enjoy the days she had left with him.

* * *

"Surely this is a jest?" Duncan asked.

"Nay, my lord," the man said, directing his answers to Connor.

"The Robertson waits for me at the MacCallum's keep?"

The messenger, who stood cold and dripping in the middle of the solar, shook his head again. "He should be there now, my lord. He was three days behind me and I left there three days ago."

Duncan walked to stand next to Connor. Leaning down, he spoke so that only Connor could hear his words.

"Could this be a trap?"

"But we are allies now, Duncan. Why a trap? Why now?"

He could think of only one reason why Iain Robertson waited for him at the distant keep—and her name was Marian. He would not even speak her name in front of his man, so he nodded to Murdoch who stood at the ready.

"See to…" Duncan raised his brow and waited for a name.

"Fergus," the man offered.

"See that Fergus has something to eat and something warm to drink while the laird and I discuss this invitation."

Once they were alone, Duncan sat in a chair and shrugged. "I have not heard back from the men I sent east. I have expected their return for the last week."

"I think they have stirred up the past and that the Robertson is calling you to put a halt to it."

Duncan nodded at that assessment. "I can see a long, cold trek through the winter storms coming for me."

"Follow the path to the shielings, at least they'll be some protection for you against the winter nights."

"Aye," he said, agreeing with Connor's plan yet dreading it at the same time.

Even if they made it to the MacCallum's in three days' time as Fergus took to get here, it meant at least a sennight away from Marian. And that was if the weather did not take its customary mid-December change for the worst.

Standing, he was already thinking of the preparations he needed to make before he could leave when the loud crash outside the solar reached them. Pulling the door open, he found Fergus lying bloodied on the floor. Marian stood across the room, looking rested but shocked at whatever had happened.

"What happened, Murdoch?"

The steward held up his hands to signify that he knew nothing of what had happened, but the guilty look in his eyes said otherwise. Turning to Gair, Duncan asked again. This time he could intimidate the younger man easier than the old.

"He called her…" Gair glanced in Marian's direction and then back at the unconscious man on the floor. Duncan understood before he explained the rest. "Weel, ye ken?"

"Aye, Gair. My thanks for defending my wife's honor, but I need this man whole and ready to ride out in the morning. See to it?"

Connor now stood at his side. Putting a hand on his shoulder, his friend said quietly, "Go to her and put things between you aright. I will see to the lass."

"Connor, there is no strife between us." The words sounded as hollow and false as they felt.

"Tell her the truth of your heart before you leave her side."

"I do not ken the truth of my heart, Connor."

"Oh, aye you do," he said with the tone of a man who knew his quite clearly. "Look at her and let your heart speak. Do it now."

Somehow, his feet moved him forward until he found himself within an arm's length of her. She stared at him until he reached out and pulled her into his embrace. Sliding his hands up to her head, he freed her hair of its restraining braid and held her face to his. Kissing her over and over, he knew only one thing—he loved this woman and needed to find a way to convince her to stay with him forever.

Chapter Nineteen

He moved like a storm, wrapping his arms around her, tugging her hair loose and possessing her mouth until she stood breathless against him. Instead of running from the onslaught, she held on to him and let him have his way. Only the sounds erupting around them broke through the growing haze of passion.

Duncan may not have realized it, but she did and so did the rest of the clan—he had never touched her this way before them. Any physical affection between them had been in the privacy of their chambers and certainly not in the middle of the hall while many of the clan looked on. This was a declaration, a simple and plain one, that everyone could understand.

And one that she would not think on right now.

He released her only to take her by the hand and lead her to their chambers. Closing the door behind them and dropping the bar, he captured her against it and kissed her again. She lost herself in the emotions and the sensations as he pressed his hard body to hers, lifting her so that she pressed against the whole length of him. The feel of his strong legs. The thick hardness that jutted along her belly as he leaned down and took her mouth again. The strength in his arms as he held her still.

He slid a knee between her legs and then higher up into the junction there and she found herself sitting on him. He tugged his belt loose, let his plaid fall to the floor and lifted the edge of his long shirt. The heat of his skin made her gasp, but it was the feel of him sliding his hand along her legs searching for a way under her skirts that made her ache.

Soon, a determined Duncan found the edge and inched his hand up along her thighs until he touched the wetness there within the curls. She leaned her head back and sighed her pleasure. He pushed her skirts out of his way, spread her legs and urged her to wrap them around his waist, which she did, opening her up to his invasion. With one thrust he filled her completely.

Then the storm stopped and he stood with her pinned to the door and stared at her as though seeing her for the first time. He kissed her gently, so softly that it made her feel like something precious and it brought tears to her eyes. He lifted her into his arms even while staying deep within her and walked them into their bedchamber. There, he climbed onto the bed, laid her down and brought her such exquisite pleasure that she cried as she felt her release.

And then he began again until there was no place on their bodies that had not been touched and kissed and tasted and felt by the other. He did not seek his own release until she cried or screamed or moaned or sighed out hers and then each time, he waited for her racing heart to calm.

And then he began anew.

The life in the keep went on around them and they remained cocooned away from it all, lost in each other and the unmatched passion that finding the person you could love forever brings.

Sometime in the day, a meal appeared on their table. The cook would be horrified to learn that they ate sitting naked but for a blanket over their shoulders and that they put some of his dishes to other uses.

The plum preserves were difficult to lick off certain places and could be removed only with a focused effort. Duncan was better at that than Marian, but he did not seem to mind that she needed more time and more strokes to lick that part of him where they smeared it clean of the sticky coating.

Later, buckets of hot water appeared and although they tried to use them to wash, the feel of the soap as Duncan lathered that place between her legs simply led to other things and the water cooled before they could use it. And she would never look at the table without remembering the things they'd done on its strong frame.

When darkness fell over Lairig Dubh and the keep quieted for the night and as they finally lay completely sated and exhausted in their bed, she knew that he would tell her of the Robertson messenger. He never stopped touching her, though. His hand rested on her shoulder or hip or even on her breast as though it belonged there. And in many ways, it felt right to have him there.

"I leave in the morn to meet your brother," he said without preface. "He awaits me at the MacCallum's keep."

She began to sit up but he held her next to him. "I will go with you, Duncan."

"Nay, you will not. The weather may not hold and you are not used to traveling. You will only slow me down."

He was correct but she was not happy about it. "What does he want? What did the messenger say?"

"Before Gair knocked him senseless for insulting you—" he winked at her then "—he said only that your brother summoned me there."

"I do not like this, Duncan. Do you ken what this is about?" She could only imagine what her brother wanted with Duncan. But, to rouse him in the cold of winter and to make him travel halfway across Scotland, it must be something important.

"I think we both ken what this is about, though you ken more than I on the subject." He sat up then and leaned back against the headboard. "What surprises await me there, Marian? Give me some idea of what he will tell me."

"He will tell you nothing, because he cannot," she promised.

"Cannot or will not?"

"They are the same result, Duncan."

The last time they'd had this exchange of words, it was so much easier not to tell him. Now, she longed to let them loose and free herself from the past and all its pain and suffering. Unfortunately sharing the truth would not free him, only leaving him would do that. And loving him as she did, 'twas the price she was willing to pay for his freedom.

"So, 'tis a fruitless journey that I undertake into the cold of winter then?"

"I fear so, unless something else has happened that would bring him so far?"

She nearly missed it, for the fleeting expression moved so quickly into and out of his gaze, but she saw it. There was something else afoot that he would not speak of. Allowing herself to be a coward for the first time in such a long time, Marian purposely turned her gaze from his, hoping to make him believe she'd not seen it.

Once he spoke to her brother, things between them would change. She knew not how, but only that it would be different upon his return. Now, though, she felt greedy about not giving him up. She reached out and touched his muscular chest. Then she slid her hand down until it reached the sheet that lay over his legs… and other interesting parts.

"Well, then, the morning comes too soon, Duncan," she said, resting her hand on the rippling muscles of his stomach and skimming it up over his male nipples and then down to the bones of his hips. "I do not want to waste a moment more fretting over what happens beyond that time."

He took hold of her wrist, she thought to stop her action, but instead he guided her down to the part of him she wanted to touch. Grasping its length, she stroked him again and again until he finally saw the wisdom in her approach.

Nothing could change what happened next, all she could control was how she spent her last hours with the man she loved.

She thought he could not bring her to another release,

but she was wrong. This last time, as he began to grow harder just before his seed spilled, he stared deep into her eyes, willing her to say the words she could not. Marian wondered if he would stop or if he would do the one thing that could end any choice she might have in the matter. In the end, he did as he promised he would do and protected her as much as he could.

In the end, he was an honorable man and his honor would be the thing that would stand between them and any chance of happiness together.

When she woke in the morn, he was gone and she felt as empty and alone as she had before she met him. 'Twas time for her to learn that feeling again.

Duncan rode as long as he could, driving himself, his horse and the messenger hard to reach the MacCallum's lands. By now, Iain waited for him and Duncan was eager to hear his reasons for this call. He was even more eager to make the bastard pay for what he'd done to his sister.

Without knowing all the details, without knowing more than he did right at this moment, Iain should be a dead man. Letting his sister watch her friend die in childbirth, forcing her from their clan and labeling her a harlot to keep some truth from being kenned were all reasons he should be dead as soon as Duncan reached him. 'Twas the still-too-many unanswered questions that would keep him alive.

They'd made good time the first day, reaching one of the far mountain shielings by nightfall. But, the storm hit the next morning and delayed them a whole day. Fergus was not an unpleasant fellow, but sitting with him and their horses in a shepherd's wee sod hut

freezing his arse off was not something Duncan wanted
to do. And especially not so soon after leaving the
warmth and comfort of Marian's arms and her bed.

Five days after leaving Lairig Dubh, they arrived at
the MacCallum's keep, nigh to frozen and wet to the
skin. Duncan handed off his horse with orders for his
care to one of the men waiting by the gates. There
would still be four or five hours of travel possible if he
finished with this matter and got back on the road. He
would need to use one of the MacCallum's horses, but
he'd done that before.

Tugging the layers of plaid loose and pulling it free
as he entered the hall following Fergus's path, he found
a servant waiting to take it. And holding a large cup of
steaming mulled wine for him. He drank nearly the
whole of it and nodded for more before looking around
the hall for his quarry. He sat at table with Athdar and
the laird, near a blazing fire that filled the front of the
expansive room with heat.

The MacCallum called out to him and walked back
to greet him. Duncan barely spared a nod to the old laird
as he downed the last of the wine, tossed the cup on the
table and wiped his mouth with the back of his hand.
Then, he punched Iain square in the face and knocked
him to the floor.

"Here now, lad," the MacCallum said, wrapping his
huge arms around Duncan and holding him back.
Duncan was nowhere near done letting this bastard
suffer for the damage he'd wrought. But, the laird,
though much older, was strong and held him tight.

Iain roused and, with Athdar's aid, climbed to his
feet, wiping at the blood that poured from his nose and
mouth. He nodded at Duncan.

"And greetings to you, my brother-by-marriage."

His cocky tone made Duncan even madder and he struggled against the MacCallum's grip. "I promised him the hospitality of my hall, Duncan. Ye canna do this."

Duncan calmed and offered a grim smile. "Well then, laird. All I can give you is my word that I will not kill him in your hall."

Placated by that much of a promise or mayhap realizing the futility of trying to stop it, the laird stepped back and called for the hall to be cleared. Duncan smiled genuinely then, for he would have his chance to wreak a bit of vengeance on Iain for those who could not or would not. And for the pain he caused to Marian.

Duncan lifted his scabbard over his head and laid it on the table, along with his sgian-dubh and another longer dagger he carried in his belt. This would be a fight with his fists, he needed no weapons to help him in this battle. Turning, he faced Iain and raised his fists in challenge.

If he thought Iain would let him pummel him without some resistance he was wrong. The man gave as good or as bad as he got, but Duncan was fighting for something more—he fought for the woman he loved. Two benches were broken, a small table was crushed, a tapestry was torn from the wall and several clay pots were shattered before Duncan knelt on Marian's brother's chest and tried to remember why he should let him live.

"Why? Just tell me why she needed to carry the weight of your lies? Why did *she* bear the punishment?" Iain said nothing, which enraged him even more; he shook the man.

"Why?" he yelled again.

"Why did she not tell you, Peacemaker?" Iain gasped out.

Not able to see or think clearly at that moment, he punched Iain into unconsciousness and then fell to the floor himself, exhausted by five days on the road and by the beating he'd taken as well. Struggling to his feet, he strode outside, smashed the layer of ice on the horse trough with his bloodied fists and dunked his head in the frigid water.

Tossing his head back, the icy rivulets dripped down his body even as steam from his sweaty skin escaped into the cold air. Duncan splashed more of the water on his bloodied hands, rubbing them clean and then he leaned down and did the same to his face.

Damn!

In all of his years as Connor's man, he had never, never lost his temper. He'd never used his fists or sword to accomplish that which his words could. He'd never attacked a sworn ally of his clan. And he'd never broken a pledge of hospitality, for once given even enemies could sit at table together without fear.

In the short time since his arrival here, he'd broken every rule he lived by and was known to keep. And due to his actions, Iain now was in no shape to answer his questions. He would have to delay at least another day before he could return to Marian.

With his temper and his body now cooled, Duncan walked back into the hall and found Tavish's people cleaning the floor and moving tables back into place. Iain was gone from where he'd left him and the laird and his son stood waiting for him.

"Do ye wish to speak on this matter, Duncan?"

Tavish asked him. Shaking his head, he gathered his weapons from the table.

"Nay. There is naught to accomplish by talking now. I would apologize for my lack of control and for dishonoring your pledge of hospitality. I acted only on my own concerns and in no way am Connor's man in this."

Instead of berating him, the laird smacked him on the shoulders and winked. "Here now, Duncan. What man hasna lost control when he loves a woman? Iain will mend. He is being seen to even now. By the morrow he can tell ye what ye need to ken."

So, old Tavish had been listening and watching the fight after all. And he'd seen what it had taken Duncan so long to recognize about his feelings for Marian.

"Edana," the laird said, calling out to one of the servants. "See Duncan to his chamber and get him some food and wine." Tavish turned back to him. "Ye will hiv the chamber ye had before."

"I can sleep out here in the hall, Tavish."

"Nay, I will not hiv Connor's man sleeping on my floor."

The laird was not going to give in, so Duncan nodded and followed the servant to the room. Just as they entered other servants were emptying the last bucket of hot water into the large tub.

Edana waited for him to remove his plaid and his shirt so she could take it to be washed and he climbed into the tub. As she closed the door and he sat down in the water, he realized that Marian was correct about two things.

He would never fit into this tub.

Iain would not tell him what he'd come to find out.

Chapter Twenty

~~~❧~~~

Duncan took a great deal of satisfaction as he watched Iain limp into the hall the next morning. Although his own lip was cracked and his left eye swollen, he'd not sustained the same injuries as he'd inflicted on his opponent. With a sense of uncharitable glee, he watched as Iain held his side as he sat down at the table and as he grimaced when placing the cup on his mouth. Stitches to close the gash over Iain's eye, the large bruise on his jaw and guessing that his rib was most likely cracked or broken simply made Duncan smile.

And although Duncan ate with enthusiasm this morn, he watched as Iain added more cream and a healthy measure of uisge-beatha to thin out the porridge in his bowl. Then, he poured it into his mouth, drinking it down. The laughter that escaped did not go unnoticed.

Finally, once those living in the keep had broken their fast and went off to see to their duties and tasks, Duncan and Iain sat alone facing each other across the table.

"You summoned me here, laird. I but wait on your word," he said, not even trying to hide his sarcasm.

"I thought you would accept the gift I gave you and be done with your questions, Peacemaker," he said quietly. Iain lifted a cup and drank deeply from it. "Instead you sent your dogs out sniffing."

"You could hardly expect me to sit back and accept your lies…or did you? Did you think the gold would turn my head as it has turned others on your behalf?" Duncan watched Iain's eyes for signs of deceit.

Iain leaned forward, resting on his elbows. "I gave you a virgin bride with a substantial dowry. I paid you for any inconvenience or insult suffered. Another man would have accepted that gift and never spoken of the rest."

"You gave me your sister, Iain. A woman scarred with the wounds of living a lie—a lie at your behest and for your good I suspect. And you had not the decency to warn me on our wedding night."

Although Iain's face flushed, he said nothing. As Duncan expected. The stalemate went on for several seconds before Iain issued his command.

"Call off your dogs, Duncan. You ken not what they may find."

Duncan slammed his fists on the table then, still wanting it to be Iain beneath them. "Then tell me what they will find. Tell me what you have forced Marian to hide. Tell me why she would sacrifice her own life for yours. How can you call yourself a man and laird of your clan if you earned it on her suffering?"

"Call off your dogs before it is too late," he repeated through clenched teeth, not responding to his insult.

The clamoring of someone's arrival in the yard interrupted their privacy. Tavish entered, calling out orders to clan and servants as a small contingent of men were escorted in and brought before the laird.

His men. And from their expressions, 'twas much too late.

"Laird," he said, rising to stand in front of the Mac-Callum. "These are my men, on their way back to Lairig Dubh. You have met Eachann and Farlen before, they have served Connor for many years." The two stepped forward and bowed to the laird. "Donald is newer to my laird's service, but he was with me on my last assignment." Donald bowed then.

"Welcome to my hall," Tavish said, waving to some of the servants. "See to their comfort."

"We need to speak," Farlen whispered under his breath. "Away from him." Duncan did not need to see who Farlen spoke of.

"Laird, if you would excuse us for a short time?"

He did not need to explain further. Men arriving in the middle of a winter snowstorm were not there for pleasure. Duncan waited while each man got a cup of wine and then led them to the chamber he'd used last night. Once there, it took only minutes before he had a clearer idea of what he faced, but there were still gaps in the story.

"She has been ill-used, Duncan," Farlen said as he finished conveying what they'd discovered. "By her family and her clan." He swallowed the rest of the wine in his cup and slammed it down on a table. "And I canna abide a man who would use a woman that way whether he be father or brother or even husband." Farlen's stare spoke of his expectations that as her husband Duncan would right the wrongs done to Marian.

But Farlen did not ken the larger aspects of this problem. If it were only a matter of declaring Marian was a virgin on their wedding night, it could be simply handled. Lands, titles, reputations, even lives hung in the balance of this matter and so much was at risk, not the least of which was Marian's and Ciara's future.

"There is something else, Duncan," Eachann said. "The manner of her death and her bairn's has never sat well with her family. There was talk of them seeking you out over this matter."

"Why would they seek me?"

"Word has spread of your marriage to the Robert…to Marian and of her having a daughter. They have put some of the puzzle together and think that the lass could be Beitris's last bairn." At his frown, Eachann went on, "There were rumors of all kinds at the time of Beitris's death and the story of the Robertson Harlot overshadowed all the others. Beitris's clan has never trusted the Robertson's explanation and seeks the truth as well."

"Can you ride now?" he asked.

At their nods, he walked out to the hall and spoke to the laird of their needs. Within an hour, they were on the road back to Lairig Dubh. Slowed down by the weather once more, it took four days to reach home. Upon entering the gates, he discovered the Broch Dubh was now an armed camp.

He jumped from his horse, intent on finding Marian, but Connor stood outside the doors to the keep waiting for him. He dismissed the men with a nod and followed Connor to a place where they could speak in private. Duncan recognized the place high on the walls, between two of the towers as a place where no one but the laird or his wife were permitted entrance to.

"They arrived two days after you left," Connor began immediately. "They demanded to see you and I offered them hospitality to stay until your return."

"The guards?" Duncan did not ever remember seeing armed guards at the doors to Broch Dubh before.

"We were caught unaware as were they. Marian walked through the yard and into the hall and they saw her. Things were said…." Connor's words drifted off then, no need to explain what the words were. "Their soldiers are now housed in the stables, under guard. Only Beitris's father, two brothers and sister are in the keep."

"And Marian?"

Connor let out a breath that lingered in the cold air around them. "She has a guard at her door. Ciara has been staying with the other bairns in the nursery, out of their sight." Connor stared up at the tower where his wife was. "And Jocelyn is none too happy over this. Margriet is the only one who has been able to spend time in their company without wanting to rip off their heads."

"Her many years in God's service taught her patience then?" he asked. Rurik's wife had been raised in a convent and had many years' experience in dealing with difficult people.

"Some, but she carries no weapons when she is with them."

Duncan smiled at the fierceness of Marian's defenders. Connor faced him then, meeting his gaze and asking him the question he did not want to answer.

"They claim the lass is theirs. They claim that Beitris died giving birth to her."

With what Connor had witnessed when Jocelyn was giving birth and what Jocelyn might have shared, Duncan knew that Connor shared their suspicions. But to say the word, to speak it aloud, would damn them all.

They stood in silence for a moment, one long enough to tell Connor so much. Duncan could not ever remember lying to Connor, whether by intent or omission, and he tasted the sourness of it though the words had not passed his lips.

The sound of footsteps crunching on the freshly fallen snow stopped their conversation and they turned to whoever approached. Marian stood at the corner where the wall met the tower.

"I gave her leave to walk the walls when she needed to," Connor explained. "Jocelyn and I have no need of them for now." Connor took a step away and then turned back to him. "You have choices to make, my friend. Choices I have faced and I do not envy you them."

He watched as his laird and friend passed Marian with a word and then disappeared down the stairs into the keep.

Duncan stared at her across the distance that separated them and waited. The fear in her eyes and in her stance was clear even from there. He hoped the love in his was as well. Then he opened his arms to her and she ran to him.

Tugging the last layer of plaid loose, he drew her close and wrapped her in it. Leaning down, he smoothed the loose hairs out of her face and kissed her as he'd longed to do. One led to another and another until, between the kisses and the cold winds swirling around them, they lost their breath.

"Come, we must talk," he said.

They walked to the tower where their rooms were and climbed down the steps. Soon they were in their chambers and, as he peeled away their plaids, he resumed the kisses he had missed so much. If there was time, he would have done so much more, but the call for him would come very soon and then…well, then everything would be forever changed.

When he faced her and saw the grim expression, he knew the changes would begin now.

She had not slept in days. Not having his warmth around her was part of it. Not having his love to keep her strong was another. And knowing that she would never have him again was the larger part that plagued her nights and her days.

It was his welcome into his arms that confirmed her plans. Marian realized he did not believe she would leave him. And that the truth she could tell him would bear out the need for him to let her go. He was caught in a situation where he could not win and neither could she. She'd come to accept the conundrum and its only possible solution months ago, but Duncan had not yet. He would now, though.

She reached up and touched his swollen lip and noticed the bruise over his eye. "Iain?" she asked.

"He looks much worse," he answered with a certain amount of pride in his words. "I suspect he will be here once he can sit a horse."

"Sit," she said, pointing to the bench. She poured wine for them and she watched as he drank his. "You must be exhausted."

He drank the cup dry and then spread his hands on the

table, rubbing its surface. The glint in his eyes told her that he was thinking on the last time he'd been at that table. She smiled, remembering every moment of it. Then she shook her head, realizing that it was all in the past.

"Just tell me, Marian," he said softly. "Speak the words."

"Beitris and I fostered together, both with her family and then mine," she began. "I was the one to first suggest her marriage to Iain. I was a selfish girl who loved her brother and did not want to lose him or my friend. If they married, I could have them both."

"Did they not wish to marry then?"

"Beitris had loved Iain for years, but Iain did not seem intent on marrying. He enjoyed all the pursuits that young men did and seemed uninterested in marrying at all. Of course, my father began to pressure him since he was heir and would need a wife. 'Twas I who convinced my father and mother that Beitris would be the perfect woman for him."

There was more, but she could not share that.

"They were married and seemed happy together, but as they tried to conceive a child, things changed between them. They argued. There were fights and accusations. My father stepped in, to push and prod them along, but it helped not. Then after two years, Beitris was with child."

Marian sat down now, unsure of how steady her legs would be through the rest of it. "Instead of finding joy in her condition, there were more angry fights. Although I think they still loved each other, something had changed between them and I did not ken and could not guess why. Beitris's health was precarious through the whole time she carried and the midwife warned of an early birth."

She closed her eyes for a moment, reliving the beginning of that horrible night. She'd been asleep when she heard Beitris calling out for Iain in the hallway outside her door. Pulling on a chemise and a robe, she opened the door to find Beitris gasping for breath and blood pouring down her legs.

"She stood in front of Iain's chambers, staring and moaning at what she saw inside until she fell to her knees there."

"What did she see, Marian?"

The thought of exposing Iain's secret to anyone and exposing the lengths to which her friend went to please her husband in his need for an heir, an heir he would never produce, had troubled her the most. But Duncan's word and honor would be questioned because of this and he had already been held up to ridicule because of her, and he deserved to know the truth. Deciding to tell him and saying the words were two different things, neither one an easy task.

"Iain did not like women," she said. Such simple words and such a terrible price paid for them. "I do not doubt that he loved Beitris, but he could not…"

Duncan's hand covered hers then. "I understand. Go on."

"Beitris was having pains and went to find him. She discovered him with two or three other men and witnessed them…" She did not really understand it, so it was difficult to accept and tell what Beitris had told her. "I do not think he realized her condition. He must have thought she walked in on them and was shocked and backed out of the chamber. He closed the door and locked it against further interruptions."

"Good God!" Duncan whispered. "And you were left to help her? Where was your father?"

The tears flowed down her cheeks now as she thought of Ciara's birth and Beitris's death. "I called for my father and helped Beitris to her rooms, expecting he would call for the midwife. Instead he broke into Iain's rooms and saw them…"

She stopped and took a breath. When she closed her eyes, she could see it all again.

"Come, Beitris, the midwife will be here soon," she'd told her friend. "Get on the bed and try to let go of the pain."

When Beitris managed to get on the bed, Marian gasped in horror at the amount of blood pouring out of her. Then Beitris moaned and drew her legs up and pushed from deep within herself.

"Nay, Beitris. Nay!" she urged. "Wait for the midwife."

Looking at Duncan, she saw his tears. "My father came in then with Iain. They'd reached some agreement about his…preferences and he said that only a true son of a Robertson would sit on the high chair."

"He said that?"

"Aye. He meant to kill the child if it was a boy, but when he saw it was a girl, he had no use for her. He pointed at me and said my screaming had brought others so 'twas my duty to keep everything quiet."

"Bastard," Duncan said. "But why did you agree, Marian?"

"She was my friend, Duncan. If I had not pushed the

matter so, she might have married elsewhere and lived a long and happy life. She would be alive if I had not convinced her to marry my brother."

"Even you do not ken that. 'Twas not your fault."

"Still, my father said that if I agreed to take the disgrace in order to spare Iain and serve the clan, he would make certain that none of the truth came out. He swore that Beitris would remain blameless. If I did not, the babe would disappear and Beitris, whose only crime was loving my brother, would be shamed even in death."

Tears flowed now making it difficult to continue. Duncan moved over and sat at her side, taking her in his arms while she cried out her sorrow. "I could protect Beitris and her bairn by accepting his plan. I had to, Duncan." She lay quietly in his arms, thinking back on that night with the wisdom she'd gained in these last years. "He played on my guilt that night. He played my love for my friend and my brother against my need to keep them from harm."

She rubbed her eyes clear of tears and sat back. "He made all the arrangements and then, without telling me what to expect, he threw me into Iain's chamber and began screaming insults. The men must have been paid or threatened to take part for they threw me on the bed, tore at my robe and poured wine and ale on me to make it seem that we were…"

"You do not need to tell me the rest, Marian. I think I ken what happened."

She could not stop the telling now that she'd begun it.

"All I kept thinking was that I was protecting Beitris

and her baby. She was discovered dead, with Iain at her side, and my father said she'd died trying to give birth. He ranted about his disgraced daughter who celebrated while his daughter-by-marriage died trying to carry out her duties. Those below stairs heard it, believed it and when I was flung naked into the great hall, they beat me and cut my hair to punish me for my sinful ways. The only thing he stopped was when someone screamed out to mark me as a whore with a hot iron."

"Holy Mother of God!" Duncan exclaimed. "I had no idea he was capable of such things."

She shook herself from the past. "So now you ken the truth and are bound by it."

"Bound by it?" he asked.

"Sir Thomas is here to ask you if Ciara is mine or Beitris's babe. Now that you ken the truth, what will you say?"

"Marian, there has to be a way out of this," he said, not giving her the words she wanted to hear.

"Think on it, Duncan. You have two choices—to lie or to tell the truth. And now when you ken the truth, when you are called upon to make that choice, I ken that you could no more lie for me than you could live without breathing, and I ken that. I have always known. Your honor is more important to you than your life."

She stood then and stepped away from the table and from him, preparing in a small way for the bigger separation to come.

"So, when the Laird Erskine asks you for the truth…"

"They already have most of it, Marian. They have suspected all along that the story told by your father was not the whole truth." He stood now and came to her side, but she backed away.

"Marian, do you love me? Would you stay my wife?"

"Aye, Duncan, I love you. Enough to understand that something is more important to you than I am and not to damn you for it."

"I want no other woman, Marian. We can find a way."

"There was a time during Jocelyn's labor when Ailsa thought they might have to choose between her or the bairn. She was losing so much blood and the bairn seemed stuck. When Ailsa put the choice to Connor, he did not hesitate for a moment. He told her that he could not live without Jocelyn and that Ailsa must do everything in her power to see her safely through the birth."

She paused and wiped her eyes once more. "He said it while gazing at Jocelyn with such love in his eyes that I had to turn away. He loves her so much that, while making such a horrible decision as that one—one against Church law, one against even nature itself—he chose her.

"That's what I want in my husband, Duncan. I want a man who will choose me above all else."

She looked at him and saw the love in his eyes, a love that could simply not erase their problems or withstand the challenge that faced them now.

"What about your daughter? What about Ciara?"

"We both ken she is not mine, Duncan. Ciara will be returned to her family and they will raise her as her mother would have. She will be surrounded by those who want her and who will treat her with love and kindness. 'Tis better this way."

Could he hear her lie now? A large part of her was

dying inside even now as she spoke the words about Ciara's fate. Once Beitris's family heard the words Duncan would speak, her life would be ripped apart at its very seams. All because she could not leave well enough alone. All because she pushed two people, neither one ready for the other, together all those years ago. All because her father thought her dispensable and his son not. All because…

She found that the reasons mattered not now. Iain's secret would remain so—Duncan's word would only reveal Ciara's true mother and the rest could still lie quietly buried in the past. The treaty between the clans would stand as Connor's assurance to her guaranteed it would, so all that would be left was to finish out their year and she would move away. Soon, there would be no trace of Marian, the Robertson Harlot, left here or in the Highlands for she planned to move far, far away.

"So, I will release you from our bonds as soon as the time comes so that you will not have to do it. You can keep your honor and your name and protect your clan as I ken you must. I only thank you for the time we had together. You have shown me another side to marriage that gives me such hope, hope for both of us."

"This is what you want, Marian?"

"I see no other choice for you or me. If we honor the promises made then…"

Marian was out of words and out of the ability to speak them. The knock at the door startled them, but it signaled an ending for them. Duncan walked over and pulled the door open a crack.

"The laird calls for you, Duncan," Rurik said. "In the solar."

Chapter Twenty-One

The guard standing next to the solar door opened it for him and he entered. The chamber, though the largest room in the keep other than the hall, was crowded with people. Connor and Jocelyn sat next to each other in the two largest chairs and then several others he did not recognize sat around them. Unfortunately this was now a matter of honor—the clan kenned it and so did their laird—and there must be many witnesses so that no questions would be raised later. He walked forward until he caught Connor's eye and then approached and bowed before them.

"Laird, I have come at your call," he said formally.

Connor stood and came over to him. Turning to the older man seated next to Jocelyn, he said, "Sir Thomas Erskine, this is Duncan MacLerie. Duncan, this is the baron of Dun." Duncan bowed to the baron. "And these are three of his children, Rory, Munro and Elizabeth." Duncan greeted each of them and waited for Connor to take his seat.

"There is a personal matter that they seek your

counsel on," Connor said. "A question involving some private information they have received and they thought it best to come and speak with you directly."

He noticed that Jocelyn appeared to be in pain. She gripped Connor's hand now tightly enough that her fingers blanched.

"Laird, is the lady needed here? With her coming so recently from her childbed, mayhap she would rest more com…" He never got the rest out.

"I thank you for your consideration, Duncan. I am well enough," she said. Apparently Connor's efforts to keep her away amounted to what his did—nothing.

"I think that with these issues under discussion, a lady's presence can soften and mitigate any harshness caused by the emotional nature of such concerns," she continued, smiling at him. There would be hell to pay for his attempts to get rid of her. "Or so my husband tells me." She batted her eyelashes at Sir Thomas who muttered something about wives obeying their husbands under his breath.

"I bow to your will then, countess," he said. Turning to Beitris's father, he said, "Tell me how I can be of service to you?"

"My youngest daughter was married to Iain Robertson some years ago and she died in childbirth," he began.

"I have heard this," Duncan said.

"We were not present when Beitris died, or her bairn with her, but we were told of that terrible night by the old laird before he died. A terrible night," the man said.

His sons looked at Duncan with open speculation and he could tell by their expressions they were thinking of Marian and not their poor dead sister.

"Rumors persisted after that…"

"About my wife?" he asked, putting it in front of them.

"Nay! Nay, sir, about my daughter's death. You see some who were in the keep that night heard things that do not follow what the old laird told us. Some spoke of hearing a bairn's cry. Some spoke of Beitris calling out and damning her husband."

The man's sources were correct about all of this, but he would not say so. "I was not there, sir."

"True, true, but your wife was."

"Should I call her here so she can answer your questions about that night?"

"Nay!" he cried out. "Nay! That is not necessary."

"I will not be in the same room as that har…" Elizabeth said loudly, rising from her seat as though Marian walked through the door.

"I would guard your tongue, lady. You speak of my wife," he said in warning.

"Elizabeth, cease or you shall be removed!" her father whispered furiously. He understood how close to insult she'd come. "I beg your pardon, sir."

"I understand how trying this must be for you, Sir Thomas. Pray, continue."

"These stories have come and gone in the five years since Beitris's death, but now other stories have come to light."

This was interesting. Dangerous to Marian, but interesting.

"A cousin confessed on his deathbed to having…" Sir Thomas looked at Jocelyn and then Connor as though choosing his words carefully. "An *indelicate* relationship with my daughter."

One of the men, having a crisis of conscience and wishing to die in peace, had confessed. "Surely not?"

"To our shame, aye. I only consider it to have any merit because he was facing the Almighty and did not want that sin on his soul."

Duncan fought to keep any accusations or information within him. If he could say nothing, mayhap this would be over?

"Unfortunate deaths. Deathbed confessions. Falls from grace. Illicit affairs. None of this sounds as though Duncan is involved. What exactly do you need of him?" Connor asked.

"You recently married Marian Robertson," he said. "Marian has a daughter."

Duncan said nothing for fear of saying the wrong thing.

"Although we have not been permitted to see her…"

"As I said, she is Duncan's child now and he was not here to give or withhold his permission," Connor said with an edge of anger in his voice.

"Oh, aye, laird. I understand your hesitation. A man has a right to decide about his children, of course."

With a certain sense of irony, Duncan realized that was exactly what this man was trying to do.

"No one can remember Marian giving birth to a babe, either before or after she left Dunalastair. I wondered if you knew of anyone who might."

"Have you spoken to the Robertson, Sir Thomas? These questions you raise are about the man's wife and sister."

Did they not realize the trouble if they did discover Ciara was Beitris's bairn? Even with the disclosure, the treaty between the MacLeries and Robertsons would stand now, but any ties between the Erskines and the Robertsons would be broken and worse, their daughter's good name thrown into disgrace.

Now he truly realized Marian's quandary.

"He will not speak to us about this matter, sir. We have not been on good terms since Beitris's death."

"So, what do you want from me? What is there that I could have personal knowledge of and not answer through hearsay or repeating the words of others?"

Sir Thomas took a breath then, glanced over at his daughter and Jocelyn and then just barked out his question.

"Did Marian Robertson come to your bed a virgin or could she truly have given birth to the bairn she claims as hers?"

It all came down to one question. His honor, his word, the trust of his laird and clan, all of it depended on his answer to one question.

The chamber grew quiet and every person there stared at him, waiting on the word he would give and the results were nothing more than life and death. He looked at Connor and read the sympathy there, for he had made similar decisions and found himself damned by many for the choice he'd made. Jocelyn's eyes were filled with tears—for him? For Marian? He kenned not which, but he could feel the pain in her heart as he was faced with this choice.

There would be repercussions and consequences for years to come because of his choice, but Duncan realized that there really was no choice for him in this matter. The truth was the truth….

But love was more than that.

"I took no virgin to my marriage bed," he said softly.

"On your honor as the MacLerie's man?"

"You have my word."

Elizabeth gasped at his words, but Sir Thomas's disappointment was palpable. He sensed a good purpose in the man, but Duncan could not think about the past now. Marian deserved a life of her own and her friend deserved to rest in peace, content that her bairn was protected by the only person who could.

Jocelyn sagged against Connor then, looking paler than she had and signaling that she needed rest. Connor stood and lifted her into his arms.

"Sir Thomas, please seek refreshments in the hall. My men are readying your horses for your journey home," Connor said. "I must see my wife to her chambers and I will return."

Connor leaned closer as he walked by Duncan. "Wait for me here," he said. "The daft woman insisted on being present and now look!"

In a few moments the room had cleared and Duncan waited on Connor's return. The movements of someone behind the servant's screen in the corner surprised him, but the man who stepped out was even more of a surprise.

"I did not think you capable of sitting a horse this soon, laird," Duncan said.

Iain Robertson walked closer. "May we call a truce, Peacemaker?"

"Peacemaker no more, I fear," Duncan answered. "But you can have your truce."

"Why no longer?"

"I have given a false oath, as we both ken. How can I be trusted again?"

"Only a handful ken that it was false," Iain pointed out.

"Aye, but I ken it, and that is all that matters."

"Why did you do it then?"

"I love her, Iain. As simple as that. I could not allow her suffering to continue and be made worse by losing her daughter."

"Beitris's daughter," he said.

"Marian's daughter, put into her hands and into her heart by her dearest friend."

Iain did not meet his gaze then, instead staring off into the distance. The past would forever lie on his shoulders.

"Why did you do it? You owe me at least that much."

Iain walked over and sat in the chair just vacated by Connor. "I was a weak man. I thought I could change. The only good thing I did was to put her in your possession."

"And now? Have you changed? Is this talk of a new marriage true?"

"I will not marry, Duncan. We both ken that, but I think I have more control over the man I am." Iain stood then, winced in pain and then smiled. "But my brother Padruig shows every sign of being a good husband and a better laird, so I have no fears for the Clan Robertson.

"You should go to her," his brother-by-marriage suggested. "She has been in your chambers waiting to hear the outcome, thinking she kens the outcome, and would probably like to hear it from you instead of others."

"Are you staying here at Lairig Dubh?"

"I do not want to get back on a horse for some time, so I have accepted Connor's invitation to stay."

Duncan walked to the door, intent on getting to Marian as quickly as possible, but Iain called his name.

"Do not forget that she makes you a wealthy man."

"I already am a wealthy man, Iain. I did not need your gold to persuade in this." Years of receiving commissions for his work for other clans had given him great wealth.

"What will you do with it then?"

"I think we will hold it for Ciara, since our first daughter together will inherit so much from her mother's family."

"Your first daughter?"

"Aye," he said turning away. "The one I plan on making with her this very night."

Rurik still stood by the door, arguing with Margriet about whether or not she could enter and speak to Marian. Duncan walked up and pushed him out of the way to get inside.

Marian sat at the table, but her head lay on her arms and her eyes were closed. Shushing the two of them and closing the door in their curious faces, he walked quietly to her side and brushed the hair from her face. He touched her cheek and then slid his finger along her chin, waiting for her to wake. He was about to resort to more provocative measures when her eyes fluttered open and she saw him.

"Duncan," she said, rubbing the sleep from her eyes. "Why are you here?" She looked past him. "Have they taken Ciara?"

"Nay, and they will not. She is your daughter, Marian, and could not be more so if you had given birth to her."

She gasped. "What has happened?"

"You said you wanted a husband who chose you above all else, Marian." He guided her to stand and pulled her close. "I am that husband. You are first in my heart and in my soul and more important to me than my honor."

"Nay!" she cried. "I did not ask for you to lie for me, Duncan. It will eat at you and you will hate me for all you give up for me."

"Shhhhh," he soothed. "As a man of honor I could not stand by and watch you suffer more pain because of others. I could not allow your friend to be shamed after her death. I could not allow another innocent to be taken from the only mother she has known."

"Duncan," she said softly. "You lied for me. I am sorry."

He slipped his arm under her legs and carried her into the bedchamber. Once there, he undressed her and himself and they fell onto the bed wrapped around each other. He touched her in all the places that made her sigh and gasp and moan until their bodies screamed for release. Then he thrust deep inside her and moved farther still until she screamed out her pleasure. With a hand under her bottom, he lifted her up and plunged to her womb.

"Be my wife forever?" he asked, staring into her eyes and praying that she wanted him as much as he wanted her.

"Aye, Duncan," she whispered. "Forever."

It took but one more thrust before his seed spilled there inside her, but the feel of her tightness surrounding him while he found release was exquisite. He held her there, not wanting to leave the warmth of her body yet.

Sometime later when they could both speak, she asked about what had transpired in the solar.

"I did not actually lie to him, Marian."

"You did not? I thought you told him I was not a virgin?"

He rolled over his side and dragged the sheets down so he could look on her breasts as they talked.

"'Twas more of a prediction really," he said, reaching out to tease the rosy tips of her breasts with the back of his hand.

"You are now a soothsayer?" Marian asked, reaching out to touch his body now.

The sheets were tossed back and they were teasing each other to arousal when he realized he had not told her what he'd said.

"I said that I took no virgin to my marriage bed."

Her indrawn breath as he moved his fingers between her legs spoke of success. Her hand around his hardness guaranteed it.

"And I plan that you will not be a virgin when we say our marriage vows and consummate those vows in my bed."

She laughed and after so much heartache it lightened his soul. "You are just twisting the words, Peacemaker."

"'Tis what I do best, wife."

Epilogue

The spring day dawned sunny and clear-skied and everyone proclaimed that it was a good sign. Father Micheil had called the banns for three weeks and the chapel door and altar were decorated with fresh spring blossoms of all colors and fragrances.

Inside Broch Dubh, the cook and his helpers worked on the foods that would make up the wedding feast. In the village, some of the women placed seeds and other fertility charms around the door of their new cottage and in the bed where they would consummate their vows. All stood ready for the marriage of Marian Robertson and Duncan MacLerie.

Except the bride, who knelt over a chamber pot heaving out the contents of her stomach.

"It must be something I ate," she said to the women who stood smiling around her.

"'Twas not something you ate, Marian," Jocelyn said, smiling. Her mirth did not fit the disgusting situation as she leaned over and heaved once more.

"It must be my nerves, after all this is marriage and not something temporary," she said, wiping her mouth with the damp cloth Margaret offered.

"'Tis not a nervous condition, either," Margriet said, her own large belly keeping her from getting too close.

"Can it be the sickness?" she asked. "This is the third day in a row…" Marian stopped and looked at the three women who stood grinning at her like silly fools.

"Nay, it cannot be!" she said, sitting back on her heels. "I am with child?" she asked, holding her hands on her still-flat stomach. "I am with child?"

She was so stunned by the thought of it that she forgot she was supposed to already have borne a child. "I mean I am with child again?"

Jocelyn helped her to her feet and called in a servant to take the pot away. "It should not be a surprise, Marian. MacLerie men seem to have no trouble begetting bairns."

Considering that these women had given birth to ten bairns among them with another one, or two more expected in the coming months, fruitfulness was not a MacLerie problem.

"Does Duncan ken?" Margriet asked.

They had been living apart, at Father Micheil's request, since the banns had been called and Duncan was not happy with the arrangement or the forced celibacy. She'd not spoken to him since the previous day and not on matters involving the making of bairns. She expected no rest this night when they returned to their new cottage in the village.

"Nay," she said, tugging her new gown into place. "I did not ken until just now."

"You should tell him now. 'Twill brighten his spirits."

They put the last of the flowers in her hair, which cascaded loosely over her shoulders and down her back. Walking with her from their chamber, they guided her to Duncan where he stood drinking with their husbands. The men all stopped and stared as she approached and Marian could feel the heat of a blush creep up into her cheeks from such an appraisal. Duncan held out his hands to her and examined her from head to toes.

"You are a sight to behold, lass," he said before drawing her close. "And you are mine."

She'd thought on how to tell him and he'd just presented her the opportunity. "Aye, Duncan, *we* are yours."

"Where is the little lass?" he asked, obviously looking for Ciara.

"Nay, Duncan," she said, taking his hand and laying it on her belly where soon he would be able to feel his bairn growing. "*We.* Are yours."

She could tell the moment he realized what she meant for he leaned his head back and howled out the news. Then he scooped her up in his arms and swung around and around until Jocelyn called for him to stop.

"'Tis not a good idea to spin her around just now," Jocelyn advised. "Her stomach just stopped heaving."

Connor and Jocelyn led the others away so she could steal a private moment with him before they took their vows.

"You are pleased then?" she asked.

"I had planned it," he answered proudly.

"On the bairn?"

"Aye. There is no one who more needs children of her own than you, Marian. I wanted you to ken the joy that Jocelyn and Margriet and the others ken. Ciara will always be your firstborn, whether you birthed her or not, but this will be our first."

"And tonight?" Would they forgo the pleasures of the marriage bed now that she was carrying?

"I plan on taking you to my bed and ravishing you the whole night through. Carrying or not, you will think it was our first time together." He shook his head. "Better than our first time together," he promised instead.

He kissed her then and it was filled with promises made and promises kept. Leaning back, he smiled at her.

"I told you that I made a prediction that day to Beitris's father. You do not come to my marriage bed a virgin."

She laughed then, and he held her close for a moment.

"I choose you today, Marian. Above all others. Above everything else in my life. I choose you."

The laird stood a short distance away watching as his cousin and friend discovered one of the most incredible joys of life—fathering a child with the woman you love. Connor turned to Jocelyn and saw the same expression on her face that he wore.

"You are greetin', lass," he said, reaching up to wipe the tears from her cheeks. "Surely, you knew about the bairn already?"

"Aye, Connor." Her eyes shone through the tears

now and she smiled. "We knew," she said with a nod to the other women standing with their own husbands, "but could not speak of it until Marian realized it herself."

"And did she share with you that this is her first?" he asked, waiting for his wife's reaction.

"Did Duncan tell you?" Jocelyn whispered as she gazed around as though making certain their words could not be heard.

"Nay, love. Duncan revealed nothing to me. I simply watched Marian during these last months. 'Twas clear to me." Connor drew her into his embrace and kissed her, understanding in that moment that she continued to amaze him. "But you should have told your laird when you discovered that truth about her."

"There are some things a laird need not know…or know first." Jocelyn pulled his head down to her face and kissed his mouth. "If I had thought her a danger to the clan…" Her words drifted off into another kiss.

Connor accepted her kiss as her apology for her actions and pressed for more, but her words bothered him. They touched on the quandary that had plagued since even Rurik's return from his journey to the Orkneys and through this situation with Duncan's behavior.

Why would a man lie or keep secrets from his laird?

Now looking at his cousins and their wives and then back into the eyes of the woman he loved, Connor knew the answer—a man who loved a woman with his whole heart and soul would do anything, even lie, to protect her.

Just as he had done ten years before.

Just as he now recognized Rurik and Duncan had done.

As a laird, he should be horrified that something, anything or anyone, should come before loyalty to clan and laird.

As a man he could accept it.

As a man in love he could relish in it.

Glancing around the hall, there was no doubt that he and Rurik and now Duncan had found women worthy of that love and that protection.

Author's Note

$\sim\!\!\!\sim\!\!\!\sim$

The practice of handfasting plays a large part in the legends of the Scottish Highlands, but it is difficult to find a factual basis for it. Most evidence is anecdotal at best and even that comes from time periods more recent than the setting of my story.

Part of the misunderstanding about the practice (if it did exist) is that it goes back to the time when marriage was actually divided (or thought of) in two parts—the betrothal and the consummation. In earlier periods, families who were high in power or wealthy with lands and money to protect would make marriage arrangements in advance with a formal betrothal and marriage contracts drawn up to divide or protect their lands, titles or wealth. At some time after that betrothal, the woman would go to live with the man and the marriage was accomplished, more through the fact of consummation and living together as husband and wife than through a formal marriage ceremony.

In the later tenth century and early eleventh century,

the Church became interested in the vast assets of noble and royal families and in gaining power through the political control of nations and asserted itself into the marriage process. Priests were required as part of the betrothal and marriage contracts (many clerks who kept the records for the wealthy, noble and royalty were in fact priests or monks) and the marriage ceremony began to take precedence as the beginning of the marriage.

Sometimes, though, marriages began without the sanction of the Church, especially in distant areas where priests were not permanently assigned to serve or unable to reach on a regular basis. Like the Highlands of Scotland? So, after agreeing to marry and planning to marry, some couples began living together as husband and wife until the priest could arrive to make it official.

It's possible that stories of trial marriages or temporary ones came from those situations and later, the stories told by travelers in the eighteenth and early nineteenth centuries speak of handfasted unions, which lasted for a year and a day and could be ended with the consent of the couple. Proving the existence of handfasting has been difficult, if not impossible, but proving it didn't happen isn't possible, either.

So…writers use this legendary practice for lots of romantic reasons (as I have in this story), yes, taking literary license to enhance the story of handfasting so that it helps to strengthen our stories. And it is appealing, isn't it?

If you're interested in learning more about the reality of marriage in medieval times, I can suggest *The Knight, the Lady and the Priest: A History of Modern*

Marriage in Medieval France by George Duby. I've found it to be an incredible source of information about the mores and customs of the times.

Happy Reading!

MILLS & BOON

Historical

On sale 2nd October 2009

Regency

THE BRIGADIER'S DAUGHTER
by Catherine March

Having married her sister's bridegroom, Miss
Alexandra Packard's sense of propriety urges her to
confess all – but her romantic, womanly side keeps her silent!
Secretly, she very much wants to find out what it would
be like to be Captain Reid Bowen's wife in *every* sense…

Regency

HONOURABLE DOCTOR, IMPROPER ARRANGEMENT
by Mary Nichols

Dr Simon Redfern won't risk his heart ever again. So
he's shocked to find himself falling for young widow
Kate Meredith! Kate longs for children of her own,
and Simon soon becomes the only man she can
contemplate as their father…

MILLS & BOON
Historical

On sale 2nd October 2009

Regency

THE WICKED BARON
by Sarah Mallory

Luke Ainslowe's reputation as an expert seducer precedes him, and innocent Carlotta refuses to become the Baron's next conquest – she has lost her heart to Luke before. However, the Wicked Baron *never* takes no for an answer!

HIS RUNAWAY MAIDEN
by June Francis

Rosamund Appleby is disguised as a youth and fleeing to London when she meets Baron Alex Nilsson. Intrigued and suspicious of this "boy", Alex seeks to protect her. But now hastily married to Rosamund, Alex wonders which is more dangerous: his persistent enemies – or the seductive lure of the woman in his bed…

ROCKY MOUNTAIN WIDOW
by Jillian Hart

The end of Claire Hamilton's marriage left her alone amidst a blizzard of murder accusations and the cold, bitter winter – until Joshua Gable saves her life. Josh's strength and closeness ignite the flames of passion, and Claire wonders if it's possible to love again…

★

◉™ MILLS & BOON®
are proud to present our...

Book of the Month

★

Expecting Miracle Twins
by Barbara Hannay

★

Mattie Carey has put her dreams of finding
Mr. Right aside to be her best friend's surrogate.
Then the gorgeous Jake Devlin steps into her life...

Enjoy double the Mills & Boon® Romance
in this great value 2-in-1!

Expecting Miracle Twins by Barbara Hannay and
Claimed: Secret Son by Marion Lennox

Available 4th September 2009

*Tell us what you think about
Expecting Miracle Twins
at millsandboon.co.uk/community*

millsandboon.co.uk Community

Join Us!

The Community is the perfect place to meet and chat to kindred spirits who love books and reading as much as you do, but it's also the place to:

- **Get the inside scoop from authors about their latest books**
- **Learn how to write a romance book with advice from our editors**
- **Help us to continue publishing the best in women's fiction**
- **Share your thoughts on the books we publish**
- **Befriend other users**

Forums: Interact with each other as well as authors, editors and a whole host of other users worldwide.

Blogs: Every registered community member has their own blog to tell the world what they're up to and what's on their mind.

Book Challenge: We're aiming to read 5,000 books and have joined forces with The Reading Agency in our inaugural Book Challenge.

Profile Page: Showcase yourself and keep a record of your recent community activity.

Social Networking: We've added buttons at the end of every post to share via digg, Facebook, Google, Yahoo, technorati and de.licio.us.

www.millsandboon.co.uk

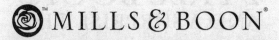

2 FREE BOOKS
AND A SURPRISE GIFT

We would like to take this opportunity to thank you for reading this Mills & Boon® book by offering you the chance to take TWO more specially selected books from the Historical series absolutely FREE! We're also making this offer to introduce you to the benefits of the Mills & Boon® Book Club™—

- **FREE home delivery**
- **FREE gifts and competitions**
- **FREE monthly Newsletter**
- **Exclusive Mills & Boon Book Club offers**
- **Books available before they're in the shops**

Accepting these FREE books and gift places you under no obligation to buy, you may cancel at any time, even after receiving your free books. Simply complete your details below and return the entire page to the address below. You don't even need a stamp!

YES Please send me 2 free Historical books and a surprise gift. I understand that unless you hear from me, I will receive 4 superb new books every month for just £3.79 each, postage and packing free. I am under no obligation to purchase any books and may cancel my subscription at any time. The free books and gift will be mine to keep in any case.

Ms/Mrs/Miss/Mr_____ Initials _____

Surname _____

Address _____

_____

_____ Postcode _____

Send this whole page to: Mills & Boon Book Club, Free Book Offer, FREEPOST NAT 10298, Richmond, TW9 1BR